Mrs K . Pillay

4003008

# THE
# STRATFORD
# STORY

# THE
# STRATFORD
# STORY

*Rosemary Anne Sisson*

A CRESCENT BOOK
Published by the Hardback Division of
W.H. ALLEN & Co. PLC

First published 1975
This Crescent edition published 1986

Set by Galleon Photosetting
Printed and bound in Great Britain by
Garden City Press Ltd, Letchworth, Herts
for the publishers, W. H. Allen & Co. PLC
44 Hill Street, London W1X 8LB

ISBN 0 491 03732 5

Not like some peevish fugitive from death,
Disputing life's completeness with the tomb,
Nor, grossly garmented in all but breath,
Treading the boards of some frequented room—
No! spirits do not show skull-dwindled faces,
Nor raise their melted eyelids out of sleep,
But gentleness still keeps familiar places,
And country memories are long and deep.
The swans, strong-beating in the evening air,
Call you, with us, to note their tuneful pride,
And doubled pleasure is it still to share
The kingcups, prodigal on Water-side.
    Waking, with you we lie and listen still
    To cuckoos calling up on Welcombe Hill.

                              R.A.S.

# CHAPTER 1

Under a blue sky, William stepped out of the house with Edmund and strolled down Henley Street. It was impossible to hurry, since Edmund proceeded by starts and pauses, turning aside to stamp through every puddle from last night's rain. But William felt no inclination whatever to hasten through his father's errand in order to return to the dark little work-shop and his accounts. Whenever he had thoughts of playing truant, William's mind turned immediately to Rufus, and so he decided to call on him now before he bought the skins for his father. He picked Edmund up and carried him through the market place, stopping to look at the stalls or to allow the country people to jostle past him with their baskets.

There were days—many days—when the small town of Stratford seemed like a prison, more terrible for its familiarity, as though he had been there for so long that everyone had become used to him being behind the bars, and never even wondered whether he wanted to escape. He had been fifteen when his father's business collapsed into ruin, taking with it his hopes of the University, and now he was eighteen. Three years of doing the work of the vanished apprentice, three years of writing poetry in secret on scraps of paper stolen from his father's account book, three years of lying awake in the raftered upper chamber that he shared with his brothers Gilbert and Richard, breathing the prison air of hopelessness and confinement, and yet all the time uncertain what it was he longed to escape to, what, after all, was the nature of his imprisonment. 'I, I, I!' cried his spirit, beating against the bars, and mocking voices answered, 'Who are you? What are you? A glover's son. What do you hope for? Why should you hope—you, of all the other tradesmen's sons of Warwickshire? What makes you different?' And he could find no answer, but only knew that he *was* different. 'I, I, I!' beating against the immovable, invisible bars.

But today Stratford did not feel like a prison. It was like a playhouse, staging a comedy for his particular amusement. In the first year that his father was bailiff, a company of players had come to Stratford. John Shakespeare, as leading citizen of the town, greeted them on behalf of the council, and the young William had been allowed to sit on a stool in the council chamber and see the play specially performed for the councillors. He remembered how he had laughed so ecstatically at the business of the clowns that they had put in several lines about 'pleasing the young gentleman in the front row'; and then everyone had laughed more than ever, and William had felt that he was taking part in the comedy, had been, for a while, almost one of the players, tasting the heady, unfamiliar wine of other men's attention and applause. So now he watched the traders in the market and the stolid country people around them, and saw them as comedians performing, for the unique benefit of himself, William Shakespeare, the inexhaustible drama of humankind.

Edmund, leaning down from William's arms to clutch at everything within reach, suddenly saw a stall of children's toys and held his hands out, shouting, 'Give! Give!' It was the word he said best.

William paused, seeing a small cart that shouldn't be too expensive. He picked it up and enquired, 'How much?'

'Fourpence,' answered the man.

'Fourpence!' said William indignantly. 'Fourpence for a penn'orth of wood and a bit of carving?'

'All right,' said the man, 'carve one yourself. And move on if you don't want to buy.'

William eyed him thoughtfully. He knew all the Stratford stall-holders by sight, and this was not one of them.

'Fourpence!' he said again, very loudly. A few people stopped to listen. 'Fourpence?' said William. He held the cart up for everyone to see. 'Fourpence for a little thing like that! Why, it's robbery!'

'So it is,' said one old country woman. 'That's a great deal of money for a small cart—and not very well made either.'

'Put that down!' cried the man, outraged. 'Put that down and move on, or I'll call the constable.'

'Ah!' cried William. 'That's what happens when you get out-of-town traders here. To be told to move on, and me in my own town!'

'Ah yes, he's a foreigner,' said another woman, and the old country woman added, 'I don't like his face, that I don't!'

'Now then,' said the pedlar, appealing with an air of exaggerated honesty to the fairness of his hearers, 'all I ask is that I should get paid for my wares. This fellow wants to take the cart and pay nothing for it. Now, I ask you, ladies, I ask you, is that right?'

The good wives hesitated, and the old country woman said doubtfully, 'He ought to get his money.'

William abandoned his fickle supporters and said to the man, 'Just because you come from Coventry——'

'Not Coventry,' the man broke in, with rash haste, 'Leicester.'

'Hah!' said William, in triumph, and went on, 'Just because you come from Leicester, there's no reason to think you can cheat good

Stratford folk out of their money. Where's the constable?'

He glanced round, saw the constable moving away in the opposite direction, and quickly stepped in front of the stall-holder so that he shouldn't observe it.

'Now, I don't want no trouble, young sir,' said the man. 'Just to show you, I'll let you have that pretty little cart for only threepence.'

'No,' said William, 'I'm not interested now. All I want is to see that poor folks aren't cozened.'

'Here, sir, this pretty little cart for threepence, only threepence. Here, little gentleman, you'd like this cart, wouldn't you?'

'No, he wouldn't,' said William, hastily removing the cart from Edmund's ready fingers. He looked at the man sternly. 'Half a groat,' he offered.

'Threepence,' said the man.

'There, you see,' said William. 'He thinks that because he comes from Leicester——'

'Half a groat,' said the man, despairingly. 'But it'll ruin me,' he added.

The small crowd dispersed and William gave the cart to Edmund, who examined it carefully, turning it round and round in his stubby little fingers.

'You'll admit that's all it's worth,' said William, as he paid over the twopenny piece.

'That's as may be,' said the man, 'but if we

11

always did trade like that, how d'you think we'd make a living?'

'By stealing sheets off the hedges,' replied William, cheerfully, and strolled away, delighted to catch a flash of startled consciousness on the man's face before he was lost in the crowd.

His friend, William Hart, always known as Rufus, was taking down the shutters of the hatter's shop, whistling to himself, his hair glinting red in the early sunshine.

'Rufus,' called William, 'I've bad news for you.'

'My master's better?' suggested Rufus. 'Or someone wants to buy a hat?'

'No, not quite so bad as that. It's only that your aunt has died.'

'Ah,' said Rufus. 'I didn't know I had one.'

'You'll still have to go to her burial tomorrow.'

'Naturally,' Rufus agreed. He took Edmund in his arms and tossed him up and down before asking idly, 'Apart from going to my aunt's burial, what else am I doing tomorrow?'

'Going to see the players at Drayton.'

'Oh Lord!' said Rufus, disappointed. 'I hate actors. Who wants to hear shabby fellows mumbling dull phrases for three hours and more?'

'Then you won't come?' asked William.

'Of course I'll come,' said Rufus.

William grinned. 'I'll ask Dick Quiney too,' he said.

'Dick won't go,' said Rufus. 'He'll say that his father trusts him and that he has work to do.'

'I don't ever hear you say that you have work to do,' said William, laughing, 'or that Master Sharp trusts you.'

''Fore God,' cried Rufus, indignantly, 'if he did I'd never work for him again! Here, are you going to Dick's house now? I'll walk along with you.'

They went together along the crowded High Street and paused outside Quiney's shop.

'Dick!' called Rufus, in a penetrating voice. 'Richard Quiney! Master Richard Quiney! Sir Richard Quiney! Lord Quiney!' Dick hurried out, much flustered, and begged him to be quiet.

'If you'd waited a little longer,' said Rufus, 'I'd have conjured you out.' He drew a circle in the road with his toe and began, 'By Beelzebub and all his small devils, by Satan and——'

'*Don't*,' cried Dick.

'Dick's afraid we'll harm his reputation,' said William. 'Then when he's a great merchant, no one will trade with him.'

'Well, neither of you wants to be successful,' said Dick, peevishly. 'But I mean to be a rich man one day.'

'Then we'll come and borrow money from you,' said William. 'Meanwhile, will you come to Drayton tomorrow to see the players?'

'I don't know,' answered Dick, cautiously. 'I must ask Father.' And he disappeared inside to consult the mercer, while Rufus said disgustedly, 'It was just the same at school. If there was a way Dick could do something without getting into trouble for it, he always took it.'

And he looked surprised when William laughed.

'I can go,' Dick announced, presently returning. 'Father has thought of an errand I can do for him at Drayton, so that won't waste the time so much.'

'And you still mean to go?' said Rufus. He was examining Edmund's cart, and added, 'Dick, go and get some thread so that Ned can pull this along behind him.'

Dick obediently went inside and came back with a length of thread, which Rufus tied to the cart.

'There you are, Ned,' he said. 'Now you won't lose it. Well, I suppose I must go back to the shop. With Master Sharp ill, I have to do all the work.'

'I never see you working,' said William.

'I never *look* for work,' Rufus answered, 'but if it comes and jostles me, I have to do it.'

He waved his hand and wandered away. Dick looked after him disapprovingly, and then turned to go inside.

'Are you coming to the cock fight this evening?' William called after him.

'No, I shall be busy,' Dick answered.

William chuckled and started back up the street, walking slowly and enjoying the sunshine. It was the time of year he liked best. The countryside was rich but not yet somnolent and the cuckoo had lost that piping monotony which he had earlier in the year. His breaking voice seemed to show that he must soon leave the choir, and his song seemed sweeter because it would soon be heard no more. William thought of Dick and Rufus, and of the comedy of the man in the market place, and saw Edmund stumbling along backwards so that he could gaze at his cart; and Stratford was this morning a place of such delight that he wondered how he could ever have longed to leave it.

By the tanner's stall, William told Edmund to play with his cart and stay close, and himself became absorbed in choosing the skins for his father. Suddenly he heard a familiar voice raised in anguished screams and, looking round, he found Edmund no longer beside him. He struggled through the crowd, following the sound, and half expecting to find Edmund knocked down by a horse or lying under the wheels of a wagon in the road. But, thrusting his way past a gossiping group, he saw Edmund at last, lying on his back beside a stall and still screaming loudly. William started forward, but a woman was before him, taking the child in her arms and setting him on his feet, and William, coming up behind her, heard her speaking in a low, country voice.

'There,' she said, 'thou art not hurt. Where's thy mother?'

She knelt beside him, holding him round the waist, her kirtle in the mud and Edmund's dirty little hand dragging at her coif. 'There now,' she added, as Edmund stopped crying, 'that's better.'

'I'll take him,' said William, smiling.

And Edmund immediately began to cry again, reaching his arms up and incoherently explaining the disaster.

'I don't think he's much hurt,' said the woman. 'His cart caught on the edge of the stall and pulled him over.' She smiled at Edmund and said, 'There, now thou hast thy father.'

'He's my youngest brother,' said William. 'I'm not married.'

'Oh,' said the woman, and blushed and seemed confused. She bent down and picked up the cart and gave it to Edmund and turned to go.

'Oh, wait!' cried William, taking a step after her. She paused. 'We haven't thanked you,' said William. 'Edmund, say thank you.'

Edmund did so, still tearful and solemn, but always obliging. The woman kept her eyes down, murmuring, 'I must go home.'

'Do you live in Stratford?' asked William, feeling that he was keeping her against her will, and yet oddly reluctant to let her go.

16

'Oh no!' she replied. 'I live in Shottery.'

'What, so far away!' cried William, laughing. 'That's a great journey to come to market!'

'It's a mile and more,' she said, gravely, so that he didn't know whether she knew that he was teasing her.

'I sometimes walk through Shottery,' he said. 'Perhaps I might see you one day.'

And then she did look up, briefly, and her face looked very young and round and defenceless, so that William in that instant dropped his tone of half idle gallantry, feeling that it was as unfair as teasing a child. He asked quite seriously, 'Where do you live?' She hesitated, and then said, breathlessly, 'I live in the house called Hewlands.'

'And what's your name?'

She hesitated again, and replied, very low, 'Anne Hathaway.' Then she murmured something else which he couldn't hear, and turned and hurried away through the crowd and was lost.

'Gone,' said Edmund, looking up at William.

'Yes,' said William, 'she's gone.'

And there was a curious oppression on his spirits, as though someone dear to him had just left him. All through the rest of the day her face remained clear in his mind, the wide, grey eyes, the broad forehead, the chin too long for beauty, but, above all, that look of defencelessness, so different from his mother's competence or his sister's self-contained laughter.

# CHAPTER 2

'Mother,' said William, at breakfast the next morning, 'can Joanne come with us to see the players at Drayton?'

'*Joanne?*' exclaimed Mary Shakespeare. She paused. Joanne could feel the arguments against such a plan forming up like soldiers in her mother's mind. 'All the way to Drayton?'

'It's not very far,' said William. 'We'll stop on the way and have something to eat.'

'Not at an ale-house!' said Mary. 'How many of you are going?'

'Dick and I,' William answered, and added, 'Oh, yes, and possibly Rufus.'

'That idle good-for-nothing!' cried Mary Shakespeare. 'No, it's not fitting for Joanne to go wandering about the country with three young men. She's not a child now and she mustn't behave like one.'

There was a brief silence, and then Gilbert took an unexpected part in the conversation. William and Joanne were old allies, but Gilbert, two years younger than William and three years older than Joanne, usually went his way and minded his own business, keeping his place as independent and sardonic observer of family affairs. But he occasionally amused

18

himself by intervening when it was least expected, and his interventions, being unexpected, were always the more effective.

'I don't think you need to worry, Mother,' he remarked. 'Joanne won't be alone with three young men. Half Stratford will be there.' He grinned, saw Joanne's look of gratified surprise, and grinned again. 'And Dick Quiney's married,' he said, 'and is such a steady fellow.'

'Well, but to see the players!' said Mary Shakespeare, yet wavering a trifle all the same. Then she went on, 'And Joanne is too much given to idleness. William, you shouldn't encourage her.'

Joanne could think of a good pert reply to that, but restrained herself, knowing that one sentence from her would be enough to settle the matter.

'The players don't often come, wife,' said John Shakespeare. 'And I have given William a holiday. Perhaps Joanne could have one too.'

'It's not the same at all,' said Mary, severely. 'What will Joanne do when she's married? Go gadding about after every company of travelling players and leave the house and the children to look after themselves?'

'*I* shan't ever marry!' cried Joanne, with all the scorn of thirteen years and four brothers. 'Men are all either stupid or villainous and——' (demurely) 'I would never marry a villain.'

'And he would have to be a stupid man to have you,' Gilbert agreed.

'Now, Joanne——' began her mother, but at that moment Richard, who knew that at all events he would not get a holiday, scrambled down from his stool, shouting, 'I shall be late! I shall be late for school!'

'If you were late for school as often as you expect it,' Gilbert observed, 'the master would be quite accustomed to it and would probably beat you if you *weren't* late.'

Richard paused to think this over, and then said earnestly, 'No, he said he would beat me next time I was late.'

'Then you'd better not disappoint him,' said Gilbert.

Richard looked at him blankly for a moment, then turned away and began to search the room, saying, 'Mother, I can't find my satchel.'

'Where did you leave it?' said Mary, getting up.

'Quick, Will!' said Joanne. 'Mother hasn't said "no" yet!' and she slipped through into the kitchen with William close behind her.

They met Dick and Rufus in the market place, arriving together.

'Oh Lord!' exclaimed Rufus, on seeing Joanne. 'If I'd known we were bringing women, I'd have asked my mother to come.'

'It's a pity you didn't,' answered Joanne, immediately. 'She's better company than her son. You should have stayed at home and sent her.'

'I would have if I'd known you were coming,' said Rufus. 'I hate chattering women.'

'I should have thought,' said Joanne, with sudden deadliness, 'that you would have got so used to it at home that you wouldn't mind.'

Rufus flushed, and the laughter disappeared from his face. He lived with his widowed mother, who was famed throughout Stratford for her tongue. She talked uselessly, aimlessly, and unendingly. She was at once a joke and a plague. People laughed at her but fled into doorways to avoid her, and she laughed at herself, yet never tried to mend her ways. Rufus teased her about it constantly, but he still hated that she should make herself a laughing-stock. He once said to William, bitterly, that he thought his father must have died of a surfeit of talk, and if he himself should go the same way, his mother would probably kill the cat with it. But he had never said as much to anyone else, and Joanne's thrust went right home as she had hardly meant it to. Rufus turned away and walked between William and Dick, and Dick then fell back to join her. She welcomed him readily, and listened to his tales of business with ostentatious interest, but she was aware all the time of Rufus, walking ahead in unaccustomed silence. She tried to be glad she had defeated him, but could only be sorry that she had found him vulnerable, and sorrier still that she had taken advantage of it.

Outside Drayton, William and Rufus paused beside a small house and William said, 'We'll go and get something to drink. Dick, sit out here with Joanne will you? We'll bring it out.' They disappeared inside, and Dick solemnly continued with his description of a bargain made with a customer.

'Master Bates (said my father), you know that I shall give you a fair price. Yes, Master Quiney (said Master Bates), I know that. Well then (said my father), here is my final offer. Take it, Master Bates, or leave it. And he took it!'

Dick leaned back on the bench and waited for her astonishment. But Joanne had missed the first part of the story. She could only say, 'Well! Did he lose by it?'

'No, no,' Dick explained, 'he didn't lose by it. But my father gained by it, by as much as twenty pounds. It was a fair price.'

'Oh,' said Joanne.

She turned to look through the open door, and saw Rufus sitting astride a bench, waiting for the ale to be brought, and William leaning against the wall just inside the door, talking to someone who was out of her sight.

'It must be rather a hard job in the winter,' William was saying.

'Dar!' said a voice in reply. 'I don't travel

22

round in the wintertime. I lies snugged up in Lunnon. You won't find me raound 'ere when the snow's on the graound. Dar!'

There followed a hawking noise and then a very determined spitting. The voice, cracked and wheezing, sounded as though it was composed of beer and evil living.

'London!' William exclaimed. 'Do you like London?'

'Dar!' Another spit. 'Powerful dull up there, 'tis. No one to gossip with. Everyone mindin' their own business. No one afeard o' me.' A wicked, cracked chuckle. 'You know what they calls me raound 'ere? Crooked John! I don't know why.' A laugh which broke off into coughing and gasping. Then, 'They says I'm a wizard.'

'And are you?' enquired William, with interest.

'Ah, lad, telling's telling.'

There followed a loud drinking noise, as of the river running beneath the bow of a boat, and then the bang of a pot being slammed down on the table.

'Have another drink?' William offered.

After a pause, the voice said in the tone of one conferring a favour, 'Ay. Ay, I will. And it ain't everyone I'll take a drink from, not in the spirit of kindness.'

'Rufus,' called William. 'Ask the boy to bring another pot of ale.'

'O' course,' his companion went on, 'there's

times I've 'ad the price of a drink an' put a curse in it for 'im as give it.'

'And did the curse work?' asked William.

'Ah, no telling. But I don't see why it shouldn't, as well as a blessing. Hah!' as Rufus brought the drinks, 'and a very good health to you, sir!' He drank once more, and then continued, 'Now, I 'member a time, not long ago, when I was passin' through——' Rufus brought the drinks out to Dick and Joanne and turned to go inside again.

'Who's Will talking to?' enquired Dick.

'Old pedlar,' Rufus answered, and left them.

'I don't know why Will likes these disreputable fellows,' said Dick, in high disapproval.

'Hush,' said Joanne, 'I want to listen,' and she moved to the end of the bench.

'So then the whoreson rogue says to me,' went on the old pedlar, 'he says, "Ye're a rascally cutpurse, an' I'll have ye set in th' stocks." So I says, "No, master, that I en't, but I knows a thing or two about you, then as I wouldn't mind tellin', if so be as the magistrate was to ast me." Then, by the Red Blood of God, if the mouldy rogue didn't give me a shillin' and tell me to be on my way, an' him as white as a lump of dough!'

'And what was it you knew about him?' asked William, laughing. Again the cracked cackle.

'Nothin'. Nothin' at all. But by th'time I'd bought a few pots of ale with 'is shillin', I could've made up enough to satisfy 'im—an' the magistrate too. An' a curse for'm in ev'ry pot!'

The old man drank again, and set down his cup, and then there was a heavy grunt as he got to his feet. 'Well, I mus' be on me way.'

He came to the door, his basket on his shoulder, and Joanne saw a brown, wrinkled face, like an old door knocker, two green eyes glinting with such joyful, unabashed wicked-ness that it was almost like innocence, and a sardonic grin that showed one yellow tooth and widened at the sight of her and Dick Quiney.

'Well, my maid,' he began immediately, 'what's your fancy? There's a lad as'll buy it fer you. Come, now, ribbons, laces, love poems, what'll you 'ave?' And he dragged his basket forward from his back, which Joanne now saw was greatly deformed with a hump.

'Hey!' called William, coming out also, 'that's my sister.'

'Ah?' said Crooked John, looking from one to the other. Joanne smiled at him. 'Ah, I see she is,' he said. 'And a pretty little maid, too. No trouble findin' her a husband.'

'Why does everyone want to find me a husband?' said Joanne. 'I don't want one.'

'What!' cried the old man. 'Are you goin' ter lead apes in hell, then?'

25

'I'd rather lead 'em in heaven,' answered Joanne.

He laughed. 'If I was Saint Peter,' he declared, 'I'd say, "You come up to heaven, my lass. Devil don't deserve to 'ave you daown in 'ell." '

He turned the contents of his basket over with his gnarled brown hand, and brought up a bunch of ribbons which he held out to her.

'Oh no,' said Joanne. 'I haven't any money.'

'Dar!' said Crooked John. 'Take it.' She still hesitated, thinking of his threadbare coat, strained over his hump. 'Take it,' he commanded. 'I'll cozen some old dame for it, never fear.' She took it and thanked him, and offered him a handful of cherries from their dinner. 'Are them fer me?' he said, delighted. 'Now, there's one thing I likes, cherries.' He took two pairs and hung them over her ears, remarking, 'Country earrings fer country roses. There's many a London lady as would like to have as good.' Then he shouldered his basket and went on his way, without another word, walking with the firm, slow, sturdy tread of the traveller who has far to go.

On the common at Drayton, the players had set up their stage, and one or two of them lounged outside the tents which stood a few feet from the curtain at the back of the stage. Joanne, William, Rufus and Dick joined the people who were already sitting down on the grass in front, and amused themselves by flicking cherry stones on to the stage.

'If they don't begin soon,' said Rufus, 'I shall go up and act a play myself. Will, do you remember that play we did at school? Lord! Those long Latin speeches! I thought I'd never learn them, and then I thought I'd never forget them, and, marry, now I can't remember one.'

'Well, thank God for that!' said Dick, with unaccustomed energy, and was rewarded by William's launching immediately into the longest speech of the play which he had once delivered to great applause.

'Will, you'd better become an actor,' Rufus remarked, when they had succeeded in silencing him. 'They say that all you need for it is a good memory and a loud voice.'

'Perhaps I will,' William answered, laughing.

Dick began a solemn exposition of the evils and discomforts of an actor's life, but he was interrupted by the beginning of the play, although he went on for several sentences after the rest of the audience had stopped talking.

The curtain trembled, and a young man in a rich costume and feathered hat stepped out from behind it, came to the front of the stage, bowed, and announced, '*The Tragedy of Prince Hamlet's Revenge*. Never before acted. As it will shortly be shown at the court in London.'

'—travelling round the countryside, far from your own parish church!' finished Dick.

27

'Oh, hush!' cried Joanne, as the curtains parted again and a King and Queen came out, dressed in jewels and ermine, and followed by a magnificent group of courtiers and a handsome man dressed in black. 'Oh, Will!'

Until the play began they had all been there merely in search of idle amusement, but from the moment that Prince Hamlet first spoke, they were swept unrestrainedly away into the tale of great events and nobility. It is true that when the ghost, having risen impressively out of the centre of the stage, followed this success by a long and tedious speech, Rufus remarked, 'Hurry up, old Mole, it's time you went to earth again!' but by the end even Rufus had fallen under the enchantment. The words of violence stirred their hearts, the action took its terrible and destined course, the King was killed at last, and the heroic Prince perished in the very moment of triumph.

Slowly Joanne returned to the sunlight and the trampled grass and the smell of warm wood. She looked at William, and he returned the look, dazed, as she was. Slowly the ringing voices faded in their ears. The players came forward and bowed, and Joanne noticed with shame a cherry-stone clinging to the King's ermine. (And was the ermine a little more soiled than she had thought?) The curtain trembled for the last time and was still, and the stage was bare once more. It was evening now, and mothers began to call the children in

28

to bread and milk and bed. Small boys swung apathetically upon the stage, exhausted with excitement, and there was a great emptiness everywhere, as follows a long-awaited victory.

'Come on,' said Dick Quiney. 'We'd better be starting back.'

'I want to talk to the actors,' said William, slowly.

'You want to do *what*?' enquired Dick in astonishment.

'I shan't be long,' said William, and turned to go.

'I'll come with you,' said Joanne, quickly, and she thought that he was pleased to have her, although he said nothing. They walked away together, leaving Dick staring after them blankly, and Rufus cheerfully remarking that they must have caught some of Hamlet's madness.

Behind the back curtain, the players were hurrying about, dodging in and out of the tents, whose flaps were caught back, giving Joanne and William a glimpse in one of them of the King in hose and shirt, looking not at all villainous as he removed his eyebrows. Hamlet, still in his black suit, was shouting directions to a boy loading a cart, his voice no less sonorous than it had been on the stage. He was a sturdy, square-shouldered man of about forty, with a fine nose, broad forehead, and blue eyes slightly bloodshot. Joanne hung back when she saw him, but William stepped up to him.

'Well,' Hamlet said, in a friendly way, 'what can I do for you, young sir?'

'We—I enjoyed the play,' answered William, looking to Joanne's eyes suddenly much younger than eighteen.

'Ah,' said Hamlet, with satisfaction. 'You enjoyed it? Good. Have you seen many plays?'

'No, sir. Only one before this, and plays at school.'

'Well, well. I'm glad you enjoyed it.'

He turned away to assist the boy, whom Joanne now recognized as the Queen. Joanne wished that William would go away now. Hamlet obviously thought that there was no more to be said, and she blushed that William should still stand there, looking embarrassed but dogged. And she herself felt painfully conspicuous, standing by the tent among the players. Hamlet returned, and glanced at William in surprise.

'Do you go back to London soon?' asked William.

'No, we have barely begun our tour. We go to Gloucester, Coventry, York, Leicester—I'm not sure after that.'

'Then the play will be presented in London later?'

'In London——?' Hamlet seemed disconcerted. 'Oh yes. Yes, we hope to present it at court—ah, later.' He looked at William shrewdly for a moment, and then said, 'Would you like to be an actor?' William took a breath, hesitated, and then said, like a man taking an oath of allegiance, 'Yes. Yes, I would.'

Members of the company were now taking down the stage, and their knocking and clattering gave to the conversation an air of unreality. It was like talking in a high storm.

'We have a vacancy in the company,' roared Hamlet. 'We couldn't pay you anything at first, of course, but I would see to your training myself. There is no greater pleasure than acting in the provinces. Better than a London audience any day.'

'If I could!' cried William.

'Well, I must change,' said Hamlet. 'If you want to come, help take down the stage and then join us.'

'But I must go home to Stratford first and tell them,' William protested.

'There's not time for that,' said Hamlet, carelessly. 'We move on in less than an hour.'

William looked at him wildly. Joanne held her breath and could feel her heart beating. It was as though she still watched a play, and the hero was William caught up in the rushing tide of fate, while she, in the audience, was powerless to stretch out her hand to save him. He had often talked of leaving home, but to go in such a way, with a company of strolling players, as though carried away accidentally in a crowd without farewell, to disappear for ever!

'I *can't* go,' cried William, with agony in his voice. 'I can't do it. I *must* go home first.'

'Well,' said Hamlet, his hand upon the flap of the tent, 'if you are ever in London, enquire for me, John Hampton, at the Theatre in Shoreditch, or at the sign of the Bull in Bishopsgate Street. If I am back in London, I will take you into the company.'

'Oh, thank you, sir,' cried William. 'Thank you.'

The actor smiled at him, with an odd look of pity and amusement.

'Well, well,' he said. 'Perhaps we shall meet again.' He hesitated, as though about to say something more, but then he stooped and went into the tent, with a cheerful, 'Good day to you.'

William stood where he had left him, staring at the ground. The King had helped to take down the other tent and was loading it on to a second cart. The Queen and an aged Counsellor, now revealed as a lad of about twenty, were lifting a basket of costumes up beside it.

'Where's the other basket?' asked the Counsellor.

The Queen jerked his head towards the invisible Hamlet. '*He's* late, as usual.'

'Having a drink?' enquired the Counsellor.

The Queen shook his head. '*Talking*,' he said, with extreme contempt. Without his wig and paint, he was revealed as a plain child,

32

with teeth that stuck out a little and sandy hair.

'Well,' said the Counsellor, 'there's time for a pot of ale, then. Ned!'

'Coming,' said the first courtier, hatless and undistinguished. They moved briskly away towards the ale-house, evidently trying to get inside before Hamlet emerged, ready for the journey. William came back to where Joanne stood on the trampled grass. In silence they walked across to where Rufus and Dick were waiting for them, and without a word William set off on the homeward journey, leaving Joanne to answer the mocking questions of Rufus and listen to the disapproving comments of Dick.

They had not gone far before they were overtaken by a cart, which drew up just ahead of them.

'D'ye want a ride? Where're ye goin'?'

'Stratford,' called Rufus.

'Come on, then.'

They hurried up to him, but William stayed where he was.

'You go on,' he said. 'I'll walk. I'd rather.'

'Oh, come on, Will,' called Rufus, climbing up and helping Joanne up on to the cart.

'Hurry up,' said Dick. 'My wife will be growing anxious.'

'No,' he answered. 'I'd rather walk.'

'I'll walk with you,' said Joanne, preparing to jump down again.

TSS - 2

'No!' said William, angrily. 'No! Mother wanted you to get back early. You go on. Dick, see that she gets home safely. Go on.'

Joanne knew that, for the moment, she was a part of that quicksand which held him and would not let him go, one of those friends who were hidden enemies to his ambitions. His anger was not against her but against his disappointment.

'I'll tell mother you'll be home soon,' she said, and the farmer remarked pleasantly, 'Ah, a walk's not so bad in the cool of the evening. Gee-up, Daisy. Goarn then.'

The grey mare stumbled over a non-existent stone, collected herself and walked sedately on, one ear pricked with a misleading air of obedience for her master's voice. When he cracked his whip, she pricked the other ear, but did not vary her pace.

'Was you at the play?' enquired the farmer.

They all told him, together, that they had been there.

'Ah,' said the farmer, 'I thought I seen you. 'Twasn't too bad, was it? 'Twas a good play. But the actors, now, they wasn't much. I was up in London, a year ago or thereabouts, and I went to see Leicester's Men act a play. They did *The Famous Victories of Henry the Fifth*, and James Burbadge was the King. Ah, that was an actor for you. Not like that fellow today!'

'But I thought he was good,' said Joanne.

34

'Well, you could hear'm,' answered the farmer, tolerantly. 'I'll say that for'm. But his fighting—there warn't nothing to it. Now, James Burbadge, you'd see'm fight a battle, right there on the stage, and calling out all the time, telling the Frenchies they warn't no good, and they warn't goin' to beat him. Ah, that was a good play, that was. I saw it at the Theatre, in Shoreditch.'

'But the actor today, John Hampton, he said he was acting at the Theatre in Shoreditch.'

'Ah,' said the farmer, cunningly, 'he might say so, I dare say. But I'll lay he don't take the chief parts up there. He's just one of the travelling ones, and then you may get the best of 'em, or you may not. Just depends, like, which of the companies you may 'appen to get. But when I went to London, 'twas James Burbadge, and he's a good one, he is. Ah, I'll never forget him calling out to the Frenchies, how they warn't goin' to beat him, and how he was a-goin' to take France away from 'em. That was a good play, that was.'

The farmer sighed, reminiscently. 'I wouldn't mind goin' up to London again,' he said, handsomely. 'I had to go up to give evidence in a Chancery case, and so did a friend of mine from Shottery. My wife was angry, though. Why couldn't they ask me to go, she says, and let you get your hay in? Well, I says, they en't goin' to ask a woman to tell the truth now, are they? They be fools in

London, but they en't such fools as that!'

He nudged Rufus in the ribs and laughed loudly, and the grey mare broke into a lolloping trot, virtuously nodding her head. By the time Rufus had abused women's truth-fulness a little further, and Dick had told them all about a Chancery case his father knew about, they were in Stratford, and Dick took Joanne home, while Rufus went to give the farmer a drink.

But William walked slowly along in the evening sunshine. In his mind was such a turmoil of grief and anger as he had never known before. He had often made plans for his future, as he walked alone by the fishing grounds, or as he sat with Joanne in the window at Henley Street, looking out into the empty street. He had planned to become the Queen's Poet, to have his sonnets read by courtiers, to stir men's hearts with his epics. But these had been only dreams, to be admired, not grasped. And now here was the opportunity, perfectly prepared, by which he could take hold of these vagrant dreams and force them into reality. For the first time, his fate cried out to him, 'This is the moment!' and he must ignore the summons, like a lover who hears his mistress calling to him and by enchantment is held silent and motionless, half mad for love of her.

William turned aside and leaned on a gate that led into a field, half minded still to go back and join the actors. Now the second tent would be coming down, soon to be loaded on to the cart. The other basket would be filled and closed. The last ale would be drunk and the reckoning paid, and soon the fellowship would set off, this little band of brothers-in-arms, who faced contempt and poverty and danger of imprisonment, to bring to quiet villages these tales of greatness. And then, when the tour was over, they would set their faces towards London, stooping like falcons to that great lure.

William straightened his back. His fortunes lay with them. This was no longer a dream, or a sharp, beckoning whim. He would return home and tell his mother and father what he had resolved, and say his farewells and ask for their blessing. Then he would set out alone to find the company, either at Coventry or, if he missed them there, at York.

He turned back into the road and went on his way again, thinking about money and whether his father would help him for such a cause, and whether Gilbert would take his place as his father's clerk. But all the while, his mind was full of echoes, the King's words, the Queen's, the Harlot's—

Ah, noble Prince, beseech you, be not mad.
We must be what we are, both good and bad.

37

Or the Ghost's hollow pronouncements—

> But yonder, Phoebus flings his golden
> rays,
> And I turn from dark nights to darker
> days.

Or Hamlet's dying speech—

> So die I now, but still am I revenged!

The words ran against each other, brilliant but confused, as though the whole play was in his mind, and needed only a shake to appear perfectly clear.

# CHAPTER 3

After Anne left William in the market place she did not go to look for her stepmother. She walked quickly down Greenhill Street, along Back Lane, and on to the footpath that led to Shottery. Her legs ached and the market bag was heavy, so presently she turned aside and sat down on the grass. The path was deserted, and the air was full of the fragrant, bitter scent of meadow-sweet, the creamy, feathery flowers nodding in the gentle wind. Anne sat motionless and contented, as a soldier snatches repose in a lull in the battle.

She felt that she never wanted to go back to

Hewlands, never again to see Catherine, her sister, smiling across the table with the easy contempt of the healthy and self-assured. She never wanted to hear Joan, her stepmother, urging her to 'be pleasant', to 'try to be more cheerful', to 'smile when a man spoke to her'. She wanted to escape, not only from them, but from the Anne who answered them, who seized upon every word as a challenge to the useless, mean and unending battle fought day by day in the cottage. It seemed that only when she was alone and away from Hewlands did she become herself again, as she once had been all the time, and she knew that every day of nagging resentment weakened the true Anne, so that she feared there would come a time when the Anne of Hewlands was the only one left. She saw herself as a plain and shrewish spinster, tied inescapably to her stepmother, with whom she was always at her worst. In the blackness of the future, all misery and humiliation, her own figure was the nightmare that cast the most terrifying shadow.

For now there were still moments when it was possible for her to remember how once she had loved and been loved. When Joan and Catherine were out, she sometimes played with the children, and liked to remember that Thomas, at least, was her own mother's child. And he remembered Bartholomew more clearly than the others, and how, before Bart's marriage, the three of them had sometimes gone out together. When she put the children to bed and sang lullabyes to them, she sometimes pretended that she was their mother and that Hewlands was her own for ever; that Joan would never return to make some such waspish comment as, 'Yes, it's all very well for you to sit upstairs singing when there's work to be done'; and that the children would never turn back into fierce little changelings, each one a spy in the enemy's camp.

But these moments of reprieve were becoming fewer every year. As Joan and Catherine became more painfully antagonistic to her, so she became more dependent upon their company, and was likely to become yet more so. She felt between herself and the other people in the village a barrier that every year grew more impenetrable. It was partly caused, she knew, by her own shyness, and partly by her unhappiness which made her seem disagreeable, but mostly it was caused by the malicious stories told about her by Joan and Catherine. So now she would walk through the village with her head down and her mouth set, neither giving nor gaining greetings, and fancying everywhere unkindness and dislike.

Even when she went farther abroad, to Stratford, she walked like one set apart from her fellow men, as though her misery was a burden of guilt that made a leper of her. And she *was* guilty of sins, which mounted every day, adding to her unhappiness and fed by it. Each Sunday at church she resolved to still her tongue and mind her temper. She would kneel thankfully in the gentle half light, whispering the same prayers she had once repeated with her mother kneeling beside her, making the same responses of humble piety. She saw herself as she once had been and as she could, surely, be again, the cheerful, busy, happy daughter of the house, delighting in cleaning and cooking and minding the children. She would clasp her hands upon her forehead, certain, as she trembled beneath the minister's blessing, that all things were possible, with God's help, and that this Sunday marked the end of the old strife, the beginning of the new peace and kindness. Then they would be outside in the sunshine or rain of the church-yard, and there was Joan talking too loudly to one of the neighbours of the latest gossip, and there was Catherine smiling her gap-toothed smile at one of the village boys and looking sideways up at him, and there were the children chasing each other down the path or round the grave stones, and suddenly she was Anne of Hewlands again, saying sharply, 'Come on. Let's get home. Children, stop that at once! Where do you think you are?' And every broken resolution, like sinking tufts of grass, plunged her more helplessly into the

41

bog, until the time came when even as she made the resolve she knew that it would not be kept. Then there was no hope for her except when she was alone, or when she met someone unexpectedly who did not know Shottery or her stepmother.

She thought of the young man in the market place. Or rather, the thought of him had been there all the time, and now she allowed her mind to rest upon it. She smiled to herself as she remembered how he had called her back, and how anxious he had been for her to stay and talk to him, and she heard again that gentle tone in his voice when he said, 'What's your name?' And then she began to frown, remembering, too, how curtly she had hurried away. If she had been Catherine she would have moved closer to him instead of drawing away, and would have looked up at him admiringly instead of keeping her face averted, and would have encouraged him instead of being shy and surly and awkward.

Anne got to her feet and went on towards home. Slowly the unaccustomed warm spring of hope rose again amidst the familiar cold waters of self-mistrust and bitterness. He had asked her name. He knew where she lived. He often came through Shottery. Next time, she would smile at him and tell him that she was glad to see him. She was smiling now at the thought of it, and was so unused to smiling that the tears came into her eyes, as though to ease the smile.

The long afternoon wore away, with Anne unsettled and happy to be so, often stepping to the kitchen door as though she watched for the coming of her love. Late in the evening, when they were all at supper, Catherine came home and they heard her voice and James Whateley's, and then a silence outside the door, and a high laugh from Catherine, with a hint of triumph in it. Anne's lip curled, and yet she was envious of that kiss in the dusk—but not from James Whateley. Then Catherine came in, burnt red by the sun, still laughing, and they heard James Whateley's heavy tread down the path.

'Well,' said Catherine, looking from Joan to Anne slantwise, like a cat, 'did you have a good time at the market?'

A rich, rare, beautiful gust of laughter shook Anne like a summer wind. She looked up at her sister and replied, 'Very good,' while Joan and Catherine stared at her in amazement.

But darkness came down fast, and the young man from Stratford still had not come. Anne went out to shut the henhouse door, and stood for a moment looking down the lane. She had determined that if he really wanted to see her again he would come that very day, and it was only now, when there was no hope of it, that she realized how much she had counted on his coming. But, she thought, there was always tomorrow. Perhaps he had been busy today. Anne went to bed and lay listening to Catherine's heavy breathing, torn between hope and despair, pleasure and anguish.

In the morning, Anne was up early, as usual, and put on her best kerchief, thankful for no comment from Joan. All day she worked in the kitchen or the front garden, and podded the peas outside the door, in full view of the lane. After dinner she sat there again, mending some of the children's clothes. But he did not come.

Joan and Catherine went down into the village to visit a neighbour. Anne gave the children their supper and put them to bed, but sang them no lullabyes.

The sky turned from red to cream and then to a deep blue. The moon came out, and her attendant star. The birds stopped singing. The kitchen was very silent. Anne went out into the garden to shut the hens in once more, and then lingered, dreading to return to the still house. There was no chance now that the young man from Stratford would come to see her. Worst of all was the humiliation she felt, to think how greatly she had hoped for it. She saw herself as Joan and Catherine saw her, plain and undesirable, and it sickened her. She went to lean on the garden gate, gazing straight ahead. She trod her life like the steps of a prison, each one leading down farther into darkness. As the shadows deepened in the garden, Anne felt the dark come down again on her soul, and did not struggle against it, but rather invited it, to know it, as a prisoner holds his wrists apart to feel the inviolate strength of the manacles. She put her face down on her arms and stayed there motionless for a long time, her mind empty of thought, knowing only that she was desperately and eternally miserable.

In the evening hush, there was a sound of footsteps coming down the lane, and Anne started back into the shadow of the hedge. The man was walking slowly and as he came level with the gate, she saw his face in the dim light. She started and said, 'Oh!' and her feet made a sound on the path. He paused for a moment, and looked round, startled, and said, uncertainly, 'Good evening.'

'Good evening!' Anne replied. The tears rushed into her eyes again and she could not keep the exultation out of her voice. He had remembered her. He had remembered her and had come to see her.

It had seemed for a moment that he might pass on down the lane, but when she spoke, he crossed over and came to stand beside the gate, narrowing his eyes. Then he smiled and said, 'Why, it's—Anne Hathaway.'

It sounded as though he greeted her after a long absence. She smiled back at him, so happy that she forgot to be embarrassed.

'How's Edmund?' she asked.

The young man laughed. 'Edmund has quite recovered.' Then, still smiling, he remarked, 'You remembered his name!'

Anne blushed at that, as though he could know how much she had thought about him, how much she remembered of their brief meeting. She said hastily, 'But I don't know your name.'

'Will Shakespeare,' he replied.

There was a silence. Anne was afraid he was offended that she had asked his name. She could think of nothing else to say, and she was in terror lest he should go away. A bat swept down, close above their heads, with its own mysterious stillness. A starling twittered in the hedge. The seconds slipped away, and Anne expected every moment that he would smile and bid her good evening, and walk away down the lane, never to return. And yet she seemed incapable of trying to keep him. The tricks that women use to keep men beside them were not beneath her but beyond her. Through some folly in her nature she found herself unable to use them. She could only stand quite still beside the gate, her hands folded upon it, looking at him. Then he broke the silence to say with the air of one making an important confidence, 'I've just been to see the players.'

'The *players*?' echoed Anne.

'Yes,' said William, 'at Drayton.' He

hesitated, and then added, 'They wanted me to join them.'

'You *talked* to them?' cried Anne, in amazement. She thought of actors as something between wizards and Spaniards.

William nodded. 'If I could have left at once I could have joined the company. But I had to go home first.'

'I should think so, indeed,' said Anne. 'It wouldn't be fit for you at all. I should think they'd be ashamed to ask you. My father used to say that players were all drunken fellows and godless, and it stands to reason they would be, too, travelling round far from their own parish and staying in alehouses.'

A thoughtful look came to his face. He gazed down as though he saw something in the grass at the roadside, and said, absently, 'But it was a very good play.'

Anne clasped her hands. The world opened up before her, and she said, 'Oh, I should like to see a play. Except that—father used to say that they were wicked.'

He looked up at her. 'The next time some players come near,' said William, 'I'll take you to see them, and then you shall judge for yourself.' She knew that he was teasing her, but she didn't mind. He spoke as though they would be meeting again.

But now that feeling which had hurried Anne away from the market was upon her again. She was afraid of wearying him, and of

47

showing him how much she wished to stay and talk to him. She half turned away and said, 'I must go.'

He stepped closer and put his hand on the gate, not on her hand but beside it, and said urgently, 'Not yet. Wait a minute.' She paused, seemingly anxious to leave. 'When shall I see you again?' asked William.

'I—I don't know,' said Anne.

'Tomorrow. Let me call tomorrow evening and take you for a walk.'

'I have to milk the cow in the evening.'

He smiled. 'Couldn't someone else do it for once?'

'Yes,' said Anne slowly, 'my sister could.'

'Well, then, shall I come tomorrow?'

Anne was silent. She did not want him to meet Catherine.

'Please,' said William. 'Please come, Anne.'

She hesitated a moment longer, and then said, 'Very well. But don't come here. Let me meet you. I'll start along the footpath to Stratford.'

'At four o'clock?' William said.

Anne smiled at him, breathless with joy. 'At four o'clock.'

She went away up the garden path, but William stayed where he was, and presently called after her, 'You won't forget?'

She stopped and turned round and looked at him gravely. Then she replied, 'I won't forget.'

# CHAPTER 4

'We used to come here when we were children,' said Anne, 'on Sunday afternoons.'

'Did you?' said William. 'So did we.'

They were standing on the bridge, looking down into the river Avon.

'There were so many things we did when we were children,' Anne went on, as though speaking half to herself. 'We used to go out into the woods to pick primroses, and in September we went blackberrying and then, later, wooding. But we don't do things like that any more. And if we did, it wouldn't be the same.' She added, 'Water runs under the bridge, but it never returns,' and her country voice gave to the old proverb a newness and truth.

William said, 'The old pleasures go, but new ones come to take their place.'

'Do they?' said Anne, bitterly. 'That's what people say. I don't remember any pleasures since my mother died.'

'When did she die?' asked William, with that gentleness which made his company such a rare thing to her.

'Twelve years ago,' said Anne. 'I've counted every one.' After a moment, she went on,

'Until then we were all so happy. We never had a quarrel in the house, no, not one that I can remember. And then mother died. And father married—he married that—that *woman*. He married *again*!'

'Perhaps,' said William, diffidently, 'so that she could look after the children.'

'But not so soon!' cried Anne, with a note of hysteria in her voice. 'Not so soon as that! Before she was dead two months!'

William could find no answer. After a few seconds, Anne went on more calmly. 'And I could look after the children. Thomas, the new baby, was like my own. He *was* my baby until *she* came. And Cathy, too.' She had not used that name of endearment for years. 'Cathy loved me until *she* came. And then she seemed to forget mother and me, because *she* spoilt her. After mother died, I looked after the house and the children, and did the cooking, and I think I was the only one who really missed her. The children were all right with me, and my brother Bart was very good with them. And then father brought *her* into the house, and everything was wrong. And father was angry with me because I wouldn't call her "mother". I couldn't,' she cried, turning on William as though she must convince him against his will. 'I *couldn't* do it.' William shook his head in silence. 'I had to help her in the house. We were always together. We did everything together. There was no way to escape from her. Even when little Joan was ill we had to nurse her together. We thought we'd saved her, and then, suddenly, she slipped through our fingers. She sat up in bed, and she said, "Open the window, Anne", and I opened it, and then she died. It was her soul went out through the window.'

William thought of his little sister, dead three years before, and caught his breath.

'And *she* was there then. We were together then,' said Anne. '*She* cried, and so did Catherine. But I didn't. I couldn't. Not when they were crying.'

She leant her elbows on the bridge and her cheek against her clasped hands and went on, wearily, 'It wasn't quite so bad while Bart was in the house. He loved me, and my step-mother, she liked him, and so he stood between us. But then he married Isobella, and he went away to live at Tredington. And now I never see him. And I miss him so much.' Her voice broke, but she recovered and went on, 'Then father died. And they none of them really minded. They cried, of course, but that was nothing. And they thought I didn't mind. But I remembered how he used to be, before he married *her*, and I seemed to lose him twice. And now there's nothing left!' she cried. She straightened up, and struck her hands together, and all her calmness fell away. She turned on William a face of anguish.

'They hate me, and I hate them, and yet I have to stay there. I can't get out. Sometimes I think I shall go mad. But I don't. It would be better if I did. Sometimes they think I'm mad, and sometimes I seem to be mad, because it's easier. It's easier to seem to be mad than to pretend that everything is all right. I can't pretend. I never could. I can't pretend that I love her, when I hate her, and I can't try to make her love me. I would rather she hated me than be like Catherine. And so I scream at them, and I break things, and all the time I know that if I weren't a Christian I'd kill myself. Everyone that I love dies, but I have to live.'

'Oh, Anne,' said William gently. 'Oh, Anne.'

He put his arm round her, and she leant her head against his shoulder, gratefully, as though she laid down a burden. She closed her eyes and sighed. Undefended by anger or suspicion, her face in repose was as simple and delicate as a child's.

But, almost immediately, she drew away from him, and said with a strange return to formality, 'It's getting late. I must be going home.'

They walked back together, talking little. William drew her hand through his arm and held it, and she leant towards him very slightly. As they turned into the lane, a woman and a young girl came towards them and nudged each other and giggled as they saw them. Anne drew her hand away and, as they came level, nodded at them but showed no inclination to stop. The girl, smiling in a way which pushed out her lower lip, called, 'Oh, Anne!' But she was looking at William. He took his cap off to them and they went on past them, and he did not trouble to look back after them.

'That was my stepmother and my sister,' said Anne, keeping her eyes down on the road.

'Oh, was it?' answered William.

She looked quickly up at him, and her face broke unexpectedly into a radiant smile. She said, laughing up at him, 'I don't believe you noticed them.'

He answered, 'I was looking at you.'

Then she took his arm of her own accord, still laughing, and looking very young and very happy.

They parted at the gate, where Thomas was swinging noisily to and fro, and not even Anne doubted that they would meet again.

'Tomorrow,' said William, 'at the same time?'

She nodded immediately. 'Tomorrow.'

'Don't be late,' said William.

She put her head a little on one side, and said with an unpractised and wholly un-disguised essay at coquetry, 'Perhaps I shall forget.' Then William came back and took her in his arms over the gate and kissed her and

53

said, 'That's to make sure you remember.'

'Oh!' cried Anne, breathless and taken entirely by surprise. 'Oh!'

She gazed after him down the lane, looking astonished and dismayed. Then presently she began to smile, and she turned and went inside to get the children's supper.

The summer weeks that followed were to Anne and William not like a dream of love but rather as though they had both stumbled suddenly upon reality. The time they spent together each day was clear and certain, while the hours they spent apart were distant and confused, like a dream. Anne was like a prisoner allowed each day to walk in green fields. When she returned to the darkness of her cell, her eyes were still dazzled and golden with sunlight. She cooked or scrubbed, milked the cow or fed the chickens, and thought all the time of William, so that her life away from him was unconsidered. She knew that if she had never seen him again after that evening by the gate, still nothing else would ever have been real to her again but the thought of him.

To William, too, that meeting by the gate had been like a sudden moment of truth. When she stood, with folded hands, and spoke of the players it was as though his picture of them shifted in his mind in that instant, and he saw not a brilliant fellowship of high adventure but bloodshot, faded blue eyes, and a purposeful hastening towards the ale-house, and tawdry finery and soiled ermine. He never decided that he would not, after all, go to join the company of players. It was simply that he did not go, and day by day the idea of joining them seemed to become more dreamlike and unreal, while Anne, all undesignedly, simply by being what she was, took hold of his heart as a young child's hand closes confidingly upon a stranger's. She met his kisses passionately and whole-heartedly, and yet there was in her nature a tincture of puritanism which made love come strangely to her, which must every time be overcome, and which gave her always an air of reserve. Her simple profundities constantly defeated him, and the opaqueness of her mind concealed her thoughts as a looking-glass conceals the wall behind it. And it was this blending of natures in her one nature, of simplicity and sad wisdom, of passion and reserve, of maturity and childishness, that bound him to her more closely every day.

William was going to take Anne to the fair, and she was waiting for him in the kitchen on a beautiful summer afternoon. He had promised to come early, and yet here it was, after dinner, and still he had not come.

'Well, you may be different,' said Catherine, 'but *I* wouldn't wait about all day for a man. I always keep them waiting for me. But p'raps yours wouldn't wait,' and she laughed at James Whateley, patiently standing by the door.

'He said he'd be late today,' answered Anne, and then was angry with herself. It was degrading to argue with Catherine on such a subject—and to tell a lie as well!

'Then why've you bin waiting for him all the morning?' asked Catherine. 'I hope he's worth waiting for.' She sauntered to the door, saying over her shoulder, 'Tell her I've gone.'

And she went off down the path with James Whateley, looking extremely pleased with herself. Better a prompt James than a tardy William.

After a few minutes Joan came clattering down the stairs, in a dress too low and with a kerchief too bright and with her hair oddly dressed.

'We ought to be going,' she said. 'Where's Catherine? In the garden?'

'She's gone,' Anne answered.

'Gone? I thought I was s'posed to be going with them.' She peered out of the window. 'How long ago?'

'Oh, not long. You can catch them.'

Joan turned on her with relief. It was no pleasure to her to abuse Catherine.

'Oh, I can catch them, can I? A lot you care! I suppose I've got to take the children, too? It'll be a nice day for me, I can tell you, taking a lot of children about with me. But you couldn't take them! Oh no! You're waiting for your fine gentleman from Stratford. Well, you'd better be careful you don't get more children than you expect, my girl, going about with him! You don't think he wants to marry you, do you? I wonder you aren't ashamed!'

Anne turned her back on her and sat down by the open door with her mending.

'Oh yes, you can turn your back!' said Joan furiously. 'Coming the fine lady over us, and then kissing and hugging at the gate in front of all the village!' She stamped out of the door but turned back to say, 'You might as well come along with me and look after the children. He won't be coming this afternoon. I'll wager he's found someone better'n you to go with.'

Anne raised her head and gave her the insolent stare which never failed to enrage her, and then went silently on with her work. Joan stormed away down the path, shouting in her shrill but powerful voice, 'Thomas, Margaret, William, John! Come along now, do. Don't keep me waiting all day.'

'It's us 'as bin doin' the waitin',' said Thomas, and was rewarded by a cuff on the ear. John began to laugh, and was in turn hit by Thomas, who raised a tremendous yell that was echoed by Margaret, who had got her foot trodden on in the scuffle. Still bawling and shouting, they all struggled through the narrow gate and deployed down the lane. Anne listened to their vanishing voices and envied them their senseless squabbles and unfeeling tears.

She sat for a while with her work in her lap, and then flung it down and wandered impatiently about the room. This was the second time William had kept her waiting. The first time she had pretended not to notice it, but now——. He had never spoken of marriage, and she had never dared even to hint at it, lest trying to hold him fast should result in driving him away. And to return to life without him would be such anguish that the very thought struck like a dagger to the stomach. She almost felt that she had been happier before she knew him, when a dull misery had held her, instead of this tormented, uncertain glory of love. She tossed about the room, possessed by a thousand devils of doubt and unsureness, murmuring, 'What will become of me? Oh, what will become of me?' Until at last the click of the gate sent her quickly back to her chair, pretending to sew.

William's voice called out, 'Anne!' Then, as she did not reply, he came up the path and smiled cheerfully at her as she sat in the doorway, saying, 'Well, sweetheart, here I am. I'm sorry I'm late.' Anne got slowly to her feet and stood looking at him, clutching her mending in her hand. She was suddenly trembling. She said, in a voice of suppressed fury, 'Sweetheart! You needn't trouble to call me that. In fact, you needn't come any farther. I'm not going to the fair.'

William looked amazed. He came up to her and made to take her in his arms, saying affectionately, 'Why, what's the matter, love? You're not angry with me?'

'Don't touch me!' cried Anne, backing away from him violently. 'If it wasn't worth coming before, it's not worth coming now. I suppose you thought I'd wait till all hours for you.'

'My father kept me,' said William. The innocent bewilderment in his hazel eyes maddened Anne more. How dared he be so secure, and understand her fears so little?

'Then you'd better go back to him!' said Anne, sharply. 'I wonder you could bring yourself to come over here at all.'

William flushed, and his temper began to rise.

'If you don't want me,' he said, 'perhaps I'd better go away again.'

'P'raps you had,' said Anne, and turned away, but there was a break in her voice at the end which betrayed her. William began to smile and came and put his arm round her.

'My love,' he said, 'we've never quarrelled yet, have we?'

'You were never as late as this before,' cried Anne, turning into his arms and abandoning all the dignity of wounded pride.

'Oh, Anne!' said William, laughing and shaking his head. He drew her down on the settle and kissed her, and Anne sighed and put her head down on his shoulder.

'This is pleasant,' said William. 'Don't let us go to the fair.'

But immediately, just like a woman, Anne started up, saying, 'Oh yes, we must. We must go at once. My stepmother will miss us.'

'Why did I mention it?' said William.

He looked about him. 'This is a good cottage. I've never been inside before.' He got up and wandered about the room and peered up the staircase. 'What's it like upstairs? Can you see Stratford?'

'No,' Anne answered, 'only fields.'

But he strolled up the stairs, and she followed him.

'Here's where the children sleep, and here's where I sleep, with Catherine.' She led the way on through the doorway. 'And here's my mother's room. *She* sleeps there now. That's my mother's bed. She brought it with her when she married, as part of her portion.'

Anne looked at it, frowning to think of Joan sleeping in it, first with her father and now alone.

'I'm to have it when I marry.'

She glanced at William, but he had gone to the window and was looking out, leaning his elbows on the window sill. The cattle drowsed in the field, motionless but for the regular swing of their tails. The trees drooped their heads, heavy with foliage, like ladies combing their hair at night. In the garden below, the bees hummed meditatively in the lavender bushes, until it might have been one creature down there, humming to itself and sending its sweet scent upwards. The magic of summer was upon the time of day, with a heat-haze on the meadows, and the air warm and sweet smelling.

'I shall hate to leave all this,' said William, 'when I go to London.'

Behind him, Anne stiffened and clasped her hands, as though she suddenly caught sight of a dangerous enemy. She asked in a voice that she could not keep steady, 'To London?'

William nodded slowly, still looking out of the window. 'My father was talking about it this morning. He thinks he can find me a place up there with a friend of his.'

'But—when?' asked Anne, and now something in her tone caught his attention, and he turned round and smiled at her, and answered, 'Soon, I hope.'

'Why?' cried Anne, still desperately struggling with the incomprehensible. 'Why should you go to London at all?'

'I can't stay in Stratford all my life,' said William, as though it were evident.

'Why not?' said Anne. 'Other folks do.'

William looked at her soberly for a few minutes. Then he said at last, 'I'm not other folks, Anne.'

She was silent for a moment, puzzling over his words, and then, abandoning them, she flung herself away from him and cried out that most honest question which lies at the root of all our questionings, all our lives, 'But what about me? What about me?'

William looked surprised. 'Why, I shall be coming back on visits. The roads to London are good now. I shan't be gone away for ever.'

'You might as well,' said Anne, violently. 'You might as well go now, and never come back again. You don't love me. You never did, or you couldn't leave me.'

'Of course I love you,' replied William, patiently, 'but that has nothing to do with it.'

'It has for me,' said Anne.

They still looked at each other across the bottomless abyss which lay between them—he with his life and his love, and she with her love, and love not enough to bridge the gap.

'I shan't be here when you come back,' said Anne, with sudden deadly calm. 'I'll drown myself in the Avon like Katherine Hamlet did at Tiddington. They said *her* lover wasn't true.'

William caught her by the arm, protesting, 'Anne, I'm true to you. I swear it, and you know it without my swearing.'

'But you don't want to marry me,' she said between clenched teeth, and had her reply in the way he caught his breath and was speechless. 'Oh, let me go,' she cried, trying to free herself. 'You don't love me. You only make a fool of me. She was right. She was right!'

'Anne, listen to me,' said William. 'You don't understand.'

'I understand,' said Anne. 'I understand that you don't love me, and that's enough.' Then she turned on him in a fury, screaming 'Let me go. Let me go.'

And before they knew what was happening they were struggling with each other like mortal foes, William shouting, 'Listen! Anne, will you listen?' and Anne saying, 'Let me go! Let me go!' Then she suddenly went limp in his arms, crying bitterly.

'My poor love,' said William. 'Everything will be all right. Come, kiss me.'

'I can't bear you to leave me,' whispered Anne. 'I can't live without you.'

'I won't leave you. How could I? You're my life, you know that.'

'No,' said Anne. 'I'm not your life, but you are mine. Oh, you are mine!'

She kissed him, with the tears streaming down her face and salt on his lips, until need turned to passion, and passion to a confused and ignorant struggle which found its way to ecstasy.

The bees hummed in the lavender, a blackbird tapped a snail shell on the path, the rooks cawed in the elm trees. The summer's magic was still warm about the cottage, and Anne and William never went to the fair.

# CHAPTER 5

'Well, Mary,' said John Shakespeare at breakfast next morning, 'we shall soon be losing William.'

They all turned to look at William, but he was staring at his father with a startled expression.

'What do you mean?' asked Mary Shakespeare, sharply.

Her husband was smiling. 'I'm giving William a chance to go to London.'

'Oh, wonderful!' cried Joanne.

'God help London,' murmured Gilbert, but not quietly enough to escape his mother's attention, who exclaimed, 'Gilbert! I will not brook these blasphemies!'

'How far away is London?' enquired Richard, who at seven years old had suddenly acquired a slow but persistent desire for miscellaneous information.

'A long way,' answered his mother. 'Now, eat your breakfast, or you'll be late for school. John——'

'Across the sea?' Richard pursued.

'Yes, across—No, of course not. John——'

'Farther than Warwick?'

'Much farther than Warwick, Richard,' his

father broke in. 'And now be quiet. You have learnt enough for one day.' He was still smiling. 'I have arranged for William to go to work with Master Harrison, in Bishopsgate.'

'But, when did you—when did you arrange this?' Mary asked, frowning anxiously. She hated to be surprised, but her husband delighted in surprises, and never seemed to have learned that she did not enjoy them.

'I received the letter from him yesterday. I wrote to him some time ago, suggesting that my son should come to work with him, but I didn't mention it for fear of disappointing William. I know he has set his heart on London.' He nodded pleasantly at William, too happy in his own benevolence to look for a response.

'But, when must he go?' asked Mary.

'I talked of the plan to William yesterday, and said that I thought it would be best if I wrote to Master Harrison, and we awaited a further reply from him. But on thinking it over, I believe William may as well leave at once, while travelling is easy. Master Harrison says he would like him to come "when it suits me to part with him". Well, that would be never, so he may as well go now as later. I shall miss him, but he's young and he has a right to see something of the world before he settles down. Who knows? He may become a wealthy man in London. They say that men make their fortunes every day there.'

65

'Yes, and lose them, too,' said Mary. 'Don't put such ideas into his head. It's enough for him to be a good honest man, and respected in his guild. Nobody wants more of him.'

'Well, well,' said her husband, good-humouredly, 'we shall see. In any case, Will, you shall go away as soon as your mother can get you ready.'

Edmund, unexpectedly, raised his face milkily from his bowl to enquire, 'Will go 'way?'

'Yes, Edmund,' answered Joanne, exult-antly. 'Will's going away.'

Whereupon Edmund turned scarlet, opened his mouth very wide and began to roar. Large tears tumbled out of his eyes, and he chanted tragically through his sobs, 'Will go 'way. Will go 'way.'

'Hush, darling,' said his mother, the tears starting to her own eyes in sympathy. She took him on her lap, whispering, 'William will come back soon.'

Edmund stopped crying abruptly and, looking very woebegone, repeated in a squeaky voice, 'Will co' ba' soon?'

'Yes, love,' said his mother, fondly, 'and then he'll buy you a nice present.'

Edmund considered the matter briefly. Then he reached his hands out to William, suggesting, 'Give. Give.'

Then they all laughed, except William, and Edmund began to laugh too, feeling that he had done something clever, though not sure what it was.

'Father,' began William, and then stopped.

He sat looking down, fumbling with a spoon on the table. Joanne gazed at him in amazement. She had expected to see his face glowing with pleasure and excitement, and instead of that he simply looked sulky, as though they were trying to force him into something he didn't want to do.

'William,' said John Shakespeare, realizing at last that his son's reception of his news lacked something of the expected rapture, 'is anything wrong?'

William looked up at him, and then down again. He took a deep breath and let it go, and said, 'Father, I can't go.'

There was a general exclamation, and Joanne stared at him as though he had suddenly been overcome by lunacy.

'You have taken him by surprise,' said Mary, with some satisfaction. 'It's never good to take people by surprise.'

'Nonsense,' said her husband, irritably. Like most optimistic people, he was inordinately disappointed when his plans went wrong. 'I talked to him about it yesterday, and he was very pleased. He said that there was nothing he wanted more than to go to London.'

'I've changed my mind,' said William.

'Will!' cried Joanne.

His father's face turned slowly red, and he said in a very different tone, 'Then you had better change it back again. Are you trying to make a fool of me, William?'

They all sat very still, and even Gilbert lowered his eyes. Their father was so rarely angry, that when he was it seemed more violent, like a summer thunderstorm after days of fine weather.

'Now wait, John,' said Mary, quickly. 'Wait a minute. Perhaps Will feels that—that it is his duty to stay and help you, while trade is so bad.' She looked at William hopefully over Edmund's fair head, but he still kept his face down, with the set, sullen expression which was so unlike him.

'If I am prepared to let him go——' began John, and then stopped short and looked at his son. 'Is that it, William?'

William shook his head and said, without meeting his father's eyes, 'No. I just don't want to go. I'm sorry, Father.'

A new flood of temper swept over his father's face. 'Sorry! So that is what I must tell Master Harrison. "My son is *sorry*" ' (with infinite contempt) ' "but he has changed his mind." Well, I can tell him something more. I can tell him that I thought that I had a man for my eldest son, but I find that he is only a foolish boy, veering with every wind that blows, like a weather cock.' He got to his feet and stood, leaning his fists on the table. 'William, there must be some reason. I insist upon your telling me the truth.' He waited, and everyone held their breath, and Edmund looked up into his mother's face enquiringly. William still looked at his plate in silence.

'Very well, then,' said his father, and turned to leave.

Gilbert raised his head and said, 'Father.'

John Shakespeare paused, still frowning heavily.

'Father,' said Gilbert, mildly, 'if it would make things better, I could go to London instead.'

William looked up at him sharply, but more, it seemed to Joanne, in anger than relief. John came back.

'You, Gilbert?' he said. 'Yes. Yes, it might answer.' He looked from him to William and back again. 'Yes. I believe Master Harrison would have the best of the bargain yet. And you were only to work for Master Perkins for a short time, until his son was old enough. Would you be ready to leave presently?'

'Yes, Father,' Gilbert answered, and then looked somewhat apprehensively at William.

His father followed his gaze.

'Now, William,' he said, 'you understand that this is your last chance of going to London? If Gilbert takes your place now, you won't find that I shall bestir myself among my friends to find another opportunity for you. If

69

you are going to "change your mind", you had better do it now.'

William looked up at him, and it seemed to Joanne that he had something of a struggle with himself before he replied with even more difficulty than before, 'No—I—I——Gilbert had better go.'

'Very well then,' said his father again. 'Gilbert, come into my workroom and I'll show you Master Harrison's letter, and some other matters.'

Gilbert tried to catch William's eye as he got up, but William resolutely avoided it, pushed his chair back and went out of the house.

During the next two weeks, Joanne felt strongly inclined to curse the obliging Master Harrison, his wife, his business, and everything that was his. It had seemed to her that William had been behaving strangely for some time—wandering off every evening for long, solitary walks, refusing to go to cock fights with Rufus, or to shoot at the butts with Hamnet Sadler, returning late and giving evasive answers to questions. But she had thought that he was working on a poem, or that he was suffering from one of his fits of restlessness from which he would soon recover. Now he was a hundred times worse. All the while Gilbert was preparing to leave Stratford, William hardly appeared in the house at all except when he was working, and he seemed all the time morose and abstracted. Gilbert had several times tried to talk to him, but always got sharply snubbed, and when John Shakespeare, in his buoyant fashion, would speak of Gilbert's prospects in London, of the great opportunities there and of Master Harrison's hopefully childless state, Gilbert glanced anxiously at William, and William pressed his lips together and said nothing.

At last the day came for Gilbert's departure. He was to travel with Master Quiney, who had business in London, and they all got up early to breakfast with him before going to Master Quiney's house to see him set off. After breakfast, Joanne ran upstairs to get a wrap against the cold summer morning. Her mother had gone into the kitchen to put final touches to Gilbert's provisions for the journey, and her father strolled round to supervise the packing of the horse, taking Richard with him.

Joanne came out of her room and stopped short. William was standing moodily looking out of the window, and Gilbert now went up to him and put a hand on his shoulder. Joanne held her breath and kept still, anxious not to interrupt them, and longing for William to say a kind farewell to his brother.

Gilbert said, softly, 'Who is she, Will?'

Then William did look round at him for a moment, before turning back to the window and answering shortly, 'You don't know her.'

'Does she live in Stratford?' asked Gilbert, in the same casual, friendly way.

William shook his head. 'Shottery.'

They were both silent for a while, and Joanne thought that Gilbert would ask something more, but at last he said only, 'Well, good luck to thee, Will.'

William turned to him then, and took his hand and said heartily, 'And to thee, too, Gilbert.'

They shook hands, smiling at each other, and William said in his old way, 'Don't make too much money in London.'

'I'll make all I can,' Gilbert promised, 'and leave the rest for you when you come.'

Then Joanne ran downstairs and their mother hurried out of the kitchen, followed by Edmund, and they all went out of the house together.

It seemed strange, walking back to Henley Street and knowing that Gilbert was already on his way to London. At the last moment, Edmund had realized what was happening, and Gilbert's parting from his family was marked by a loud wail which followed him down the road and in which could be distinguished the words, 'Gil co' ba' soon?' Joanne and William walked slowly back, side by side and in silence, except when Joanne, in an unlucky moment, exclaimed impulsively, 'Just think! Gilbert might be Lord Mayor of London, like Richard Whittington! I wish it was you going, Will.'

He turned on her. 'Don't you suppose *I* do?'

'Then, why didn't you——?' began Joanne, but stopped herself in time, and neither of them spoke again.

Gilbert's going made a great breach in the household. His was the first departure, except for the involuntary partings of death, and it caused a general feeling of loss and ending. They all missed him, his strong face with the clear features and steady eyes and dark hair, his voice at table, mocking, good-humoured and calm, and his friendly detachment which had always evened the balance of their family disagreements. At sixteen, his judgement had already been sound, and his advice given without heat. And perhaps they missed him more because, with his departure, William, too, seemed to have gone from them into some distant country of his own.

Joanne often thought of that conversation between William and Gilbert.

'Who is she?'

'You don't know her.'

'Does she live in Stratford?'

'Shottery.'

She echoed the first question to herself, wondering if William had explained it to Gilbert before she came out of her room. 'Who is she?' Whoever she was, thought Joanne, if she kept William from going to London, I hate her. And if he marries her, Joanne thought, I'll never speak to her. But, after all, she might not have understood what they were talking about, and if William was really in love with a girl he would be always talking about her and praising her, as he had with Judith Staunton. So Joanne forgot about it, as August slipped away, and autumn came, and red leaves fell, and winter trod upon the autumnal heels.

## CHAPTER 6

It was intolerably close in the cottage. The children, shut in all day because of the drizzling rain, were noisy and quarrelsome, and the room reeked of the smell of cooking and the damp odour of the unclean youngest. Anne was sewing, trying as usual to patch some decency into their clothes, and Catherine was making herself a linen cap, assisted and advised by Joan. Now and then they would whisper to each other and giggle, looking across at Anne. She felt their glances and wondered vaguely what mischief they were hatching, but she was too much engaged in trying to sew through a throbbing headache to trouble about them.

At length, Catherine said, 'Your *gentleman*

hasn't been over for a day or two, Anne.'

Anne nearly did not answer, but that old weakness betrayed her into saying, 'This weather isn't fit for walking in.'

'Oh, you think he'll be coming again, then, when it's finer?'

'Of course,' replied Anne.

'Oh,' said Catherine, and nudged Joan and giggled.

'I shouldn't think he'd bother,' said Joan, 'now he's got what he came for.'

Anne could feel her heart beating and her breath shortening. She had to stop sewing because her hand had begun to tremble. But she kept her eyes down on her work and asked, as calmly as she could, 'What do you mean by that?'

'What do I mean by it?' echoed Joan. 'That's a good one! What do I mean by it! I mean what the whole village is talking about, my girl. That's what I mean by it.'

This time Anne refused to answer, and, after waiting for a minute, Joan went on, 'I suppose you won't try to tell us you're not going to have a baby? I saw you letting your kirtle out, my girl, even if you did try to hide it. And you'll find a baby is one thing you can't hide.'

Anne had given up all pretence at sewing and was gazing into the fire, trying to look as though she wasn't listening. Joan raised her voice. 'I met Mrs Bowman this morning. She

75

said to me, "How's Anne?" she said. "Feeling a bit sick in the mornings?" she said. Well, I tell you, I didn't know how to answer her, that I didn't.'

'It's no business of hers,' said Anne.

'Oh, isn't it? I suppose you'll say it's no business of ours either?'

'No, it isn't.'

Joan and Catherine looked at each other, and Catherine pouted her full lips and said, 'Well, I think it is. I'm ashamed to walk through the village now, and I don't know what James thinks. And you was the one,' she went on, with sharpened voice, '*you* was the one as said *I* made myself cheap with all the village! I'd like to hear you say that now!'

'Yes, that's right, she did,' said Joan triumphantly. 'She was always keeping on at me because she thought you stayed out too late. Well, now we can see who made herself cheap!'

Anne gave her sister one look of hatred and then turned her head away again.

'I don't know how you think Catherine's going to make a good marriage,' Joan went on, 'when you make this house look like a bawdy house. And she's always been such a good girl. I wonder you aren't ashamed. But no, not you. You don't care.' She paused, and then went on in the same harrying tone, 'Well, when's he going to marry you? You needn't think you're going to stay in this house, my

76

fine lady! He got you in the mess, and he must marry you.'

'P'raps he won't,' said Catherine, smiling.

'Is he going to marry you, Anne?' demanded Joan.

'Yes.'

'Oh, is he?' said Catherine. 'When?'

Anne looked desperately from one to the other, and then turned to look once more into the fire.

'That's easy answered,' said Catherine. 'Never. I'll tell you what it is, he never meant to marry her. Look how much older she is! She had to do that, to get him to go out with her, but he never meant to marry her. Don't worry, you won't see him round here again.'

'Yes, that's right,' said Joan. 'I could see what he was like, the moment I set eyes on him. Just out for what he could get, that's all.'

Anne got to her feet and gasped out, 'Be quiet! Be quiet!'

'Quiet!' shouted Joan. 'Ah, you're the quiet one! Coming the fine lady over us, and then carrying on like that! You're nothing better than a harlot. I'm ashamed to have the children in the same house with you.'

'Well, you won't any longer,' said Anne, choking. 'I'll never set foot in this house again.'

She ran heavily to the door, scattering the children and their toys, pulled the latch and stumbled outside, and the wind blew the door shut behind her. In the silence that followed they could hear the rain beating on the windows.

'Well!' exclaimed Joan, indignantly. 'Where does she think she's going?'

They both sat looking at the door, as though expecting Anne to reappear.

'Oh, she's a fool,' said Catherine. 'I suppose she thinks we'll go after her.'

'She's always the same,' said Joan. 'Try to say a word for her own good, and she flies out at you. Now did I say anything that wasn't true?'

'Some people can't stand the truth,' said Catherine.

'That's right.'

They were both still looking expectantly at the door, and presently Joan said, uneasily, 'I'd better go after her. She'll get so wet.'

'She'll come back when she's had enough,' answered Catherine, carelessly.

'Still, I don't want her to make herself ill,' said Joan. She clicked her teeth and shook her head despondently. 'P'raps if Thomas went out after her. She'll only be in the garden crying.' But before Thomas could refuse, which he undoubtedly would have, they were interrupted by a loud knock on the door.

'That's not Anne,' said Joan, startled. 'It sounds more like—— Open the door, Catherine.'

Catherine straightened her dress and ran

her fingers through her curls and licked her lips and went to open the door. William stood in the rain outside, and she smiled up at him and said, 'Oh! Come in,' and brushed against him as he stepped inside and she shut the door.

He looked round the room and saw Joan sitting by the fire looking frightened, and the children staring open-mouthed up from the floor. Catherine stood close beside him, degradingly attractive, with her dress tight over her breasts, and her gap-toothed, beckoning smile. On the floor, as though it had been dropped in a sudden departure, was a child's shirt. The room was close and smoke-filled, and smelled dirty.

'Where's Anne?' he said sharply.

He saw a quick look pass between Joan and Catherine, before Joan answered, 'In the garden.'

'What, in this rain?' he exclaimed, and glanced at the window, as though he needed to learn that it was raining.

'P'raps she wanted to drown herself,' said Catherine, and in her spiteful voice and flickering eyes he saw that she knew the truth.

He looked from Joan to Catherine and back again, and then, with a muttered exclamation, turned and thrust the door open, kicking it shut behind him.

The garden lay under the grey dusk of the winter's evening. The rain fell steadily, beating on the path and dripping through the leaves and the bare spikes of the lavender bushes. He walked round the corner of the house, and found the garden empty.

'The river!' he thought. 'Oh God, not the river!' He stood still, with his hand on his wet forehead, trying to think what he ought to do. He felt suddenly that he was too young to be faced with such problems as these, the sleepless nights, the troubled meetings, the guilt and secrecy. As he stood there alone on the corner, with the wind and rain beating against him, he felt the burden intolerably heavy. For a moment, even the immediate single task of looking for Anne seemed more than he could manage. He thought of Katherine Hamlet, dragged down in the weeds of the river at Tiddington, and the breath came sobbing in his throat.

It seemed a long time before he moved, but in fact it was only a few seconds. On an impulse, he did not go down to the lane but scrambled up through a gap in the hedge into the fields, his feet slipping in the mud. He looked round the waste of sodden stubble and was about to turn back, when he saw her, crouching down by the hedge. He ran across to her, calling her name, but she did not look round, and when he reached her, he saw that her head was down on her knees. He knelt beside her in the wet grass and took her by the shoulders so that she raised her head, but she did not look at him. The wet ran down her face and her hair clung to her cheeks but she wasn't crying.

'Anne,' he cried, 'you must come in. You'll catch cold.'

'I wish I could,' she said. 'I wish I could die of it, and the baby too.'

Then there was a sudden cloudburst, and for a few minutes it was like a nightmare, with William trying to raise her to her feet, and Anne resisting him, and the rain, the rain pouring down on them until it was as though they were struggling in the sea with waves breaking over their heads. And their words were disjointed too, like the words of swimmers in deep waters. William did not know what he said, but he heard Anne crying out, 'I can't bear it, oh, I can't bear it!' and he saw the calm of her face, which had first made him love her, broken and distorted, with a look of madness upon it, and her grey eyes wild and staring, blinking against the rush of the rain.

At last he got her to her feet and his cloak round her, and he half carried her across the field and down into the garden. At the door of the cottage, she began to struggle again, saying, 'No! Not in there. No, I won't'

'You must, Anne,' he said, in a voice of desperation. 'Please, my dear love, come inside.'

Then she yielded and let him take her

indoors, and she crouched on the settle, looking into the fire with narrowed eyes like one in mortal pain. William took her shoes off, kneeling in front of her, and tried to warm her feet in his cold hands. Catherine stood on the other side of the room and looked at them, saying nothing, making no movement, and by the light of the flaring tallow he could see the children's faces, standing by the table staring, like curious calves by a gate.

Joan Hathaway came downstairs carrying a blanket, and William stood back while she put it round Anne's shoulders and poked the fire into a blaze. Anne seemed quite unconscious of her presence, and of William's.

'She'll be all right now,' said Joan, in an unexpectedly kind voice.

William hesitated. He hated to leave her in such company, but it was getting late.

'I'll get her to bed as soon as she's warmer,' Joan added. 'You leave her to me.'

William bent over to kiss Anne, and she reached up and clung to him, pulling him down on one knee.

'I must go now, love.'

'No, Will, don't leave me.'

'I must,' he said. 'I'll be here tomorrow.'

She still clutched him fiercely, and whispered, 'Will, you've got to take me away. You've got to tell them today.'

'Well, I'll try,' he said, doubtfully.

'You've *got* to,' she cried. She put her head

down on his shoulder and sobbed wildly. 'Promise me you will. You said you'd take me away before Advent. Promise me you'll tell them today.'

'I promise,' he said.

He lifted her up, and she leant back against the settle. William took his cloak and hat and went silently to the door. He looked back and saw Catherine still motionless, watching him out of the corner of her eyes, and Joan heating something at the fire, and Anne leaning back, crying hopelessly, with her eyes shut. Then he went out and shut the door quietly behind him and set off homeward.

He had been wet before, but he was soaked through long before he reached Stratford. The footpath, which he had trodden so often through meadowsweet and grasshoppers and summer fragrance, was now a morass in which he slipped and stumbled painfully between dank grasses.

By the time he reached Stratford, it was nearly dark. From each overhanging upper storey a rush of water fell, and on the corner a sharp gust of wind flung the rain against his face, contemptuously, like a housewife flinging a bucket of water down her steps. As he turned into Henley Street, he slipped on the cobbles, and the gutter, running high with rain-water, splashed him nearly to the waist. He swore out loud and pulled his cloak more tightly about him, and walked on heavily and wearily, more like a man of fifty than a boy of eighteen. He stood for a moment outside the house and looked up. There were no stars, but heavy clouds ran across the sky like enraged armies seeking a battle.

He pulled the latch and went silently into the house.

# CHAPTER 7

It had been an annoying day for Mary Shakespeare. Directly after breakfast, when she saw what the weather was like, she had resolved to put her store cupboard in order. With this intention she gave Margaret, the maidservant, her orders for the day, told Joanne to look after Edmund, and settled down for some quiet hours with those inanimate objects over which she had complete control. It was her habit always to tidy her store cupboard or her linen chests when the affairs of her family were in some disorder. It was some compensation to her to feel that those things at least which were within her power were perfectly ordered and her household objects ranged each in its proper place.

She managed her house, as far as possible, in the style of her father's house, Asbies, at Wilmcote. It had always remained in her mind as a standard by which she judged all housekeeping. The big, shining kitchen at Asbies, the spotless dairy, the row of preserves on the shelves, the herbs and spices, these were the things she missed when she left home, and she had never had a house large enough to reproduce them. She missed her stepmother, Agnes, with her dark hair and her old-fashioned gown, directing her household like a queen her ministers—the men and maids and her seven stepdaughters. No one had ever seen Agnes angry, or even surprised. She never raised her voice. Her husband had been a friend of Robert Arden's, and the little Arden girls had always loved to visit her, to be given sweetmeats and to hear the stories of the great wars which she had heard from her father. (Agnes never forgot that her father was a gentleman, just as Robert Arden never forgot that he was related to the old family of the Ardens of Park Hall.) And when Robert was made a widower, and Agnes was widowed, nothing could be more natural, or seem more fitting, than that they should marry, enjoying a mutual respect and the quiet affection of his seven home-loving daughters.

Into the calm of this well-ordered household had come the disquieting proposal of marriage from John Shakespeare. Mary was kept behind after her sisters had gone to bed, to discuss the matter.

'You will remember the young man, Mary,'

said her father. 'He came to the house last week for the Harvest Home, and I think you talked to him.'

'Yes, Father,' Mary answered.

She had not thought about him since that night, but she certainly did remember his fair, curly hair and beard, and his fresh complexion and blue eyes.

'He seemed a worthy young man,' said Robert Arden, 'and his father is a good tenant. That Snitterfield property is much improved since he took it. I have made enquiries in Stratford, and I find that young Shakespeare is well thought of. He is a freeman of the Mystery of the Glovers, Whittawers and Collarmakers, and it seems likely that he may one day be a prominent man in Stratford.'

'But, of course,' Agnes put in, in her delicate voice, 'he is not a gentleman.'

'Ay, there's the point,' Robert agreed, heartily. 'There's no denying I'd hoped for a better match for you, Mary.' He leant back in his chair, clasping his fine, aristocratic hands, a little swollen with rheumatism. 'At first I thought of refusing his father's proposal immediately. But then, I considered that I am a man with seven daughters and not a large property, and it seemed that it merited some discussion at least.' He turned to his wife and enquired, 'What do you think, my dear?'

Agnes answered slowly, 'I think as you do, that it is not all we could have wished, but it is not to be lightly refused.' She added, kindly, 'What do you think of it, Mary? Can you like this young man?'

Mary sat for a long time, thinking. She thought of his handsome face and good dress. She thought of the pleasures of town life, with shops and crowds and excitement. Above all, she thought of the way John Shakespeare had talked to her, of his ambitions and his certainty that he would make his way in the world. Had he not already moved far away from his father's smallholding at Snitterfield? Was he not already known and respected in Stratford? And, even though they might never be more than yeomen themselves, yet at least their children might marry well, and their sons be gentlemen.

'Yes,' she said. 'Yes, I think I might like him.'

'Very well,' answered her father. 'We will think more of the matter.'

Robert Arden did not live to see the marriage take place, but Agnes, grieved but not grief-stricken, made the final arrangements, and Mary left Asbies for her own small house in Stratford. She had never really regretted it. John's business continued to improve. He was chosen as Chamberlain in Stratford, and made himself so useful that he acted as Deputy Chamberlain for the next two years. The year after William's birth he was chosen Alderman, and then he was actually chosen to be Bailiff. That was the most triumphant day of his life, and Mary was no less proud. With what dignity that year did he preside over the councils and act as Justice of the Peace! With what pleasure did Mary hear him spoken of as 'the Bailiff', instead of merely as 'Master Shakespeare'! The year that Anne, their younger daughter was born, he was chief Alderman, and once more Justice of the Peace. He bought two more houses in Stratford, and gave lavishly to the poor. And then——

He had been drawn so reasonably into disaster, led by good sense as well as by ambition. He bought the skins of his trade from farmers, and so it was only policy to lend money that they might buy more land and better beasts. He supplied wool to cottage weavers, allowing them to make their cloth at his expense and to pay him as they sold it, himself at once patron and partner in their labours. And when his ventures proved successful he had undertaken commissions to lay out money for other men, enjoying the sensation of involving his fellow-citizens in his own prosperity, and in the prosperity of the country.

But the tide of success, which had carried him so cheerfully along, ebbed with alarming suddenness, leaving him floundering on the shore, and others involved in his disaster as in his triumph. Disease among the cattle and sheep and the consequent foreclosure of some mortgages meant that farmers could not pay him what they owed him, and he could not pay others. Some weavers failed to sell their cloth, and others betrayed their trust, spending the money they should have used to repay him, and this, combined with the loss of his own trade to foreign glovemakers, first stretched his resources, then exhausted his credit, and at last brought him to the edge of ruin.

Mary, on the evening when he sat down and told her, looked at him in astonished disbelief. How could a man who had been bailiff of Stratford-upon-Avon now be in imminent danger of arrest for debt, and for a debt which he saw no possibility of paying?

'Everything is lost,' said John Shakespeare, putting his head in his hands. 'I shall have to sell this house and the shop, and then how can I make a living? My poor children!' and he wept.

Mary sat in silence, looking at him. She perceived, with an unexpected flash of ironic amusement, that the very quality which had brought him to the highest civic honours had also carried him into this danger, which a man less gifted, but also less sanguine, would have escaped. And, at the same time, she felt a sudden warmth towards him, greater than she had ever felt for him before. He needed her now as he had never needed her in the years of easy, assured prosperity.

'Come, now,' she answered, comfortably. 'It's not so bad as that. There's my property at Wilmcote and my interest in Snitterfield. We've land to sell or mortgage.'

'No, no,' said John. 'We always meant that to go to the children. I won't rob them of their inheritance.'

'The children,' replied Mary, coolly, 'would rather lose their inheritance than be turned out into the streets.' She eyed him with some impatience, as he still sat with his face in his hands. 'Come, come,' she said, as though he were one of the boys, 'bring a pen and paper to the table, and work out how much you owe and what we need to dispose of. No doubt if we do mortgage the property we can get it back in a few years, when business has improved.'

'Yes, that's true,' said John, brightening with alarming swiftness. 'Business will not always be as bad as it has been this year. If I can only pay off these debts, I have a plan which will make my fortune. I was talking to Adrian Quiney yesterday, and he said——'

'Let us have no more fortunes,' said Mary hastily. 'Let us earn our bread, and pay our debts, and live like honest folk.'

Mary's inheritance had tided over the troubles, but John Shakespeare's affairs had been in low waters ever since. She often had recourse to her store room, comforting herself with cool, orderly shelves, and all the signs of a provident housewife.

The worst time of all came a year later when Anne died. When Mary came back from the burial, she felt for a moment that she could not take up again the burden laid upon her. Already pregnant once more, she had never felt less desirous of bearing a child. Richard was overflowing with five-year-old noise and high spirits, always rushing about and shouting. John was passing through one of his fits of depression, and crept about the house looking guilty and melancholy, and although she told herself that he wasn't enjoying it, yet she had a secret conviction that he *was*. When she walked into the house after the funeral, she wondered what they would all do if she stood still in the middle of the room and started to scream. Joanne had gone straight upstairs to the little bedroom she had shared with Anne, and was sobbing there, wildly and hysterically. Mary knew that she should go up and comfort her, but horrified herself by a strong desire to take hold of Joanne and give her a good whipping instead. Richard had picked up a stool and was banging it monotonously and intolerably on the floor, while Gilbert, lounging at the window, watched him but made no move to stop him. Mary found his air of detachment and reserve almost as annoying as Joanne's abandonment to grief. John had tip-toed through into his workroom and shut the door, leaving her to take up the threads of family life again, as though nothing had happened. For a moment Mary stood quite still, struggling against that violent dislike of her family which, once in ten years, overcomes every good mother. The gusty April wind sighed through the windows in the intervals of Richard's knocking. Then William came into the house. He had stayed behind to talk to Mistress Hart and to dispatch her safely homewards, and he came straight up to his mother, put his arm round her shoulders and guided her to the chair by the fire. He took the stool away from Richard, said over his shoulder, 'Gilbert, you might take Richard out to the kitchen, and tell Margaret to hurry the dinner,' and went upstairs.

The dreadful crying stopped at once, and Mary, lying back in the unaccustomed luxury of idleness, knew that the worst moment was past. Warmth came slowly back to her chilled feet, and she closed her eyes, weary with troubled and wakeful nights. She could hear Richard's voice, young and exuberant in the kitchen, and upstairs she could hear the quiet murmur of William's comfort to his sister. That was William's great gift, she thought, that ability to understand other people's feelings, even while he suffered himself. One might almost say that people were his trade, that he knew and loved them as John knew and loved a fine pair of gloves or a good skin. But to William, all people were good. He would never throw them aside, as John did a spoiled glove, for this fault or that weakness. It was almost as though he loved them for that very failing which to others made them seem worthless. He would listen with every appearance of interest to Adrian Quiney's interminable business anecdotes, because, he said, poor Master Quiney had nothing else to talk about. He never ran from Mistress Hart, as the rest of them did, because, he said, she made him laugh. He even bore with his Uncle Henry Shakespeare, with his bawdy tales and his nudges and his crafty, twisted ways in money matters. And yet he didn't overlook their faults, or even endeavour to moralize upon them, but rather seemed to note them with an amused fondness that had in it nothing of patronage or of superiority, only understanding.

Ah yes, thought Mary Shakespeare now, wiping down the shelf with a clean cloth, but you didn't make money out of people, as you did out of a good pair of gloves. It was William's future that was causing her anxiety at the moment. She had never been much troubled about the other boys. Gilbert had always been the most brilliant of the family, the most certain to succeed, uniting his remarkable intellectual gifts with an independence of spirit which seemed to show, even from childhood, that he would be able to make his own way in the world. And Mary felt confident about Richard's future for entirely different reasons. Richard was always much slower than the others, constantly a little bewildered by their laughter, though never disconcerted by it. He was, in fact, extraordinarily like his grandfather, for whom he was named, Richard Shakespeare. Unambitious, and of an easy temper, he was likely to succeed because he would never attempt too much. Mary was quite convinced that he would become a respectable tradesman and live and die in Stratford. As for Edmund— Mary's face softened, as it always did when she thought of him. Edmund was undoubtedly her favourite and he was the only one of her children whom she had ever spoiled. It was not simply that he was the baby, and six years younger than Richard. It was not only that he had come to take her mind off Anne's illness and death, setting up his loud and buoyant wail in the house of mourning. No, it was rather that Edmund, more than any of the others, demanded spoiling. He was beautiful, sturdy and determined. He always knew what he wanted and went out to get it. He learnt to crawl very early, and very fast, scuttling about the room like a vociferous crab. But, crawling being still too slow for his needs, he very soon learnt to walk, stumping about with an unsteady firmness and clutching any taller person who came near him, with an engaging certainty of his welcome. And now he was talking, much earlier than had any of the others, and more irresistible than ever with his squeaky voice and grave mimicry. Oh, Edmund would be great, thought Mary. He would be a famous man one day.

But William, dear as he was to her as the eldest son, reliable and gentle and always to be trusted, William was not like the others. She knew that he was ambitious, and, but for his father's money difficulties, she would have hoped that he might go to the University. But, with that ambition, instead of Gilbert's self-sufficiency, or Edmund's self-assertiveness, he seemed to have a curious yielding quality in his nature, a tenderness that boded ill for his success in times when, as the saying went, it was 'every man for himself and God for us all!'

Mary had been pleased when Gilbert went to London instead of William, feeling that he, with his reserve and coolness, was more fitted for such a venture, though she still wondered why William had refused to go. But, since Gilbert's departure, William seemed to have become more and more restless as time went by. He took long walks alone, avoiding all company and enquiries. He looked ill, and suddenly older, and was less sweet-tempered than he used to be. Mary began to think that it might be a good idea if John sent William to visit Gilbert in London. She was considering this, and dusting the second shelf in her store cupboard, when Joanne ran in, whispering with a look of mingled mirth and horror,

'Mistress Hart has come, and Margaret says she wants to see you.'

Mary cast her eyes up to heaven. 'No!' she said. 'Not this morning!'

'Shall I tell her you're out?' enquired Joanne, always ready to abet mischief.

Mary sighed resignedly. 'No, I'll come.'

Mistress Hart greeted her delightedly, her round, red face beaming like a too zealous sun. 'Well, it is nice to see you! I haven't come to stay.'

No, thought Mary, bitterly, you never have.

'I just ran in to see what news you had of Gilbert in London. Such a wonderful opportunity, going to London! I often say to William—my William, that is—that if he worked harder, he might get chances like that. But then, Gilbert is so clever—and William, too, of course—your William, I mean. But my William just says to me, well the Shakespeare boys and Dick Quiney work so hard that no one else in Stratford needs to, but, of course, I say to him, that's nonsense, William, I say.'

'Won't you sit down?' asked Mary, over the last part of the sentence.

'But when William was a little boy—oh, thank you, but I'm not going to stay. I know how busy you are. I just called in to see if there was any news of Gilbert.' And she settled herself comfortably by the fire. 'When William was a little boy, he was just the same.

He'd rather do anything than work at school. I remember once Mistress Stone saying to me— you remember her, she was left a widow with three children, or was it four? No, I think it was four, but one had died, so it was three. I heard that she married later, in Warwick. She went to live with her brother there, or was it her sister? No, I think it was her brother, because I remember she used to tell me that she never liked him, and it seemed so strange to me that she should go to live there, if she never liked him, but you know how it is, I suppose she was glad to go there, because he was quite a rich man, you know. Well, when I say rich, he wasn't poor, you know. Though of course it might not have been her brother. It might have been her sister's husband. But still, I heard she got married again, but who it was she married, I never did know. But, of course, she hadn't much portion, and then with three children, or four, but, no, I'm almost sure it was only three, because her youngest died when she was living next door to me. Well, she said to me, if William worked, he could be quite a clever boy. Yes, I said, if he'd work, but you know how it is, Mistress Stone, I said, you have children of your own, and they *won't* work if they can help it.'

Then, there's Joanne, thought Mary Shakespeare. The time will soon come when we must find her a husband.

97

'No indeed,' she agreed with Mistress Hart, 'they won't.'

With Joanne's sharp tongue and shrewish ways, she thought, we mustn't leave the matter too late. When her younger sister was alive, Joanne had been quieter and more obedient. But since Anne's death she seemed to have a kind of wildness, as though she had buried her gentler self with her sister, and now faced the world armed against tenderness, ready to repel it with wit and mockery. And she was too much encouraged in this by her father and her brothers. In a year or two, thought Mary, we must get her married. There weren't many men in Stratford of the right standing and character, but the most likely would be Robert Brown. He was industrious and sober minded, and it was a good thing that he was considerably older than Joanne, because he would have more control over her than if they were of an age.

'I know that when my poor husband was alive,' Mistress Hart was saying, 'he used to say that William got just as tired through trying not to work as anyone else did by working. I remember once—dear, how we laughed!—his father was going to haul some logs in, and he wanted William to help him. Well, of course, William didn't want to, and so on the morning when he thought his father was going to do the job, he went off very early in the morning, and never came back all day. I

98

think he'd gone poaching with your William. Those two boys! The mischief they get up to together! Oh well, they don't do much harm, I dare say, and you're only young once, aren't you? Well, William came back, late at night, tired out and covered with mud, and empty-handed into the bargain. And he said to his father, he said, "Did you haul the logs all right, Father?" And then his father said, "Oh, we weren't going to do that today, William. You needn't worry, we'll be able to do it together tomorrow." You ought to have seen William's face! Laugh! How we laughed!' Mary smiled absently. It would be a good thing, she thought, if Will did go to London, for then he would see less of Rufus, who had always had a bad influence upon him. And bad for Joanne, too, to go about the town with Will and Rufus. All that jesting and laughing was bad for Joanne's reputation. A young girl should be sober and silent, not witty and shrewd.

'But, there! he's a good son to me,' said Mistress Hart. 'Since my poor husband died, William's been a good boy. I suppose he'll be finding himself a wife one of these days. Though, of course, it's early days yet, and William has never been one to run after the girls. The truth is, I don't think he's ever been in love, and that's a fact. Not like your William. Bless the boy, how he used to pine for Judith, before she married Hamnet Sadler.

I hear she leads him such a life now. Mistress Perkes was saying how she scolds him from morning to night, and tells him he's so slow and stupid—well, of course, he is slow, there's no denying it, but still, a man has a right to speak in his own house. Of course, my husband used to tell me that I talked too much, but still, we never did quarrel, and he didn't like to talk much himself, so I used to say, well, I talk for both of us, and I suppose I still do, for the Lord knows he's silent enough now, poor soul, but still, it's what we must all come to, in the end, isn't it?'

'Yes, it is,' Mary agreed.

She would have to persuade John to break his word about that having been Will's last chance of London, and he could be obstinate when he had once made a decision. But she could usually bend him when she made up her mind to something. It should be easy enough to find some pretext for William to go up to town—some business letter that he could carry up to Master Harrison. And then, after the visit, he would settle down again. He loved Stratford too much ever to want to live his life in London.

'Though I did hear that William had found a new love,' said Mistress Hart, with a gleam in her eye. 'But still, you never know how true these things are—I heard that Robert Brown was getting married two years ago, but nothing ever came of it. But, of course,

William's very young yet, and I didn't hear anything else, but that he'd been seen with a girl during the summer, and folks wondered if anything would come of it. But, I dare say you've heard all about it?'

Mary Shakespeare started at the direct question, and answered hastily and at random, 'No, no I haven't.'

And then she wondered for an instant whether Mistress Hart might have been talking of Will, and not of Rufus. She couldn't now enquire, which of them it was, because that would show not only that she hadn't been listening, but also that she had answered without knowing at all what Mistress Hart was talking about. She began to listen now with unusual attention.

'Of course, I often say to William' (Ah, it was Rufus, thought Mary with satisfaction), 'you want to be like my William, I say, and snap your fingers at all the girls.' (Or *was* it?) 'But then, William says, oh, he says, the danger isn't in too many loves, he says, but in one.'

She broke off to laugh, leaving Mary entirely confused and hardly able to produce the faintest smile. But it *must* be William Hart, she thought. A secret love affair was just the sort of mischief that Rufus would indulge in. But yet that doubt joined to William's refusal to go to London, to his sudden ageing and his long absences from the house, and made a small whirlpool of disquietude in Mary's mind, drawing her thoughts uselessly and against her will.

Mistress Hart rose reluctantly, saying, 'Well, I must be going. I only called in to see how Gilbert was getting on.'

'Very kind of you,' said Mary, dryly.

'Yes, well, I always say, neighbours should take an interest in each other's affairs. Ah, there's Joanne'—who was caught in mid-flight half-way up the stairs—'well, I am glad to see her. What a fine girl she's growing, isn't she? We shall have her married soon, with all this talk of lovers. Well, Joanne, how are you, my dear? That's right, you look well. Goodbye, Mistress Shakespeare. You must come and visit me some time, and then we can have a long gossip.' And off she went at last, her face glowing with satisfaction and friendly feelings.

'My whole morning wasted,' said Mary, looking murderously after her.

'Poor Rufus,' said Joanne. 'If I had her for a mother, I should run mad.'

'Oh, would you?' said Mary, turning on her. 'Well, when you get a little older, you'll learn more patience. And, as for William Hart, he shouldn't speak disrespectfully of his mother.'

'But he doesn't!' cried Joanne, suddenly flushing.

'I should think not,' said Mary. 'She's a better mother than he deserves. That idle good-for-nothing!' and she went briskly back to her store room, feeling obscurely gratified.

But no sooner was she there than screams from the kitchen announced that Margaret, the maid, had upset boiling water over her arm, and Mary had to bind it up, scolding her for carelessness as she did so. Then Mary had herself to finish cooking the dinner, and serve it with Joanne's haphazard assistance. Then Edmund refused to stay with Joanne, and insisted on coming to help his mother, disarranging all that she had done, and upsetting a pot of preserves on the floor. It was nearly suppertime before she had sent Edmund off to bed and reached the last shelf. She had just replaced the big jar of salt, and was straightening her aching back, when she heard the front door open softly. She stepped quickly to the door of the sitting-room, and was in time to see William go out, pulling his cloak about him and hastily shutting the door behind him. For an instant she thought of calling after him, to ask him where he was going, but she knew that she would be too late. By the time she reached the door and had opened it, he would be out of earshot, walking swiftly, perhaps, in order that he might escape such questioning. His father, surely, would never send him out on an errand at this hour, and in the rain too. Mary stood motionless in the doorway, the cloth still in her hand, feeling that something which she had depended on for a long time was crumbling away.

William was late home that night. The supper table was laid and they were all sitting down before he silently opened the door and came dripping in from the dark street.

'You're late,' said Mary. 'Where have you been?'

William was shaking his cloak and didn't seem to hear her. He came forward, asking, 'Is Edmund upstairs?'

'Yes,' said Mary. 'Didn't you say good night to him before you went out?'

'No,' said William, awkwardly, 'I didn't know—I——. I'll go up now.'

'Yes, you'd better. And take off your wet clothes. Where did you get all that mud on them? Put your father's gown on. And then come down again at once,' she called after him as he started upstairs. 'We should have had supper before this, if we hadn't had to wait for you.'

In the chatter of Joanne and Richard and the cheerful talk of John Shakespeare, the silence of William and his mother passed unnoticed. He looked so young in his father's furred gown, and so weary, that she hadn't the heart to question him any more, and decided to leave matters as they were for a while. The children went off to bed, and John took a candle, saying that he had a little work to finish. Mary moved about the room, tidying up, and William sat by the fire. But, as John opened the workroom door, William stood up and said, 'Just a minute, Father. There's something I want to tell you.'

Mary looked up at him sharply, Richard's little wooden sword in her hand.

'Tonight?' she said. 'Your father has work to do, and you should be in bed. Leave it until tomorrow morning.'

'No!' said William, in a kind of suppressed fury. 'No, it must be tonight.'

His father paused in the doorway, the candlestick in his hand. They both waited for William to speak, and he stood and looked at the floor, like an actor with all eyes upon him who has forgotten his lines. At last he said breathlessly and with an air of desperate improvisation, 'I want to be married.'

There was a long silence, and then his mother said, with a rare, shrill note in her voice, 'Who is the girl?'

William answered constrainedly, 'You don't know her.'

John shut the door and came back into the room and put down his candlestick.

'Well, well, we shall have time to get to know her,' he said, cheerfully. 'Does she live in the town?'

'No,' William replied, 'at Shottery.'

'And how long have you known this girl?' enquired his mother. 'It seems strange that we have never met her.'

'Since June,' William answered.

His father laughed. 'What, met the lady in

105

June, and already talking of marriage? No, no, that's too much haste. We must meet her parents and see if they would consent to a betrothal, but you must remember that you are young yet, Will. The old saying is true, "Marry in haste and repent at leisure."' William looked straight at his father, flushing hotly.

'We want to be married this month, or next,' he said.

There was another silence. His father was suddenly grave. The old clock ticked noisily, and in the street the nightwatchman made his first round. Mary Shakespeare rapped on the table with the broken wooden sword and said fiercely, 'William, do you *have* to marry this girl? Have you got her with child?'

She saw him wince, but he did not answer. She felt the day's irritations mounting within her, until at last they broke into sudden, violent rage.

'You must be mad!' she cried. 'How dare you come here and say you want to marry this country wench, who, because you have tumbled her in the hay, must needs claim that you're the father of her child! I'll have you remember that you come of good stock, William Shakespeare. No wonder she wants to trap you, but you weren't the first, I'll be bound. There were others before you. Let them marry the girl!'

'But, it—it wasn't like that,' said William,

106

with difficulty. 'She—you don't know her.'

'I know enough to know that she's no honest woman, for if she were, she wouldn't be with child.'

He was silent again. Mary struck the table once more and shouted at him, 'I had rather see you in your grave than married to a whore!'

William turned on her a face that frightened her and took away all her anger. He said in a cold, deadly voice that she had never heard from him before, 'Mother, if you ever speak of Anne like that again, I will leave this house for ever. Anne is to be my wife. Her child is my child, and all the fault was mine.'

They stood looking at each other across the room, and Mary felt a great sickness and weariness, as though she had been poisoned. Or rather, it was as though they were both deathly sick, imprisoned together, and unable to help each other.

John cleared his throat. 'Now, wife,' he said, in his calm, cheerful voice, 'now, let us sit down and talk this matter over. Sit down, William. This has been a shock to your mother. This is a serious affair to broach like this, unexpectedly and late in the evening.'

William leant against the settle. Mary Shakespeare sat down, heavily, her hands in her lap, and gazed at the dying fire. She thought that John had never before seemed so dependable, so reasonable and judicial. 'First, what is her name, William?' he asked. 'And do we know her father?'

'Her father was Richard Hathaway, sometimes called Richard Gardener,' William answered. 'He died last year.'

'Then who does she live with now? Her mother is alive?'

'No, she lives with her stepmother. She's very unhappy with her. They dislike each other, and——'

'Why should she dislike her stepmother?' Mary broke in. 'That is no commendation. I have no patience with such nonsense.'

'Mary,' said her husband, 'give me a few minutes, please. Now, William, let us get this clear. You have been meeting this young girl since June, without your parents' knowledge, and she now bears your child?'

William nodded silently.

'And has she other guardians than her stepmother?'

'She has one brother, Bartholomew, a year younger than she is.'

'A young, fatherless, unprotected girl,' said John. 'William, this is not what we would have expected of you.' He paused, and something more than the fire was dying in the quiet room—a long trust and confidence, a close family relationship, a mutual esteem. They all three felt it die, and grieved for it. John continued, 'When is the child due to be born?'

'In May.'

Mary moved quickly, and broke in, 'But there is no need to marry her, Will. The matter can be patched up. Perhaps we can find a husband for the girl.'

'No!' said John. And he was no longer William's father, but the former bailiff of Stratford. 'The child is William's, and he must marry the girl.'

'Oh, God!' cried William, in a choked voice. 'I *want* to marry her. I love her.'

'A fine love,' said John, coolly, 'to betray her innocence! We must see the minister, and have banns put up as soon as may be.'

'Anne wishes to be married outside Stratford,' said William, too quickly.

'Anne wishes!' exclaimed his mother. 'Let her be thankful to be married at all!'

'Mary,' said John again. 'The girl has a right to choose. But I'm afraid we shall not be able to have the banns called before Advent season.'

'We thought that we could get a licence,' said William, and then, as his mother looked up, he corrected himself. 'That is to say, *I* thought that I could get it. And also, it might be thought that the child was born before its time, if we had been married nearly six months.'

'I see you have it all planned,' said John, drily. 'One might think you were old in the art. Well, we'll talk more of this tomorrow.

You had better bring the girl—Anne—to see us. Then we will meet her stepmother and brother and arrange a settlement. I suppose she has no dowry?'

'She has a small inheritance,' answered William, doubtfully. 'I don't know how much.'

'Not much, if I know anything of the matter,' said his mother. 'Shottery folk were always shiftless.'

'Enough, enough,' said John, wearily. He took his candle and went towards the stairs. 'Come to bed, Mary,' he said. 'Such things are best discussed in the morning when we are not tired.' He looked towards his son, and sighed. 'Put out the light, William, and come up to bed. This is a sad business, but we will mend it as best we can.'

'Good night, Will,' said his mother, but she made no move to kiss him, as she usually did.

She went up with her husband, and they both undressed in silence, because there seemed to be nothing worth saying.

'I haven't heard Will come upstairs,' said John, at last.

'I'll go and see,' she replied.

She went out on the landing, in her nightgown, with her greying hair in its thick plait down her back, and saw William sitting by the embers of the fire, with his head in his hands.

In a quick rush of tenderness she went

downstairs and put her arms round him, and he turned with a sob and rested his face against her bosom, whispering, 'Oh, Mother, Mother.'

'There, Will,' she said, 'there. Everything will be all right.' He raised his head to say, urgently, 'I love her, Mother.'

'There, of course you do. We will take care of her. She shall be just like another daughter to us.'

She stopped short, remembering that other Anne, dead in her child's virginity, timelessly innocent. Could they put this woman in her place? But William was still clinging to her thankfully. She said, gently, 'Come to bed, Will. You need some sleep. Don't worry any more. All will be well.'

They went upstairs together, and she kissed him, and heard him go quietly along to the bed he shared with Richard. She lay down with a warmth about her heart still, to think how he had clung to her. But presently that left her, and she lay awake until morning, listening to her husband's snoring, and the rain beating on the window, and the watchman's voice, thinking of the girl, and of William, ill-matched at eighteen, and wondering how it could have been William who had done this—of all people, William!

# CHAPTER 8

'Come in, come in,' called John Shakespeare. 'Come in out of the snow. William, take Master Quiney's hat and cloak. Joanne, do you not see? here is Mistress Quiney and Mistress Hart. Our maid is in the kitchen, seeing to the dinner. I'll wager you had rather she stayed there, hey? The children will take your things. Joanne, shake the snow off before you hang them up. Here, Richard, you're not too young to help. Come in, come in. It's good to see you.'

His hearty voice, and the bustle of arrivals, filled the room. Behind him stood his wife, and Anne, silent.

'Now, Mistress Quiney, here is my wife, and here is my new daughter, Mistress Anne. Anne, here is Master Quiney. What, is young Dick not here?'

'He's coming with his wife,' replied Adrian Quiney, with the solemnity that attended all his remarks and had given him the reputation of being a very wise man.

'Ah, yes,' cried John, 'I forgot that he was married. How these children grow up, Adrian! Was that another knock at the door?' And he hurried away.

112

'You don't come from Stratford?' enquired Mistress Quiney, a pale-eyed, mournful woman, with the air of one perpetually upon the brink of a deep sleep.

'No, from Shottery,' Anne replied.

'Are your parents here? I don't see them.'

'No, my—my stepmother and my sister are coming here later. They had to go home in between, to see if the children were all right.'

'But couldn't she trust them to the servant?' asked Mistress Quiney.

'She hasn't a servant,' said Anne.

'Oh,' said Mistress Quiney, opening her tired eyes for a moment, with the faint approach to surprise that was her equivalent of emotion.

There was a silence. Anne looked round desperately for William, but he was talking to Rufus by the door. Mary Shakespeare interposed to remark to the Quineys, 'We are hoping that Robert Brown will come today. He should have arrived home yesterday, but the snow may have delayed him.'

'Ah yes, he will have some news of Gilbert,' said Adrian. 'A very good young man. I dined with him when I was last up in London.' Mistress Hart bore joyfully down upon them from the other end of the room, releasing Joanne at last.

'Well, Mistress Shakespeare,' she called. 'Where is William's wife? Is she not here? What, is this—? Oh. Well, my dear, I'm glad to see you, I'm sure. Well, well, fancy William a married man already. How old is he? Not more than nineteen, I'm sure. Or, wait a minute. Rufus and he are of an age—or is Rufus older? No, wait a minute. Yes, I believe Rufus is older. These young folks, how they grow up! I shall soon lose Rufus, I know. Though they always say that you don't lose a son, but gain a daughter, but I don't know. It never seems like that to me, for they go off to live in their own house, don't they?'

'Well, Anne and William will be living here for a time at least,' said Mary Shakespeare, smiling.

'What, here?' said Mistress Hart. 'How will you fit them in? Especially when the children come along.'

'There is plenty of room for all of us,' said Mary, still smiling, stiff lipped. 'It will be pleasant for us to have them in the house.'

'Oh yes,' said Mistress Hart, with hearty disagreement in her face. 'Of course it will.'

'Here are the Sadlers,' said Mary Shakespeare, in relieved tones. 'Judith, this is William's wife. Anne, this is Mistress Sadler, and Master Sadler.'

As Mistress Hart started talking again, Judith, a little, dark, pretty woman, with a lively hazel eye, took Anne's hand and drew her slightly aside.

'You are very welcome,' she said. 'Here's another bachelor turned into an honest married man! Hamnet, how slow you are. You know that Anne is a bride, and so you may kiss her. He's always a day behind the fair. There, that'll do. Once is enough!'

'I hope you will be very happy, Mistress Anne,' said Hamnet Sadler, his blue eyes twinkling. 'I'd kiss you again, but I'm afraid of my wife.'

Anne looked from one to the other doubtfully, hardly daring to trust to this pleasant new sensation of being welcomed with laughter and friendliness.

'Now, that's what I like to hear,' cried Judith. 'Afraid of his wife. That's very good. Anne, let me give you some advice, in good time. Don't let Will have his own way in anything. For once you start, there's no holding them. They want to rule you in all things, and that would never do.'

'Hamnet,' called William Hart, coming up in time to hear this, 'can't you stop her? Have you no control over your wife?'

'None whatever,' replied Hamnet, spreading his great hands out helplessly, his round face beaming like the sun.

'I should think not indeed!' said Judith. 'Go away, Rufus. This is no place for bachelors. Come back when you've found a wife.'

'I'll kiss the bride first,' said Rufus. He took Anne by the hand and kissed her gently, saying, 'You've made a sad mistake, but as it's too late to warn you, I can only wish you well.

I could tell you things about Will—but there, I won't.'

'But I took him for better or worse,' said Anne, venturing at last the beginnings of a smile. 'And I know the better of him, so perhaps you should tell me the worst.'

'He daren't,' said Judith. 'They've been in such mischief together ever since they were at school that they are like thieves up before the judge. They keep silent, not out of loyalty but for fear of what the other might tell.'

'How glad I am that I have such good friends to speak up for me!' said William. 'Ah, but here's Dick. *He'll* give me an excellent character.'

'Dick never gives anyone a good character except himself,' said Rufus. 'He'd say that the Recording Angel was idle and that Saint Peter forgot to grease the locks. Oh, Lord, there's his wife! If I speak to her, I shall mock her, and we're all supposed to behave well today. I'm off. I shall go and tease Joanne instead.'

'Is he never serious?' asked Anne, looking after him.

'Never,' said Judith. 'When he's tired of mocking everyone else, he mocks himself. But Joanne is nearly a match for him. He's wittier, but she is sharper, and when she's had more practice I think she'll be able to put him down.'

'But, he's—he's not unkind, I think,' said Anne.

116

Judith smiled at her. 'You're very quick,' she said. 'Most people think that he is, when they first meet him, because he laughs at them.'

They stood together in silence for a few minutes, and Anne was warmed by a glow of friendship and companionship and even the faint beginnings of self-confidence, as though there might, after all, be a place for her among Stratford people.

'Now, are we all here?' called John. 'Everything is ready, and the dinner is spoiling. Mary, are we all here?'

'Mistress Hathaway isn't here yet,' she answered.

Anne turned round, still smiling, and said quickly, 'Oh, don't wait for them. They may be very late.'

'But, Anne, of course we must wait for your *mother*,' said Mary, with a surprised, disapproving look. 'The dinner will keep.'

There was a second's awkward silence, and then the conversation began again. But Anne had stopped smiling and was suddenly silent and sullen. Judith tried in vain to bring her into talk with Dick and his wife, who was a tall, pale girl, so like her mother-in-law that, as Rufus once remarked, the marriage had about it an air of highly respectable incest. The minutes dragged by interminably, with John fretting and looking towards the door, with Margaret coming out of the kitchen and

117

raising despairing eyebrows at her mistress, and with Mistress Hart whispering loudly that she always got wind if she was too hungry.

At last there was a knock at the door, and everyone stopped talking in relief. In the silence, Joan Hathaway and Catherine came in.

Oh, God, thought Anne, Joan would be wearing that gown! And she was decked out with gewgaws from every fair she had been to since she was fifteen. Catherine, sublimely confident, was already looking round the room to see if there were any young men there, and did not even hear John Shakespeare asking her if she was very cold.

'Oh, no thank you,' Joan answered for her, in a high, mincing voice. 'We had our *best* cloaks on. We were *quite* warm.'

Everyone here knows as well as I do, thought Anne, that they only have one cloak each, and that neither new nor warm. She watched them in an agony of shame as they came forward, all wrongly dressed, Joan's manners too constrained and Catherine's too free, Joan's eyes glancing quickly round the big room, and Catherine's seeking out the men. Mary Shakespeare came forward to greet them, and Anne thought that she would never admire her mother-in-law more than at that moment. *Her* affairs would never be shouted down the street, like those of Shottery folk. She might be shocked and disappointed at the marriage, but no one outside the household should ever know it. She welcomed Joan into her house as though she had been the queen, seated the guests at the table, and then went smiling into the kitchen to see to the serving of the dinner, while they all laughed and talked, taking their part in the pretence, and only Anne sat silent and frowning between William and his father—Anne feeling sick and afraid of betraying it.

Before Anne came to Henley Street she had never thought of William's family as real people. First, they were obstacles to the marriage, and, later, when they had consented to the marriage, they were simply a part of William. She looked forward to seeing them as she looked forward to seeing the house and furniture. She wasn't afraid of meeting them, because they were only shadows. She would love them, as she loved William, and they would love her in return, as they loved him. She thought that she would remember with horror and pain to the end of her days that moment when she stepped inside the door and William said, 'Mother, this is Anne.' She saw a tall, commanding woman, with strong features and clear hazel eyes. She saw the eyes widen a shade at the sight of her, and the smile grow for an instant set. And then she remembered what she had for a time forgotten—that she was eight years older than William—and she realized that

William had not told his mother this. She had thought for a brief moment that Mary was going to kiss her, and if she had, she thought that she would have flung her arms round her and burst into tears. But then there was an involuntary but perceptible withdrawing, and Mary took her hand, that smile of welcome now forced, held only with difficulty, and led her towards the fire, saying in that clear, town voice, so like William's, 'Come and warm yourself. You must be cold.'

And now Anne saw what she had done, and saw herself as she must appear to this citizen's wife, with her country voice, and her hair blown by the East wind, with her shabby gown and her fustian kirtle. She saw what it had meant to William to bring her into this home, a husbandman's daughter, neither young nor beautiful nor chaste, and bearing an unlawful child. And because she wanted desperately to make Mary like her, she could do nothing but sit by the fire, with her head bent down, looking sullen and disagreeable, and hating herself more than ever Mary Shakespeare could.

The talk limped on, and Anne heard herself making the wrong answers and speaking in the grudging voice which came to her like an old enemy. William tried to answer for her, and tried to hold her and warm her with his smile, but she avoided him as a drowning man struggles against his rescuer, and yet at the same time she suffered for him as well as for herself.

'You should have brought your mother with you,' said Mary. 'We want to meet her, and your brother too.'

'She isn't my mother,' said Anne, quickly. 'Only my stepmother.' Mary stiffened.

'But she stands in place of your parents,' she said.

Anne knew that she should agree, but made no reply, and William broke in with a discussion of the best sureties for the marriage bond.

They were interrupted by a young girl who came in from the street and stopped short.

'Ah, Joanne,' called Mary Shakespeare. 'I'm glad you're back. This is Mistress Anne Hathaway, who is to be William's wife. Come and welcome your *sister*.'

The little girl looked sharply at William, and then back at Anne. Anne caught her breath. She was back in Hewlands, standing by the baby's cradle, and her father was saying, 'This is your new mother.' She wondered what she should do if the little girl put her hands over her face and screamed, 'No! No!' and ran upstairs. But Joanne was made of sterner stuff. She looked at Anne for a moment, with open contempt in the curve of her lips and the droop of her eyelashes. Then she took hold of her skirts and swept Anne a deep curtsy, a curtsy so unsuited to the occasion and to Anne's station in life that it was in itself an insult. And she looked up with malicious amusement in her eyes while Anne, who had stood up with some notion of moving over to kiss her, could only watch her, helpless and defeated.

Mary made some movement, but before she could speak, the kitchen door was pushed open and Edmund staggered into the room, carrying, with the diligent purposefulness of childhood, his stool, which he set down in the middle of the floor.

Anne `looked up at William, her face suddenly alight, crying, 'It's Edmund. It's Edmund!' And she went across to him, without thinking, and knelt down beside him and said, 'Edmund, do you remember me?'

The child looked at her gravely for a second, and then clutched her sleeve and remarked, looking up at William, 'La'y pick me up?'

'He remembers you,' said William, laughing, and Edmund laughed too, in sympathy, showing his funny little baby teeth. For a moment, the three of them were apart together, and happy. Then Mary asked, with an acid note in her voice, 'Where did Edmund see Anne?'

'When we first met in the market,' William answered, 'Edmund fell over and Anne picked him up.'

The breath of illicit meetings and unlawful

love came into the room. Anne was grave again, standing up and dusting down her skirts. Then she thought that this seemed to reflect upon the cleanness of the floor, and stopped, and didn't know what to do with her hands. Joanne came forward and took Edmund up in her arms, seeming to draw him away from Anne as from a patch of mud, and saying softly, 'I'll take him to the kitchen.'

And suddenly Anne knew that she must get away, that she could not bear any more. She turned to Mary and said, incoherently, 'I must go now. I must go home now.'

'But, Anne,' said William, in astonishment, 'Father will be home soon. You'll wait to see him?'

'We had hoped that you would stay and have supper with us,' said Mary, polite and gracious, with a coldness in her smile.

'No, no,' said Anne. 'I must go home now. It's getting late. I must go.'

She put on her hood, while Mary stood by with tightly clasped hands, and thrust the door open before William could do it for her, and muttered some sort of thanks, and then she and William were out in the street, with the East wind tearing at them fiercely. William took her arm, but she pulled it away and walked on with her head down, all the strength of her love turned to anger against him, and she did not know why.

★

Matters between them had been like that ever since. Through all the arrangements of the licence and the bond, through the meetings of the families, through the ceremony in the chill, empty church, Anne and William had been like strangers, forced to travel in each other's company, but alien and unfriendly. And so at last came this wedding feast, in which the Shakespeares proclaimed that their son was marrying with their consent, and that the bride was henceforth a Shakespeare, a respectable woman, whose child, its presence now unacknowledged, would be born in wedlock. Anne sat between William and his father, and listened to Joan, on John's other side, laughing too loudly as the wine went to her head, and watched Catherine leaning her shoulder against Rufus and looking up at him with her loose smile, watched Mary directing the meal, caring for the comfort of the guests, trying to keep the distaste out of her face, and saw little Joanne, opposite Rufus, trying to catch his eye with that look of malicious amusement which Anne dreaded more than anger.

Joanne had been careful to place herself opposite Rufus, so that she could watch him teasing that woman's sister and so that she could laugh with him at the spectacle of her father trying to make conversation with the woman herself—and she so stupid and ignorant that half the time she didn't know what he was talking about! But Rufus, for some odd reason of his own, refused to join in the fun. Catherine, with her languishing airs and her silly remarks, should have been easy sport for him, but he was listening to her with perfect gravity, and answering her politely— not with that elaborate, mocking courtesy of his which Joanne knew of old, but with sober civility, as though she were a person of good sense and good standing. And then he was deliberately refraining from joining Joanne in mockery of that woman, for once she did succeed in catching his eye and looked meaningly towards the head of the table, but when she looked back at him, he had turned his head away. It was most provoking of him, thought Joanne, just when she most needed his support and laughter, and she could see no reason for it, unless he liked Catherine. But that wasn't possible, thought Joanne. No one could like *her*. Except that William had evidently once liked this woman, Anne. Perhaps lunacy was catching.

Joanne sighed and looked again at the head of the table. She would never forgive that woman, she thought, never as long as she lived. It was she who had prevented Will from going to London. But for her vulgar ambitions and scheming, William would have been established by now, on his way to becoming that rich merchant who was to win fame and admiration and return to astonish his fellow townsmen. And now he would instead be tied to Stratford for ever, never to escape, burdened with the maintenance of doltish children and a wife he did not love. For there was no doubt, thought Joanne, that they did not love each other. She looked at them now, sitting side by side, silent, never looking at each other, never taking hands or smiling together. This woman had forced him into marriage, to father her child. Already they were indifferent, and soon they would hate each other. And I must laugh at her and make a jest of it, or I shall cry my eyes out, thought Joanne. Oh, Will! Oh, Rufus, laugh with me! Please laugh at her!

'Very true,' Rufus was saying, gravely. 'But then, if everyone lived in the towns, there'd be no one left to till the soil and grow our food and milk the cows.'

'Oh well,' said Catherine, giggling, 'the old folks could live in the country, because they wouldn't mind, and us young folks could live in town and enjoy ourselves.'

And Rufus actually laughed with her, to Joanne's disgust, as though she had said something clever.

It was a relief when at last they moved from table and towards the fire. In the disturbance, Joanne managed to get next to Rufus and whisper, 'I hope you enjoyed your dinner. I never thought to see you held so rapt by a woman. I suppose we shall be eating your

126

wedding feast next. Will you live in the country and milk the cows for her, or live in town and dance with her?'

Rufus smiled for a moment, and then he looked towards Anne and answered, gravely, 'No, Will has chosen the best.'

Joanne looked up at him, hoping for a gleam of mockery, but found none and turned away in a rage, only to fall victim to Dick Quiney, in search of a listener to one of his longest stories, which his wife had already heard.

Some of the guests had left, and John Shakespeare was yawning and looking hopefully towards Joan and Catherine, when there was a knock at the door, and a tall man came in without waiting for it to be opened to him.

'It's Robert Brown,' cried Joanne, joyfully, leaving Dick in the middle of a sentence and running forward.

'Why, Joanne,' he said, in a quiet, affectionate tone, 'it's good to see you.'

'Oh, Robert,' cried Joanne, 'I'm so glad you're back.'

He laughed down at her, and then came forward into the room, while she still clung to his arm.

'I've brought a letter from Gilbert,' he said. 'And, Will, Gilbert asked me to tell you that he had received your letter, and that he wishes all joy to you and to your wife.'

'Ah yes,' said John Shakespeare, with

flagging enthusiasm. 'Anne, this is Robert Brown, Gilbert's good friend, and a friend of all of us. Robert, this is Will's wife, Mistress Anne.'

Robert took Anne's hand, looking down at her with kind blue eyes.

'I have a brother's kiss to deliver from Gilbert,' he said, smiling at her and kissing her on the cheek. 'And for myself, I wish you all the happiness which I'm sure you will both have.'

'Come to the fire,' said John, heartily. 'Have you eaten? Wife, what can we offer him? There's cold turkey-cock, or a piece of pasty. What will you have?'

'No, no, I've already eaten,' said Robert. 'I only came to bring you news of Gilbert.'

'A glass of wine, at least,' said John. 'Come, we will all have a glass of wine, and then you shall tell us Gilbert's news.'

'Is he well?' asked Mary anxiously.

'Very well,' answered Robert, smiling. 'I've never known Gilbert to be otherwise. He stalks about London as though he owned it, and is just inspecting his estates. He's thinking of bringing in some improvements. He finds the streets too noisy, and he thinks it would be better if shopmen cried their wares for only two hours a day. He says that the watermen swear too much, and that London folk don't know how to cook cabbage or carp. But he likes the London beer!'

'And how does he like Master Harrison, for that is more to the purpose,' said Mary. 'Or rather, how does Master Harrison like him?' Robert's lips twitched. 'They sit and discuss their business affairs like two wise old counsellors,' he said. 'Master Harrison confided to me that he'd had apprentices before, but never one like Gilbert! Mistress Harrison is afraid that Gilbert's too good, and that he'll die young, because he never brawls and doesn't care for bear baiting.' He stopped and laughed. 'I asked Gilbert if he could go with me to a sermon at Saint Paul's one morning, and I heard him getting permission from Master Harrison. "Sir, I have to go out," he says. "Will you be able to manage without me this morning? Don't forget that Sir John Falk is calling today. Oh yes, and you should prepare those accounts for the Company. I'll check them for you when I get back." "Yes, Gilbert," says Master Harrison. "Will you be back for dinner?" "Yes," says Gilbert, "and perhaps I might bring a friend of mine with me, if that will be convenient?" "Certainly," says Mistress Harrison. "We have a fine piece of veal, and artichokes." And then Gilbert takes his cap and walks out, glad to know that he's prepared his master, as far as possible, for the hazards of a morning spent without his assistance.'

They all laughed (except for Joan Hathaway, who had missed the point of the story, and

129

Catherine, who wasn't listening).

'It must be a great pleasure,' said Mary, 'to be able to hear so many good sermons.'

'Yes, we enjoyed it more than anything else in London,' Robert agreed. 'There's nearly always a notable preacher at Paul's, and Gilbert and I went to Saint Clement Dane's once or twice.' He turned to William. 'And we went out to the Theatre at Shoreditch. We wished that you'd been with us, Will, and Gilbert said that he thought that *you* could have written a better play than that when you were at school.'

'You're best go up to London, Will,' said Rufus, laughing, 'and try your hand at writing plays, so that Gilbert will be satisfied when next he goes to the Theatre.'

'Oh no,' cried William. 'That would take more courage than I possess. Gilbert was always a hanging judge on plays. Do you remember the tragedy we saw at Drayton? We thought it was quite a good play, and very well acted, but Gilbert only said he was glad that all the characters died at the end, and he wished the actors had too!'

'Well, Gilbert didn't like the chief actor,' said Robert. 'He said he ranted too much——'

But he was interrupted by Joan Hathaway, bored by a conversation in which she had no part, who remarked, bridling, 'Well, *I've* never been to see a play, and I'm sure I never want to—wicked inventions of the devil, my husband used to say.'

130

There was a moment's awkwardness, during which Anne blushed scarlet, and then Robert said, with the true courtesy of kindness, 'There are many in London, Mistress, who think as you do.'

Joanne was delighted to have Robert Brown back in Stratford. She had missed him very much during the four months he had been up in London on business, and of all the boys' friends, he was her favourite—except for Rufus, of course, but that was different. Oddly enough, although he was a good deal older, he had always been Gilbert's friend, and not William's. They had both enjoyed angling, a sport which had never much appealed to William, and used to go off for whole days which they spent sitting solemnly and silently on the banks of the river, looking, Rufus said, like a pair of melancholy herons, but always returning very contented and with a basketful of fish. Another of their favourite amusements was chess, a game that Robert first taught to Gilbert, and at which Gilbert now usually beat him. Rufus always said that they enjoyed each other's company because they both practised not the art of conversation, but the art of silence. But Robert could be talkative enough with people he liked, and he had always been more ready than Gilbert to allow Joanne to come with them on their expeditions, giving her a stick and a piece of thread to fish with, and carrying her home when she was tired. She always felt that she could say exactly what she felt with him, and that he would always be gentle and indulgent, and never shocked. She was sure that he would sympathize with her about this family catastrophe, and that his sound judgement would condemn the marriage as heartily as even she could wish.

Soon after five o'clock, Dick and his wife made a move to go, but John Shakespeare pressed them to stay for supper, and Mary lent her persuasions too, chiefly, Joanne felt sure, because she dreaded the moment when the family would be left alone with this unwelcome stranger among them, as she now would be, all the time. Joanne was careful to sit next to Robert, and seized the first moment of general talk to say to him, 'Robert, isn't this a dreadful business? How could Will have chosen her? I don't know why people want to get married. It's always a mistake.'

Robert smiled. 'I don't think I'll condemn marriage,' he said, 'because I might want to get married myself one day.'

'You!' cried Joanne, in consternation. 'Oh, *no!*'

'Most people marry,' her remarked. 'I don't think I want to live and die a bachelor.'

'Oh, Robert, don't get married,' Joanne begged. 'You are much better as you are.'

He looked down at her, and his face was

serious for a minute, and then he started to smile again, and said, 'Well, I won't get married just yet, if the idea displeases you.'

'It does!' said Joanne, vehemently. 'Will's marriage is bad enough. She's so plain and disagreeable, and not a fit wife for him at all.' She paused and looked up, but Robert made no reply, so she persisted, 'Don't you think so?'

Robert looked down at her gravely, and said, 'Perhaps she's not quite the wife one would have hoped for him, but since she's Will's choice, we must all make the best of it and try to help her.'

Joanne flushed and looked away. She felt a little ashamed of herself, and sorry that she had forced him into saying that, when she knew that he had tried to avoid it. But she was more than ever angry with Anne, feeling that she had stolen away not only William, but also Rufus and Robert. She had come across this men's loyalty before, among her brothers, and had never failed to find it annoying, but it was still more annoying when they joined with a strange woman against her. She felt no pleasure now in Robert's company, and wanted only to get away to her own bed and to be alone. Then she remembered that even this satisfaction was denied her, because she now had to share a bed with Margaret, the kitchen maid, so that William and Anne could have a room to themselves.

At last supper was over, and the guests were leaving. They took a long while to go, because it had to be decided who should take Joan Hathaway and Catherine home, since they had stayed so late. But Robert volunteered for the long, cold walk, and Rufus said that he would go, too, and hear the latest London gossip on the way back. Catherine giggled and rolled her eyes at them, sure that they were both going because they had fallen victims to her charms. As they all put on their outdoor clothes by the door, Joanne saw William take Anne's hand, as they stood side by side in front of the fireplace.

'Courage, love,' he said, in a low voice, 'it's nearly over.'

He loves her, thought Joanne. The realization came to her like a blow. The tone of voice and the gesture were unmistakable, even to her, and the words, 'Courage, love, it's nearly over,' as though he alone knew her feelings, as though there was something between them which was shared by no one else. Anne made no reply, and in a moment drew her hand away. *She* doesn't love him, thought Joanne, and in that instant hated her more than ever.

The guests were finally gone, and Joanne went upstairs and lay on her back, desperately tired, but too unhappy to sleep. She thought how the family had broken up, that family which had once seemed to secure and carefree. Now, little Anne was dead, and Gilbert gone, and William married, held for ever in the grip of a woman who had taken him for what she could get out of him, who did not love him, and who would always make him miserable. His life was over, and it seemed to Joanne that hers was too, for who could have faith in the future when such things could happen?

William and Anne went into their own room, and Anne sat down on the bed, her hands in her lap and her shoulders drooping. William came and knelt in front of her and took off her shoes.

'What a day!' he said, smiling. 'I thought that they would never leave. If Mistress Hart had talked for five minutes longer at the door, I swear I would have turned her cloak up over her head and carried her home myself!' Anne still sat and looked at him, with troubled face. 'My poor love,' he said, kissing her, 'you're tired out. Come to bed.'

Anne cried out suddenly, 'Oh, Will!' and turned and clung to him desperately, utterly defenceless, with no hope except in him.

'My wife,' said William. 'My dear wife.'

'Will, I love you,' said Anne. 'I love you.'

The one sure, certain thing. The one steady rock in shifting sands. All that night, which should have been their wedding night, she lay still in his arms, and for both of them it brought something more precious than fulfilment of love. It was the beginning of that sharing of griefs and pleasures and confidences which is the richest gift, after all, of married life, and the most lasting.

# CHAPTER 9

It was surprising to Anne to find how quickly she settled into the household at Henley Street, and how the members of William's family, those shadowy figures, became suddenly the moving force of her life, while Joan and Catherine seemed quite insignificant, all their malignancy vanished now that she was no longer in their power.

Once more she lived two distinct lives, each utterly separate from the other. In the daytime she worked in the kitchen or the living-room or the store room, under the controlled disapproval of Mary Shakespeare and the contemptuous dislike of Joanne. But in the evening, after supper, she and William would go upstairs into their own room, and shut the door, and immediately it was as though they stepped on to an enchanted island. As they undressed, and afterwards as they lay in bed in the silent house, they would talk in low tones of the small events of the day, and of the

Stratford gossip, and William would tell Anne about the lives and families of those Stratford people who had been familiar to him as long as he could remember, so that she, too, could enter into his interest in whether John Parsons would marry Timothea Jones, and whether Henry Williams, who used to spend every day drinking at the tavern, would maintain his astonishing reformation. And they would talk about their childhood, and tell those small anecdotes which make each family a world to itself, speaking its own language. Perhaps much of the magic of those hours of hushed talk came from their feeling of being, in some measure, aliens, drawing closer together in a hostile, or at least a strange country. It was as though every day was a city wall which they must climb, in order to meet at night secretly and alone outside the city bounds, whispering together in the darkness. The household whirled about as before, and Anne's presence in the house and the fact of their marriage was a constant irritation, a disturbance of the pattern of family life. But no matter how much during the day Anne might feel that William was on the opposing side, identified with the rest of the Shakespeares who resented her intrusion, as soon as they had climbed the stairs and shut the door of their room, he became once more hers alone, and everything became at once simple and her troubles bearable because he shared them with her.

137

When she first came to the house, Anne had looked forward to showing off her housewifely ways. She remembered how proud her mother used to be of her, and how well she had kept house after her mother's death, and how infinitely superior she had been, in all such matters, to Joan Hathaway. She had thought how pleased Mary would be to find that she had a daughter-in-law who kept things clean and tidy and who was a good cook. But now she found that housekeeping in a citizen's house in Stratford was very different from housekeeping in a cottage at Shottery. Margaret did the cooking, except for a few special dishes and preserves which Mary made herself, and Anne found that all her long practice of working in the house went for nothing, since everything must be done in one way only, with no variation from Mary's own customs, which she had inherited from her stepmother. Anne had once been proud of her candle making, but now she found that Mary's way was different, and she was awkward at it, so that Mary would often take it out of her hands with an impatient gesture, leaving her standing by looking foolish. She did not know how to make beds properly, according to Mary's standards, shaking up the feather beds and smoothing the coverlid tightly over them. She was always enraged by Mary's habit of coming to inspect a room after she had swept and dusted it, running her finger along the ledges of the furniture, and moving chests to see if there was any dust behind them. But, above all, a daily irritation was the setting of the table for meals. At Hewlands, Anne had been accustomed to put the food on the table, while everyone took a spoon, or a knife and spoon, drew a stool up, and set to work with no more ado. She herself used to say grace, but frequently Joan and Catherine didn't trouble to wait for it, and the children always tried to get their fingers into the dish before she had finished. She found that it was very different at Henley Street. There must be a tablecloth, and a place set for every person, with stools drawn up to the table and chairs for John and Mary. And, if she remembered the salt cellar, then she forgot the napkins, while if she remembered the napkins, then she forgot that bread must not be on the table, but set on a trencher. At the beginning, Mary reminded her of all these things with an air of strong forbearance, only murmuring that *surely* this was how she set the table at Hewlands? But, as time went by, and Anne still occasionally made mistakes, Mary would click her tongue and say, '*Anne*! The napkins!' or, 'Anne, you have forgotten the mustard! You know that we are having beef today!' Then Anne would have to get up from table, clumsily now, because of the child, and sullenly, because she thought that it was more fitting that Joanne should run errands than that she should. She knew, in her heart, that Mary gave her these tasks in an endeavour to acknowledge her as a daughter of the house, but when her legs and back ached, as they seemed to do all the time now, she did not feel like appreciating Mary's excellent intentions behind the daily chiding. At Hewlands she had been supported by a strong sense of superiority. The quarrels had always been over Catherine's laziness, or Joan's sluttish ways, and Anne's consciousness of right had given her a certain miserable satisfaction. It was very different at Henley Street, with Anne always in the wrong and always humiliated, and where her shortcomings were treated with such restraint and forbearance that it seemed impossible for her to try to justify herself. She sometimes felt that she would give anything to be back at Hewlands for an hour or two, where there was no concealment and no restraint, and where she could relieve her feelings with a good burst of temper, in which she would be heartily joined by Joan.

It was some weeks before Mary finally abandoned the pretence that she and Anne were on the best of terms and that she was entirely satisfied with her son's wife. They might have kept up such a pretence if they had been living in different parts of the country, or might even have maintained it during a weekly visit. But they were living in the same house. For Anne there was the constant annoyance of being always set right and of living in a household where everything was unfamiliar, and where she had none of the powers of a wife but all the duties of a daughter-in-law. For Mary, there was the fact of William's marriage, and its circumstances, the realization that she had not only lost him to a strange woman, but to one who was not chaste. She could never see him put his hand on Anne's shoulder or take her hand without a pang of jealousy and anger, all the sharper because she would not admit it, even to herself. Anne's country voice and cottage ways enraged her, and her sullenness under correction—so unlike the Shakespeares with their quick, easy tempers. And, at last, Mary's restraint broke down.

It was a bitterly cold day in March. After the deception of an early fine spell, black frost had gripped the country again and everyone's temper was edged by the renewal of winter. It seemed to Anne that she could not remember a time when she was not carrying the child, and her bulkiness and weariness seemed to shut her off from all the others who were going about their affairs in normal health and spirits.

They were all invited to dinner with Mistress Hart, but Anne had insisted on staying at home. She was embarrassed now in company, and she felt tired and ill. Mary, after a few minutes of exasperated persuasion, gave it up, saying only, 'Well, as Margaret is away today looking after her mother, perhaps, Anne, you'll get supper ready. We shan't be late back.'

Anne replied, in a voice which she did not mean to sound grudging, 'All right. Will you leave Edmund behind? I'll look after him.'

'Oh no, Mother,' Joanne broke in, quickly, 'we *must* take Edmund. Mistress Hart asked us to bring him, and he'd enjoy it.'

'Yes, of course we'll take him,' said Mary. 'Mistress Hart will be surprised not to see Anne. We don't want to look as though half the family has decided to stay at home. Come along, Richard, don't dawdle. Edmund, take Joanne's hand. Will, are you ready?' They all set off, but William lingered to say to Anne, 'Do you feel ill, love? Are you sure you wouldn't like me to stay with you?'

'No, of course not,' Anne answered, crossly. 'I just don't want to go.'

William opened his mouth to say something more, but then sighed and went out, hurrying up the street after the others.

And Anne, with the familiar pain in her throat at having once more hurt William, made up the fire in the kitchen and sitting-room, and went upstairs to lie down. For some time she was too cold to sleep, but at last, still aware of the chill in her hands and feet, she dropped into an uneasy doze. She stirred once, and opened her eyes, thinking that she should get up and begin to prepare the supper, but then, still feeling very tired, and deciding that there was plenty of time before the others returned, she fell asleep again, sinking thankfully down into the silence and calm of the empty house.

She was awakened by the latch of the front door, and started up with her heart beating wildly. For a moment she was afraid that it might be Mary Shakespeare, but then she was sure that it was William, come back early to see if she was all right. She struggled to her feet and shuffled to the door, still dazed with sleep, and out on to the landing. It was Mary Shakespeare. She was standing inside the door, looking at the dark room, the dead fire, the supper table not set out. Anne put her hands up to her face, horrified but incredulous, as one feels after breaking something. She came downstairs, trying to smooth her hair and her dress and still not quite awake. She said, breathlessly, 'You're back early.' Mary turned at her voice, and answered sharply, 'Early! It's nearly six o'clock, and the fire is out, and supper not ready! What are you thinking of, Anne?'

Joanne came through the door from the kitchen, carrying a rush-light, with Edmund trotting along behind her.

'Is the kitchen fire out, too?' demanded Mary.

'No, it's just alight,' Joanne answered. She glanced up at Anne, but anxiously, not with the elation that Anne might have expected her to show.

'But nothing's ready,' Mary repeated, with rising annoyance. 'Anne, did you put the children's porridge on the fire?'

'No,' Anne answered, simply, 'I didn't.'

She knew that she should explain that she had felt ill and had gone to lie down, but somehow she couldn't. She wanted to apologize, but she couldn't find the words, and felt, anyway, a kind of hopelessness, as though anything she did was sure to be wrong. Mary watched in silence while Joanne lit the candle, waiting, perhaps, in case Anne should say something more. Then she spoke in a louder voice, as though the silence had increased her anger.

'Anne, it's too bad,' she said. 'I really don't know what to say. We've all tried to help you to feel at home here, but you don't seem to make any endeavours yourself. It isn't fair to William for you to behave like this. If you had any affection for him at all, I should think that you would try to do better. Do you think he wants to be ashamed of his wife?'

Anne said nothing, standing at the foot of the stairs. Mary looked at her for a moment with pursed lips, and then turned on her heel and went towards the kitchen, saying as she went, 'Joanne, you had better put Edmund to bed and then come and help me. The others will be home presently.'

Joanne picked Edmund up and carried him upstairs, going past Anne with her face turned away.

Left alone, Anne moved slowly towards the fire, thinking that she would try to rekindle it, but there was not a glimmer left in it, and the tinder-box was in the kitchen. She stood looking down at it with a nightmare helplessness and feeling of disaster, unable to move or think. And then the numbness suddenly left her. She knew that she must get away to her own room and turned and went up the stairs slowly, step by step, with her breath sobbing in her throat. Just before she reached the top she stumbled and sank down, holding on to the rail and leaning her forehead against the bars in an agony of silent tears.

Through the open bedroom door, Joanne heard the sound of Anne's crying, and stood still for a few minutes, listening to it. She was surprised by a rush of pity and shame, as though she saw Anne for the first time as defenceless and vulnerable, and as though she herself was to blame for the tears, and not her mother. She stood, clasping her hands tightly, and wishing that the dreadful, heartbroken, subdued sobbing would stop, so that she wouldn't have to do anything about it. But she couldn't stifle the feeling of guilt, and the crying didn't stop. She gave Edmund something to play with and went out softly to the head of the staircase.

Anne was sitting on the third stair from the top, with her face in her hands, and Joanne hesitated, helpless before that human mystery of tears, second only to death in its inaccessibility.

'Anne,' she said, doubtfully. 'Anne, don't cry.' There was no reply. Joanne came nearer. She had difficulty in finding words, as though Anne was a foreigner, discovered by chance destitute in the street. She glanced down at the door, wishing that William would come, and yet dreading his arrival since he would blame them for unkindness. She knelt down beside Anne and said, 'You mustn't mind mother. She's never angry for very long. She'll have forgotten all about it in an hour's time.'

Anne shook her head and sobbed out, not to Joanne but to herself, 'William. Oh, Will!'

'He'll be home soon,' said Joanne, encouragingly.

But Anne said wildly, almost angrily, 'She said I didn't love him! Oh, Will, Will!'

'She didn't mean that,' said Joanne, vehemently, in a flood of guilt. 'Mother didn't mean that.'

'Yes she did,' Anne sobbed, 'but I do love him. I do! I do!' And she clasped the bar again and laid her head down on her wrists and cried with a new abandon, but still quietly.

Joanne was suddenly silenced, suddenly young and foolish, as though behind these tears lay something of which she had no experience. This, then, was marriage, and not as she had always thought of it. It was not only a public taking of hands, but also a secret compact. It was not merely a declaration that the man wanted an heir, not just an occasion for jokes about cuckolded husbands and jealous wives, about Menelaus and Juno, not just a long sleeping in the same bed from the bridal chamber to the recumbent tomb. Instead it was, perhaps, a journey made by two sworn comrades into a land where no man could follow them, nor any know what happened on the voyage or how each bore himself towards the other, except by hearsay. And would she, too, one day kneel down and cry for love of a man? No, never, for sure! said Joanne to herself. And yet she felt an odd sort of envy for Anne, crying there so bitterly. And with that envy, her compassion flowed freely, no longer held back by shame and awkwardness. She put her arms round Anne and, as she touched her for the first time, it was strange to find her warm and soft, as though she had her own sister in her arms again.

After a few moments Anne drew away. It was the same gesture with which she had withdrawn her hand from William's after the wedding feast. But this time Joanne saw it for what it was—a mixture of pride and diffidence, and a fearful refusal to admit that her affections were engaged, just as a general will not speak, even to his lieutenant who knows it as well as he does, of the vulnerable point in his defences. She stood up, wiping her eyes, and said, 'I must try to light the fire.' Then she added with a note of despair which brought more tears with it, 'And it always goes out when *I* light it!'

Joanne felt suddenly very lighthearted. She said teasingly, 'It'll certainly go out if you try to light it now. Your tears will douse it every time.' Anne regarded her gravely. '*You'd* better put Edmund to bed, and let *me* light the fire,' said Joanne, laughing. 'But, don't drown him.'

'But—will—your mother mind?' said Anne, doubtfully.

'*She* won't mind——' said Joanne, '—if she doesn't know anything about it! Only hurry! I can hear her rushing about in the kitchen like a Pursuivant, and if she comes out before we've lit the fire and laid the table, we shall both have to take sanctuary in the church!' She chuckled, glad to be back in her accustomed position as conspirator against authority rather than officer of justice. Anne half turned away, and hesitated, and then came back and bent down and took Joanne's hand and kissed it, and went quickly away, leaving Joanne startled and shocked, but still strangely happy after all.

After that evening's incident, trivial as it was, and soon forgotten by Mary, the pattern of life in the Henley Street household changed gradually but unmistakably. With Joanne and William both protecting Anne, Mary found herself, quite against her will, playing the part of tyrant. When she asked Anne to fetch something, it was Joanne now who jumped to her feet and ran for it. It was Joanne who showed Anne how to do her household tasks, and endeavoured to conceal her shortcomings. It was Joanne, as well as William, who covered Anne's obstinate silences. With Richard engrossed, as always, in his own small truancies and amusements, and with John amiably unconscious of any cause for annoyance, there was a kind of mad justice in the fact that Mary now seemed to find herself often an intruder in her own house, shut out from a fellowship which included Anne. 'But still,' she would think to herself, 'I have Edmund. *He* loves me still.' And yet Edmund would be always struggling to escape from her encompassing arms and to follow the others, as though 'Ned come too!' was to be the motif of his life, as it now was his constant cry, and as though he was doomed to be always staggering up to a closed door of which the latch was too high for him to reach. 'But he always comes back to me,' Mary would think, watching him, 'when the others fail him. *He* will never disappoint me, as William has. *He* will always love his mother more than all the world, and when he has conquered the world he will come to lay it at my feet.' Then he would turn away from the door and come back to her, indeed, with his face screwed up and tears rolling down his cheeks, and she would say, 'There, my love. There, my lovely boy. We'll get you a sweetmeat, shall we, and you'll stay and help mother?' And he would smile up at her, a smile of ravishing sweetness, such as he gave, she would think, to no one else, and she would hold him to her, smiling, too, and saying to herself, 'He will be great. Oh, Edmund will be great and famous one day!'

The time grew near for the birth of Anne's baby, and she felt a superstitious dread of it, as though her sin and William's was now to be repaid. But when at last Susanna was born, on a fine May morning, it was as though in that birth their marriage was consummated, as though that birth was God's blessing on their love. All the months of guilty humiliation were laid aside now forever. She was no longer Anne Hathaway, but now Anne Shakespeare, his wife, and this child was no longer the shameful hold she had over him, but a true lovers' knot. As Susanna had a look about her at once of Anne and of William, so, too, their fortunes were inextricably intertwined in her, and, like the Prince's Jewel, she was a token that William must acknowledge as his own and redeem with love and faithfulness. The spring sunshine came in warmly through the window, and the cuckoo's song was so clear on

Welcombe Hill that he seemed to be singing in the room itself. Anne lay with the little girl in her arms and thought, 'Now at last he is truly mine!'

# CHAPTER 10

One misty afternoon, more than a year after Susanna was born, Rufus came softly into the Shakespeare house, with a conspiratorial air, and found Joanne minding Susanna, while Richard and Edmund played together in a corner, very much at cross purposes, Richard setting his wooden soldiers up and Edmund knocking them down.

'Well,' said Joanne, as soon as she saw him, 'what mischief are you up to now?'

'Mischief?' said Rufus, with dignity, 'I want to see Will on—on business.'

'Business!' said Joanne, scornfully. 'If you ever get to heaven, which seems most unlikely, you will spend your time trying to tempt Saint Peter to steal the jewels off the walls of New Jerusalem.'

'And when you get to Hell,' Rufus replied, gracefully, 'where all maids with sharp tongues are sure to go, you will spend your time pulling the Devil's tail.'

'Huh!' said Joanne. 'The Devil will never let you into Hell, for fear *you* should tempt *him*.'

'Yes,' said Rufus, eyeing her thoughtfully, 'well, I've no time to spend gossiping with you. Where's Will?'

Joanne jerked her head towards the workroom. 'In there. Don't tell me you've run out of words so soon!' she called after his retreating back. 'What an epitaph they will write over you—"Here lies William Hart, who used up a lifetime of conversation before he had grown a beard!"' She laughed, and Edmund amicably laughed too, to keep her company, knocking down four soldiers with a backward sweep of his hand. Richard shouted with rage, but set to work diligently standing them up again, while Rufus carefully shut the workroom door behind him.

A short time later, William and Rufus came out again, and William said carelessly, 'Oh, Joanne, I'm going out for a little while. I shan't be late back.'

'Where are you going?' asked Joanne, suspiciously.

'Oh, just—out,' said William.

'There's no creature on earth so inquisitive as a woman,' said Rufus.

'Except a man,' said Joanne, but absently. She was watching William as he got his bow and arrows from behind the door. 'It's too late for archery,' she said, thoughtfully. 'Will! You're going out to steal deer!'

William and Rufus looked at each other and then at her.

'We are going out to practise archery,' said Rufus, firmly.

'Yes, on another man's deer,' said Joanne.

'Never you mind about that,' said Rufus. 'Let other men worry about their own harts. You can stay at home and hope that Cupid will practise on yours. Concern yourself with Cupid's dart, and let ours fly where they will.'

'Cupid's arrows will trouble me no more than those *you* shoot will trouble the deer you shoot at,' said Joanne. 'You couldn't hit a barn door at twenty paces, and your arrows are certainly more likely to fly where *they* will than where *you* will.'

'At least I hope his arrows won't fly *at Will*,' said William, laughing.

Richard had listened to this exchange with an air of sober confusion, but now, pursuing the one relevant point, he rose to his feet, announcing, 'You're going to shoot deer. I'm coming too.' He then struggled into his warm jerkin, got his bow and arrows and declared himself ready.

'No, no, Richard,' said William. 'You can't come. It's not safe. We might get caught.'

Rufus glared at Joanne. 'This is your fault,' he said, crossly. 'Why must your tongue always wag so loudly?'

Edmund viewed the departure of his reluctant playfellow with strong disapproval and went firmly across the room to attach himself to Richard, saying affectionately, 'Ned come too.'

'Yes,' said Rufus, warmly. 'Edmund must come too. And what about Susanna? We can't go without Susanna!'

'They can none of them come,' said William, looking amused. 'No, Richard, we're going out to Charlecote, and that's too far for you. Besides, we might have to run, if Sir Thomas's men see us.'

'I can run as fast as you,' said Richard. 'Take *me*, Will.'

'No,' said Joanne. 'You can't go, Richard. They are both fools to go. Do you want to go, too, and be fool's mate?'

'I don't see why Richard shouldn't go,' said Rufus, at once. 'He *can* run fast, and he can shoot, too. Let's take him, Will. I'll look after him.'

'Well, all right,' said William, doubtfully. 'No, Edmund, you can't come.'

'Ned come too,' said Edmund, clasping Richard round the waist.

'No,' said Richard, and then, with irritation, 'no, no!' He gave his small brother a firm and well-calculated push in the stomach and slipped round the edge of the door after William and Rufus, while Edmund sat down on the floor and raised his voice in the familiar and hopeless roar of, 'Ned come too!' until Susanna woke from her sleep and began to cry also, while Joanne sat and scowled at the closed door.

When Mary and Anne came back from a visit to Judith Sadler, the three had still not returned.

'Where's Richard?' demanded Mary at once.

'He and Will went out,' Joanne answered.

'Why? Who did they go with?'

Joanne hesitated. 'With Rufus,' she said.

'Hm!' said Mary. 'Up to some mischief, I suppose. Where did they go?'

'I don't know,' Joanne answered, crossing her fingers against the lie.

But Mary, with her annoying and unerring instinct for wrong-doing, looked immediately towards the corner behind the door.

'Oh,' she said, 'they took their bows with them. Have they gone deer stealing?'

'They didn't say so,' Joanne answered, cautiously and truthfully.

'Hm!' said Mary again. 'I suppose it was William Hart's idea. You'd think that Will, now he's married, would settle down and leave that idle good-for-nothing alone. He's always at the bottom of every piece of knavery in the town.'

Joanne found herself reluctant to allow Rufus to be blamed and Will acquitted, and she said, unwillingly, 'I did hear them both talking about it a few days ago.'

'Yes,' said Mary, 'after John Perkins came

home with that good piece of venison, I suppose. And they could think of nothing better to do than to copy him like a pair of grinning apes. I've no patience with it! And, when all's said and done, it's still thieving. It may be a fashionable crime, but it's still a crime. I'm surprised at Will. I should have expected William Hart to engage in such folly, but not Will.'

She looked at Anne, as though expecting some support, but Anne, as usual, maintained an air of bland abstraction. She never intervened when Mary was blaming William, either to defend him or to agree, and now she merely sat down by the fire to feed Susanna, murmuring endearments as peacefully as though she was alone in the room. But when Mary had gone through into the kitchen, Anne looked up at Joanne and said, 'Will they be all right?'

'Yes,' Joanne answered stoutly, 'Rufus is always all right. He never gets caught—or if he does, he talks his way out of trouble.'

'And they wouldn't have taken Richard if there had been any danger,' said Anne, reassured.

But John Shakespeare came home, and supper was ready, and the sportsmen were still not back.

'We won't wait for them,' said Mary. 'Perhaps when they go supperless to bed they will realize that an honest meal is worth more than stolen venison.'

'I hope they haven't been caught,' said John, uneasily. 'Sir Thomas is a hard man when he's angry, and he has the right to impose large fines for deer stealing. These young men seem to think it's a joke, but it's not such a joke when they must find the money, or when they must go to prison. Will must have been mad to risk it.'

'It's that William Hart,' said Mary. 'He finds no amusement in a sport unless there's danger in it too, and he lures Will into going with him just to share the risks.'

'Well, perhaps one day Will will learn——' began John, and then stopped as the door opened, and they all looked round. Rufus came in, his hand on Richard's shoulder, and closed the door behind him. Anne put her hand up to her mouth but said nothing, and it was left to Mary to demand, 'Where's Will?'

Rufus stood and looked at them. He had lost his cap. His red-brown hair was damp and curly, his clothes were wet, and his legs were cased in mud up to the knees. He was out of breath, and, for the first time in his life, perhaps, wholly at a disadvantage. He caught Joanne's eye and looked quickly away and down at the floor and replied shortly, 'He got caught.'

'What do you mean?' enquired Mary. She leaned forward. 'What do you mean, *"he got caught"*? Weren't you with him? Wasn't it your plan to go in the first place? How was it "he got caught" and you didn't?'

Rufus took a quick breath, raised his eyes to Mary's face and answered with a kind of angry desperation, 'I would have stayed to fight it out, but he told me to get Richard away. So I told Richard to run, and I went to help Will. But there were three of Sir Thomas's men holding Will, and he called out that we didn't want a riot, and, anyway, there were some more of Sir Thomas's men coming up——' He stopped.

'Well?' said Mary.

'Well, Will called out again to get Richard away, so I—so I——'

'So you ran away,' Joanne said, without mercy.

Rufus looked at her and was silent. For an instant the two of them might have been alone in the room.

'And we ran, and we lay down in the reeds by the river,' said Richard, excitedly. 'And the Lucy men ran after us, and they came right by us, but they didn't see us. And then Rufus stood in the river and lifted me across, and we ran half the way home.' He laughed, with the undiscriminating ten-year-old zest for adventure.

'What will Sir Thomas do with him?' asked Mary, anxiously, of her husband.

'The Lucy men said that Sir Thomas would have him whipped,' said Richard, importantly.

Rufus shook him by the shoulder he still held and said, savagely, 'Be quiet!'

Mary, who had stood up, sat down again suddenly, her hands clasped in her lap. Anne covered her face and whispered, 'Oh, no, no!'

'He can't!' said John, with sudden fierceness. 'Sir Thomas has no right to have him whipped.'

'But, if he caught Will on his grounds——' began Mary.

'He can't have him whipped, only imprisoned. Unless he can prove riot——' He looked at Rufus. 'Was there a struggle?'

'Will resisted them for a few minutes, but there were three of them——'

'And you took no part in it?'

Rufus flushed scarlet but answered simply, 'No.'

'Then imprisonment is the only legal penalty,' said John, triumphantly.

'Yes, I dare say,' said Mary, impatiently, 'but will Sir Thomas care for that?'

'He is a justice of the peace.'

'And they were on his land and chasing his deer.'

There was a long silence, while they all thought painfully of William, with his gentleness and dignity and laughter, in the power of the great Sir Thomas Lucy, and so much in the wrong.

At last Mary got up, saying with a sigh, 'Well, Richard, you must take off your wet clothes and get to bed. William Hart, you had better go home. Your mother will be anxious for you.'

159

'Mother never worries about me,' answered Rufus.

'No,' said Mary, venomously, 'I see she has no need.'

And she had the satisfaction of seeing the shaft go home.

# CHAPTER 11

William was hustled up the avenue towards the Great House, hating to be pulled and tugged at by rough hands, he the son of the former bailiff of Stratford, he, Will Shakespeare, dragged along like a slave in the power of common men.

'We'll teach you Stratford people a lesson,' said one of Sir Thomas's men, hitting him between the shoulders to hurry him along, 'Coming sneaking an' thieving here. We saw you last night, and we would have caught you then but that you sneaked and thieved away before we could lay our hands on you.'

'I've never been here before,' William protested, trying to look back at him. 'It wasn't me last night——'

'We ain't going to argufy about personifications,' said the man who had hold of his right arm. 'We got you now, and that's all that's immaterial to us.'

'That's right,' said the little man who was on his left, 'and that's all that Sir Thomas will care for. We caught him on his land——'

'*In statu pupillari*, as the parson said on Sunday,' agreed his partner, 'or, red-handed.'

'Not red-handed,' William said, with a momentary flash of amusement. 'We hadn't even seen a deer yet, let alone shot one.'

'Ha!' cried the Educated Man. 'That's an admission. He says he came to shoot deer. We must edify Sir Thomas with that!'

'Well, get along with it, Master Newbury,' said the impatient man, pushing William from behind so forcibly that the little man on the left tripped over his own feet and nearly fell. 'Let's 'ave no more talk. We all know what Stratford men are like for *talk*. Maybe this fellow'll talk when he gets up on the gallows with a rope round 'is neck. Sir Thomas'll do all the talkin' that's needed now.'

Outside the door of the house, the Educated Man, who was also evidently chief among them, surrendered William's right arm to the impatient man, and went inside. The change was effected with great anxiety, and exclamations, of, 'Ready now? Careful! Got him?' as though William was a Hyrcanian Tiger, straining to devour them and held at bay only with difficulty. Then Master Newbury returned and beckoned them inside, saying in a respectful whisper, 'Bring him through to Sir Thomas's study.' William was feeling so

161

frightened that his mouth was dry, and he felt as though he had difficulty in breathing, and yet his fear seemed to sharpen his perceptions, so that he saw everything with tremendous clarity, as though he looked at a stage. He saw the great hall, with its fine panelling and high ceiling, and saw Lady Lucy sitting at the other side, by the fire, with the Chaplain, and another tall man, in his middle years, standing beside her. He had time to wonder why they were not at supper, and to decide that they probably had it later than at Henley Street, and even had time to be amused at the efforts of his captors to take off their bonnets and make some peculiar sort of obeisance towards the fireplace, without letting go their hold on his arms. And then he was in the study, and was conscious of nothing but Sir Thomas, looking up at him with a calm, expressionless face and very cold, clear eyes.

He was a handsome man, of fifty years of age or a little more, with a nose rather short and thick for perfection, but a good forehead, a rounded face, very fresh-coloured, moustaches curling over well-shaped lips, and a neat beard, cut straight across at the end. His Puritan leanings were shown by the plainness of his dress, but he gestured with a very white, ringed hand, and said quietly, 'Let him go.'

His men obeyed him at once, and stood aside, clutching their caps in their hands.

'Where did you take him?' enquired Sir

Thomas, without moving his eyes from William's face.

'Down by the far copse, sir,' answered his tenant, no longer garrulous.

'Was he alone?'

'No, sir.' Master Newbury gained courage. 'No, there was a whole pack of them there, sir. They assisted arrest, sir, very hard, and all we was able to take hold on, sir, was this fellow. The others all got away, sir, but I sent Page, sir, and some other men after them, and I hope they'll comprehend them, sir, and I told them to bring them straight up to the house, sir, hoping as I done right, sir.'

Sir Thomas's eyes wandered for a moment to his face and then back to William's. William no longer felt amused at the Educated Man.

'Quite right,' said Sir Thomas.

'Sir,' began William, in a breathless voice, 'there were only two of us, and a boy, and there was no violence.'

Sir Thomas raised his thin eyebrows. 'Only two of you? What is the name of the other man?'

William hesitated, and then said in desperation, 'I've heard that there is honour among thieves, sir, and, being taken like a thief, I must follow the rules of my trade. I dare not tell you that.'

'Hum,' said Sir Thomas, apparently unimpressed. 'What is your name, fellow?'

William flushed at the contemptuous voice,

but answered, 'William Shakespeare, sir.'

Sir Thomas straightened his back in awakened interest. 'Ah,' he said, 'son of John Shakespeare, the glover?'

'Yes, sir.'

'I know your father,' said Sir Thomas, 'a very worthy man, and a good citizen.' He leant back in his chair, resting his hands on the table, very much the Justice of the Peace. 'It is so much the worse,' he said, 'that you, being his son, should come here in this thieving manner, to trespass and steal. If you were some ignorant fellow, or hungry, there might be some justification made, but in you it is a far greater crime. What, isn't your father an Alderman?'

'Yes, sir.'

'And has been Bailiff and Chief Alderman. And I suppose that you hope one day to learn by his example, and to become alderman yourself. A fine respect you will have from your fellow-townsmen, if this is an instance of your behaviour! They will say, quite rightly *Quis custodiet illos—er—illos——*'

Master Newbury leaned forward hopefully, glad to add to his store of learning, but Sir Thomas coughed and became suddenly disconcerted and much more human, searching his mind for the ending of this familiar tag, which now so annoyingly escaped him. William, not at all sure whether he would more please or anger the Justice by his interference, ventured softly, '*Quis custodiet ipsos custodes*, sir?'

'Ah,' said Sir Thomas, looking up at him with something like a faint smile, 'you know some Latin, then?'

'A little, sir.'

Sir Thomas nodded, slowly. 'I remember you now. You wrote a play which was acted by the boys at the school. It was a good play, and you made a speech at the beginning of it, in very good Latin. Yes, I remember now. I spoke of you to your father, and said that he should send you to the university. Did you go there?'

'No, sir. My father's affairs wouldn't permit of it.'

'H'm. A pity.'

Sir Thomas turned his chair round sideways, abandoning his magisterial pose, and put his hand up to stroke his moustache, gazing thoughtfully on the ground. William stood very still, and Master Newbury and his companions, evidently disappointed at the slowness of Sir Thomas's vengeance, shifted uneasily on their feet and glanced at each other. William found time to look at the big books on the shelves and to wish that he could own a house which contained a quiet, comfortable study for himself, where he could write his poems and read his Ovid in peace.

'Can you write a fair hand?' asked Sir Thomas, suddenly.

'Yes, sir, I believe so.'

'What work do you do for your father? You work for him, I believe?'

'Yes, sir, I keep his accounts, and write letters for him, and attend to some of his business.'

'H'm,' said Sir Thomas again.

There was a knock at the door, and one of Sir Thomas's men presented himself, carrying a bow and something that looked like a small bundle of damp cloth. Master Newbury hurried back to intercept him, and interrogated him in a hoarse whisper, reminiscent of a church-warden rebuking a member of the congregation during the service.

'Master Page says,' he announced to Sir Thomas, after a brief, agitated conversation, 'that the others have escaped.'

'We lost them by the river,' Master Page explained eagerly. 'We were hard behind them, and then, quite suddenly, they disappeared. Just like witchcraft,' he added, darkly.

'Yes, yes, Master Page,' said Master Newbury, waving his hand. 'Sir Thomas en't goin' to be interested in the matter of their escaping, but only in the manner of it. They got away. Suffixit.'

Master Page, his spirits somewhat dashed, held out the bow in silence.

'Did they leave that behind?' enquired Sir Thomas.

'No, sir,' Master Page replied, defying all efforts of Master Newbury to take the message from him and interpret to Sir Thomas, 'I found this on the grass where this other fellow was taken, and a cap too. The other cap I found near the river.'

Sir Thomas sat in silence for a few minutes, while Master Page still stood to attention, holding the bow out in front of him like a pikeman at an inspection of troops.

'Well,' said Sir Thomas, at last, 'give them to Master Shakespeare.' He became magisterial again. 'True equity,' he said, 'which is the end of all law, is to temper justice with mercy. Though you deserve punishment, both for the trespass and for intent to steal, yet for your father's sake I will for the time remit it. But there must be no more such misdemeanours. Will you go bail for your companions on it?'

'Yes, sir,' William replied, though with some misgivings as to his influence on Rufus's behaviour.

'Very well,' said Sir Thomas. 'Master Newbury, Master Page, you have done well, and I thank you.'

Master Newbury looked reproachfully at his master for a moment and then took the bow and the damp caps and gave them to William, eyeing him sternly the while, as though to show that Sir Thomas might be deceived, but he wasn't. Then he enquired, 'Shall I take him to the gates, sir?'

'No,' Sir Thomas answered. 'I wish to speak to him further. There is no need for you to remain. I thank you all.'

Master Newbury bowed and herded his neighbours out of the room, but himself returned to remark anxiously, 'He's a very violent man, sir. Would you like me to stand by the door?'

Then Sir Thomas did smile, but replied courteously, 'No, I thank you. If I should need any assistance, I can call for the servants, but I hardly expect that I shall.' He waited until the door had shut, and then he got up from his table and came round to stand in front of the fire. 'There is a place for an usher at the school,' he said, in his calm, clear, gentleman's voice. 'If I were to recommend you to Master Aspinall for the office, would you accept it?' William looked at him stupidly and said, 'Sir?'

'You would be expected to assist Master Aspinall,' Sir Thomas continued, 'and also to teach the petits, preparing them for the school. Could your father spare you?'

'Yes, sir,' William answered.

'Master Aspinall has been unable to find anyone suited to the post, and, although your errand here tonight would hardly seem to indicate your fitness for it, yet I am inclined to believe that it was simply a piece of folly for which you are now sorry.'

'Yes, sir,' William agreed, heartily.

168

'Well?' enquired Sir Thomas.

'I should like it, sir, above all things.'

'There is a cottage for your use,' Sir Thomas remarked, casually, 'but probably you will not want to take it until you marry.'

'I am married, sir, already.'

'Are you?' said Sir Thomas. 'Then it may be you will be glad, after all, of the cottage. Well, I will write a letter to Master Aspinall, and you can take it to him in the morning. He will explain your duties to you and make all arrangements with you.' He sat down at his desk and wrote a brief letter, folded it, gave it to William, and rang a small bell for a servant. In no time at all, it seemed, William had made his bow to Sir Thomas and passed through the hall where the servants were now setting out the table for supper. He caught once more that swift living picture of Lady Lucy sitting by the fire in her green gown, laughing, and the chaplain nodding and smiling, and of the gentleman in the wine-red suit looking down at them both and saying something, and then the servant had shut the door upon him, and he was outside in the fresh night air, still half dazed with the suddenness of the change in his fortunes and longing to get home, to tell them of it.

They all exclaimed delightedly, though Mary looked a little grave, trying to reconcile her pleasure with her sense of justice.

'Oh yes,' William added, laughing, 'and Sir

Thomas said that he understood that we hadn't shot a deer, and so he would only call it a *venial* crime, since our *venery* hadn't prospered.'

'Sir Thomas is a very pleasant, witty man,' said John Shakespeare. 'I was sure that you would come to no real harm with him. He was very affable when I had dealings with him on the town's behalf. Still, I'm glad you got home in time to save me a journey. Rufus seemed to think that you might be in some danger, but I was sure that once Sir Thomas knew that you were my son, there would be little to fear.'

'Where is Rufus?' asked William, looking round. 'I thought I saw him here when I first came in.'

'He went out,' said Joanne, 'just after you arrived.' It was the first time she had spoken since she had completed Rufus's sentence.

'Ashamed to stay, most likely,' said Mary. 'I should think he *would* go, and I hope he never comes back.'

'Don't be angry with Rufus, mother,' said William, smiling. 'See what good has come of our adventure!'

'The good that came of it,' said Mary, severely, 'came from you and from Sir Thomas's respect for your father. If you had got a whipping, it would have been William Hart's.'

# CHAPTER 12

The cottage was found to be a small, neat, thatched house in Chapel Lane, and the energies of the entire household now seemed to be turned to installing William and Anne in their new home. Anne took a less active part in the affair than most of the others, because she was expecting another child in February, and already, before Christmas, she was very large.

'But then,' remarked Mistress Hart, commenting upon this, 'but then, Susanna was a very big child, wasn't she? *Very* big, indeed, considering she was only a six-months' baby.'

Anne blushed and Mary, uncertain as always with Mrs Hart whether she was being malicious or merely stupid, was extremely annoyed.

Mary was the general, in command of the move, and Joanne was her lieutenant. William found himself in the position of the commander of an allied army—invited to attend councils of war, but not expected to make too many suggestions nor to have much attention paid to those he did make. Robert Brown proved himself invaluable, but Rufus, as Mary said, was worse than useless. He would lounge about in the doorways, or sit on the window-seats, offering inferior advice while William mended a broken shutter, or giving kindly encouragement to Robert and Hamnet Sadler as they strained to move a heavy chest, though neglecting to mention to them that their efforts were entirely in vain since the chest was lodged against the corner of the wall. There was between Rufus and Robert a certain antipathy, obscured by Robert's restraint and by Rufus's joking, but still there. When they were together, Rufus was always more idle and irresponsible, and Robert was often to be seen perfectly sober and faintly disapproving while everyone else was laughing at something Rufus had said. No one had noticed this feeling between them, except William, and he looked upon it as a very different thing from the cheerful wrangling of Rufus and Dick Quiney. But then, he knew Rufus better than anyone else did, and it was not Robert's temper which concerned him, but Rufus's rare, red rage.

As soon as she knew that she was to live in her own house, Anne was determined to have the bed which had been given to her mother as a wedding present, and which her father had promised she should have on her marriage. One afternoon, she and William set out to walk to Shottery, to arrange that Hamnet's cart should fetch the bed during the next week. They found the cottage in its usual state of grimy disorder, and Joan doing a little haphazard washing, putting the clothes out on the hedge to dry. Anne's brother, Bartholomew, was there, having come to help Joan in the garden. Since the house and property would come to him on Joan's death, he had some interest in its upkeep, but he would probably have come to help his stepmother in any event. For all his placidity, Bartholomew had a strong sense of duty and of family propriety. He didn't like Joan any more than Anne did, but he never criticized her, and his kind heart could never bear to think of anyone being in want.

They all went indoors, and Anne thought, with a warm pride, that it was very pleasant to know that she need no longer dread going into Hewlands, now that she had her own husband and her own beloved child. Her stepmother had no more power to humiliate her. Secure in her position as mistress of William's house, and in the kind affection of his family and friends, she had left behind her for ever the old pitiful shrewish Anne of Hewlands. They all found, with some difficulty, places to sit down, and the three younger children, Anne's half-sister and two half-brothers, stood and stared at them, as usual, with runny noses and dirty, tangled hair while Anne, with kindlier feelings than she had ever before entertained towards her stepmother, opened the matter of her mother's bed.

'Hamnet Sadler, the baker, will fetch it with

his cart next Wednesday,' she said. 'I expect William, or someone else, will come with him to help take it down.'

'Well, I don't know,' said Joan, unexpectedly. 'I don't know as I can part with it. Where d'you think I'm going to sleep?'

'There's the bed I used to sleep in,' Anne answered, with a little sharpening to her voice. 'You've only got to move it through.'

'Yes, but why should I?' demanded Joan. 'Your father left the house and furniture to me, and even if he hadn't, I got a right to it by law, as long as I live. I know my rights, and it's just as well I do, I should think. There's always someone wanting to cheat a widow.'

'There's no matter of cheating here, mother,' said Bartholomew, in his deep, country voice. 'The bed was a wedding present to our mother, and——'

'Well, what if it was?' said Joan. 'I married your father, didn't I? I'm an honest woman, I suppose? There's nothing about that bed in the will. Maybe your father did mean Anne to have it after I die, but——'

'He didn't, he didn't!' cried Anne, with that old, dangerous lift to her voice which she had thought was forever laid aside. 'He said I was to have it when I got married. He said it on his *deathbed*.'

Joan shifted her ground. 'Well, why should you have it, anyway?' she said. 'If anyone was to have it, instead of me what's got a right to

174

it, I should think it ought to be Catherine. *You* married a rich gentleman, didn't you, with his fine relations in Stratford. Catherine's just married James Whateley, she knows *her* place in the world. She may be poor, but she's honest, at least, and she didn't have to marry in a hurry, like some I could mention. I should think she's got more right to have the bed than what you have.'

'Catherine's got nothing to do with it,' said Anne, tears of rage in her eyes. 'My father said I was to have it when I married.'

'Yes, after I was dead,' Joan persisted. 'I suppose you'd like me to die, wouldn't you? You've always hated me. I suppose you wish I *was* dead.'

'Yes, I do!' Anne shouted, all restraint gone at last. 'I wish you were dead, and you deserve to be, too. You're nothing better than a common thief. That's what you are, a common thief!'

'Anne, Anne,' William broke in, in a pitying, yet reproachful voice.

Anne and Joan still stared at each other, and the men, too, exchanged glances across the table. William stood up and said gently, 'We can talk about this another time. There's no hurry.'

He started towards the door, and Joan went after him, saying, 'Well, I got myself to think of now. I'm all alone in the world, and it's not right I should be turned out of house and home. Anne's always the same, never thinks of anyone but herself. You know as well as I do that——'

Her plaintive, self-justifying voice faded down the garden path. Anne looked at Bartholomew and he shook his head.

'She'll never let it go,' he said. 'I'll see you get it after she dies, but you'll never get it now.'

'But she might live for forty years,' Anne protested.

Bartholomew nodded his head, philosophically, as he might nod his head over ruined crops or a mildewed haystack. 'She might,' he agreed, 'but there it is. There's nothing you can do about it. Best put it out of your mind.'

'I could take her to law,' said Anne.

'Cheaper to buy a new bed,' said Bartholomew. 'Besides, you'd never win it. There wasn't no one else there, only him and you and her, and no one's going to take your word for it.'

'But you believe me?' said Anne.

'Yes,' answered Bartholomew, placidly, 'I believe you. But Chancery Judge might not. No, I'll try to talk her round to it, but I don't believe I'll succeed.' He stood up, smiling at Anne with a friendly, brotherly amusement. 'Once she starts talking about being a widow,' he added, cheerfully, 'you might as well give up hope. If all the widows in the Bible had 'bin like her, I don't know as they'd have needed so much protecting.'

They went slowly out of the house, Anne unreconciled, but hopeless. William and Joan were standing by the gate talking, and there were tears running down Joan's cheeks, but she was smiling up at him. Anne was surprised by a sudden bitter feeling of jealous resentment. She had never seen a woman looking at William in that way before—in that confiding and admiring way, as though he was a handsome young stranger. It gave her an unexpected feeling of uncertainty and unsureness, as though for an instant he was not her Will, but someone quite different, someone whom any woman might love. She went quickly down the path and brushed past her stepmother without looking at her again, and so out into the lane, without waiting for William. She heard him say, 'Hamnet will come on Wednesday. If I can't get away to come with him, mind you get him to help you move the other bed through.'

'All right,' Joan called back. 'I'll have it all ready.'

William hurried to catch Anne up. She was breathless and panting, with the weight of the child and with angry emotions.

'She says she doesn't mind letting us have it,' said William. 'I think we took her too much by surprise about it, that was all.' Anne was enraged by the tolerance in his voice.

'She's no call to make a favour of it,' she said. 'It's mine by right. Father ought to have mentioned it in his will, and then there wouldn't have been any question of whether she'd let it go or not.'

'Well,' said William, laughing, 'when I make my will, I'll include a special mention of the bed, so as to be sure there's no mistake after I die.'

'*Don't*, Will!' cried Anne, violently. 'That's not a joking matter.'

'Death?' enquired William, dispassionately considering it. 'Oh, Anne, death is so laughable a thing that no man, thinking of it, could ever be a grave man.'

Anne didn't answer, not understanding him. The light of battle had died out of her heart. She felt once more shamed and despairing. Nothing was changed. She was still the same woman who had once made every day hideous in the cottage by sordid and useless quarrelling. Her marriage and her love for Will and for her dear, sunny-tempered child had changed the situation, but not her. She remained the same, still ready to accept the challenge to a dishonourable skirmish, still defeated and put to flight. And, worst of all, she thought, William would always remember her as she had been that day at Hewlands, screaming and railing at Joan like any common woman.

When the bed arrived at Chapel Lane

cottage, and Hamnet Sadler and Robert Brown panted upstairs with the bed and its furniture and set it up again in the narrow little bedroom, Anne looked at it with something like hatred. This bed, where she herself had been born, where her mother and father had died, and Susanna had been conceived, this bed of her mother's, a disproportionately fine wedding present in the midst of humble possessions, had come to be a symbol to her of the rich continuity of a family, something to link death and life, end and beginning. She had looked forward with pride to think that her son and William's would be born on that same bed where her own life had begun. And now it was tainted and marred with the memory of that miserable scene with Joan, just as her young girlhood had gone down, trampled in that same mud. What had happened to her in those years, she thought, would be with her until she died, and here was the bed, won thus hardly, to remind her that this was so.

But the preparations at the cottage went forward quickly. Mary found it rather irritating to notice that all those friends of hers and of her husband and of William who offered cupboards and chests, stools and dishes, seemed to do so not only for their sake, but also, eagerly, for Anne's, as though they not only accepted her as William's wife, but liked her for herself. But then, thought Mary, grimly, they had never tried living in the same house with her. Before Christmas, Anne and William and Susanna had made the great journey from Henley Street to Chapel Lane and Anne felt like a king who, after long exile, comes at last to be crowned and to enter into his kingdom. She swept and dusted, cleaned and polished, and in the evenings when she sat and sewed and listened to Susanna singing her wordless little song in bed upstairs, and waited for William to come home, she was astonished to find herself so happy. And not the least part of her happiness was that William seemed so contented. It was as though Master Aspinall, the schoolmaster, with his learned talk and his rich library of books, had stilled at last that restlessness which had seemed to try all the time to drag William away from Stratford and from her. William would tell stories of the little boys with their pert answers and grave follies, and of the news which Master Aspinall always heard of the outside world, and of the long talks they enjoyed together when school was over. And Anne, stepping about in her own house, putting his supper before him, sitting across the table, or across the fireside, would smile and nod, thinking, 'Now, at last, he is mine. Now at last I have him safely mine.'

# CHAPTER 13

At Christmas, John and Mary invited their friends as usual to supper at Henley Street, including the Quineys, the Sadlers, Robert Brown—and the Harts, because if they didn't invite Rufus, he would come without an invitation. More than once in the past two years, when Mary had carefully excluded him from an invitation, he had strolled casually into the house a few minutes after they were all assembled, saying that he was looking for William. Then he would start back with anxious courtesy, crying, 'Oh, but you have guests!' and then, with a cheerful glint in his eye, place himself next to Joanne and wait for Mary to ask him to stay. And civility always compelled her to do so, with a powerful sense of defeat which wasn't lessened to any noticeable degree by Rufus's polite and astonished acceptance.

When Joanne was younger, Mary had always been rather doubtful of her chances of marrying. Men, she knew, disliked a shrewish woman above all things, and would far rather have a pleasant stupid woman than a quick sharp one, unless, of course, she was an heiress, and then it didn't much matter what she was like. But Joanne's portion would be a very small one, and her beauty was negligible, a good hazel eye and a trim figure, nothing more. Mary had anxious forebodings of herself and her husband trying to scratch together enough money to persuade a man to provide for a thirty-year-old scold of a daughter. And now Joanne had two suitors, and Mary was still not satisfied with her. Mary had a clear picture in her mind of the right behaviour for a fifteen-year-old girl in that position. She should be quiet and modest, showing no preference to either of the men (though, of course, not discouraging their attentions), until her parents informed her of their choice of a husband for her. Then she might, perhaps, be a little more free towards the chosen one, though always careful not to overstep the bounds of modesty. Joanne's behaviour bore no resemblance whatever to this ideal. She seemed to take a delight in setting them up one against the other, herself veering in between them like a weathercock in a landsman's wind. One minute she was abusing Rufus for his laziness, or jeering at his new Italian doublet. The next minute she was joining him in a laugh at Robert's expense, or impatiently cutting in on Robert's slow, thoughtful speech. It was not that Mary was seriously concerned lest Joanne should marry the wrong man. Joanne had always liked Robert Brown, and she was, after all, her mother's daughter. It wasn't likely that she would even consider marrying Rufus, who was infamous throughout the town of Stratford for his wildness and follies, and who had no money at all, nor any prospect of ever acquiring any. No, it was simply that Joanne, as usual, offended her mother's sense of propriety and right deportment. She thought with relief that Robert and Joanne would soon be married, and that Joanne's behaviour would then be her husband's responsibility. Meanwhile, Mary must watch Rufus disporting himself under her roof, with his own infuriating air of self-satisfaction and amusement.

Rufus was at his best during that Christmas evening. He kept the table laughing at his nonsense and his stories of the triumphs of idleness throughout the ages, he organized a game of forfeits in which even Mary Shakespeare forgot to look disapproving, and then, when they all sat down to rest, he sang love songs to the lute in his light, careless, untrue voice, with a sentimental quaver, and the light of mockery in his eyes. Joanne watched him, seeing the firelight striking red from his hair like a smith's anvil, his eyes red-brown under dark red lashes and straight devil's eyebrows, his brown skin touched with freckles, as he lazily strummed the lute and sang out of tune while he smiled at her, and she caught her breath suddenly under the knowledge that she could have loved him. If he had not been Rufus, the idle jester of the town, she could have loved him.

When Rufus put the lute down and stretched his arms above his head, someone suggested dancing, and Robert immediately moved to clear the room, helped by William and Hamnet and Dick Quiney. Rufus sat still and watched them, gratified by the sight of so much exertion.

'Ah yes,' said Joanne, with more than her usual sharpness, 'you're well enough as a musician. No doubt you've always been *light-fingered*. But when there's a man's work to be done, then someone else must do it.'

'Much may be gained,' Rufus answered, blandly, 'by being light-fingered. However, I'm also very light-footed, as you shall see. Let us cut a caper together.'

'You can cut one by yourself,' said Joanne, 'and eat it, too, with mustard, to heat your blood a little. I'd rather dance with a man of mettle.'

And she smiled at Robert, who had come to stand beside her. Rufus, still tipping his stool back until he leant against the wall, looked up at her, and a little flush came into his face, almost like anger, except that Rufus was never angry.

'Take care it isn't base metal,' he said, softly.

Joanne, moved by some undefined un-easiness, some instinct of danger, turned away as though she hadn't heard, and Robert took her hand and led her gravely into their places for the dance. After the music had begun, she looked back, half afraid, half hoping that Rufus would still be looking at her. But he was talking to Anne, and making her laugh, too, as she never did with anyone else, so that Joanne's faint disquiet vanished.

As they danced, Robert kept his eyes on her face, still with that impenetrable gravity. She wished that he would laugh more. Lately, she thought, he had not been nearly such pleasant company as he used to be. Sometimes she thought that he didn't like her as well as he used to. He had never been very talkative, but they had always been at ease together, and now he would often seem abstracted and would forget to answer her, falling into an awkward silence as though something had put him out of temper. And then she had the feeling all the time that she was trying to ward something off when they were together, though she didn't know what it was—she told herself that she didn't know what it was. But in an endeavour to avoid these silences and this sense of tension, she would find herself talking and laughing more than usual, and wondered if it was this which annoyed him, because certainly he was not as pleasant with her as he used to be.

When the dance ended, Joanne looked round for Rufus, but he was holding Judith's hand, ready to lead her into place, and loudly arguing with Hamnet about the next dance. Hamnet, who played the viol, was placidly repeating that he didn't know the dance which they wanted, and Rufus was insisting that he *must* know it, and it went like this—with a hasty whistled snatch, quite drowned by the noise in the room. The controversy was settled by Mary Shakespeare, who called in her penetrating voice, 'The next dance a "hay". Come, everyone into place for a "hay"!' and herself led Adrian Quiney into the middle of the room.

'Lord, I love a "hay"!' cried Mrs Hart. 'It's the best dance of them all. I wish I wasn't getting too old to do it, though. Oh, Will, are we going to dance this? You don't want to dance with an old woman like me. Can't you find a pretty young girl? Oh, but I mustn't say things like that to you now, must I? I keep forgetting you're married. Dear, dear! Of course, Anne can't dance now, can she? That's what I always say with children. They're all right when they've come, it's when you're carrying them that they're so much trouble. I remember with Rufus, there was a haymaking out in the croft, and I said to my husband, let's go along, he said, well you won't be able to dance, what's the good of going? I said, well, I'd like to watch it, even if I can't dance. So we went along, and my feet were tapping the ground, and I said, Oh, if only I could dance. I'd give anything to dance. And my husband said, I knew how 'twould be, I knew you'd want to dance if you came here. And it seemed like all I could do was to eat cherries. The cherries I ate that day, and sour! But that was all I wanted to eat. Cherries.'

Joanne grinned and turned to look up at Robert. But he had not been listening to Mrs Hart. His eyes were still upon her face.

'Shall we take our place?' said Joanne, quickly.

Robert took a sudden breath. 'No,' he said. 'Don't let's dance.' He drew her over to the window. As the music struck up and the dancers began to jog and thump up and down the room, they were cut off in a little cave of silence, the two of them alone.

'Look at the moon,' said Robert. Joanne glanced up at it, and then down again, but made no answer, recognizing that she was at last defeated. 'Joanne,' said Robert, 'I've been trying to speak to you for three days now, but I never seemed to be able to begin. You must know that I love you.'

Joanne looked up at him and said on a quick impulse, 'No, Robert!' He was looking out of the window still and took no notice. Perhaps he didn't even hear her.

'I have loved you,' he said, slowly, 'since you were a child. I have never wanted anyone else for my wife. I've waited to speak until you were older, until the difference in our ages would be less felt. I know that you're fully young still, but I dared not wait any longer.' His voice suddenly dropped and became husky. 'I *could* not wait any longer.'

All Joanne's elation and excitement had fallen away from her. She said breathlessly, 'Robert, I don't know.'

'I've spoken to your parents,' he said, reassuringly. He spoke more easily now. 'They've given their consent, and the match would make my father very happy.'

Joanne's mind was tossed by confusion and doubts. She found herself saying inwardly, 'God help me. God help me. What shall I do?'

'I love thee, Joanne,' said Robert, with that new violence which seemed so alien to his nature.

She met his eyes, and shook her head, wordlessly, and saw an intentness come into his gaze. He asked slowly, 'Could you not learn to love me?'

She shook her head again, and said, trembling, 'No. No, Robert.'

The music whirled round like a living thing above their heads.

'If my parents ordered me to marry you,' said Joanne, in a low voice, 'then, of course, I should obey them, but——'

'You know that I would never have you marry me for such a reason,' said Robert.

'No,' said Joanne. She did know it, and had known it before he spoke, and perhaps she wished that he would insist that her parents should make her marry him. Then it would be all settled, and she would have nothing to do but to submit.

After a moment, Robert said, in a voice more like his old one of brotherliness and kindness, 'I think perhaps I've spoken to you too soon. It's my fault. But if we wait for a few months, or even perhaps a year, then you may feel differently about it. Let's leave it there. I'll tell your parents that you are not ready for marriage yet, and in a little time you may feel that, after all, you could come to love me.'

He spoke with some confidence, but still waited anxiously for her reply. Joanne stood with her head turned away from him, looking at the familiar room and the moving dancers. She saw Dick's wife going stiffly round like a dull puppet, and Rufus laughing at Judith, his red hair clinging to his forehead with the heat. She saw William, with his smooth brown face and wide, observant eyes, watching Mrs Hart with quiet amusement. She had a feeling of haste and urgency, and yet she did not seem to be able to drag her mind back to a steady and undistracted consideration of her answer. It would be so easy, she thought, noticing Anne going upstairs to Susanna, to agree, and to leave Robert with that hope for the future. It would save so much argument and disagreement with her mother and father. And then, perhaps, it would be kinder to Robert to be a little indefinite in her answer. With an effort, she turned her head back, away from the noisy room, and looked up at Robert. And she knew at once that this was not a man to be lightly borne in hand, and that his love was too steady and honest to be cheated. For all her pretence, for all her twisting and endeavours to escape, she had known from the beginning that he would ask her to marry him, and had known what her reply should be, and that the reason, hidden as it was (or perhaps rather a secret from herself), was a reason which could not be set aside.

'No, Robert,' she said again. 'No. It can't ever be. You must find someone else.'

'There is no one else!' he said, with a note of suppressed fury in his voice, a fury not against her but against the situation. 'There has never been anyone but you. There is no one else for me.' The tears rushed into her eyes, and she said helplessly, with a sob in her throat, 'I'm sorry, Robert.'

He looked down at her with his steady blue eyes, and began to smile. He was just as she had always known him, kind and dependable. Nothing was different except his pain.

'It's all right, Joanne,' he said, very gently. 'Don't let it trouble you. It's all right.'

'I wish it *could* have been so,' cried Joanne, with all her heart. The music stopped, and everyone began to laugh and talk, standing strangely patterned where the dance had left them. Joanne and Robert still stood side by side, a little removed in body, vastly removed in spirit from all the others. Joanne thought that she had never been so unhappy.

Robert stirred. 'All's over,' he said. 'Don't think of it again.'

Rufus's voice rose above the rest in a shout of laughter, and Joanne fancied that Robert's expression hardened for an instant, but then immediately he was himself again. He added, 'I have to go away next week, up to the north, on business for my father.'

'Oh, no, Robert,' Joanne cried, 'don't go away!'

He smiled, a little oddly, with his brows drawn together. 'I'll be back before long,' he answered. 'This journey was arranged some time ago. If you need me, I shall be here.'

And then Dick Quiney came importantly up to them and told Joanne that she could dance with him. The music struck up Sellinger's Round, and Joanne with Dick, and Robert with Dick's wife moved forward and back, set and turned, with the width of the room between them. Joanne's face ached so much with the effort to keep a smile on it, that she half expected by the end of the evening to find it visibly bruised.

The guests went at last, laughing and noisy, and calling back thanks. William and Anne went home, with Susanna sweetly sleeping, her round, delicate little face resting against

William's shoulder. And still Joanne must help Mary Shakespeare to tidy the room and clear away the last of the glasses before she could go to bed. And she thought that her mother seemed very much out of temper, too, so that she wondered if Robert had made an opportunity to talk to her during the evening, and to tell her that the marriage would not, after all, take place.

She finally escaped upstairs, and undressed and lay down on her bed. Her familiar bedroom looked strange to her, because she herself felt so different. She had always held a very good opinion of herself. She had her faults, of course, but they were good, round, admirable faults. She had even felt that they gave her some distinction. She did not really want to part with them. But now, for the first time in her life, she felt deeply and miserably ashamed of herself. There was nothing to admire in her behaviour towards Robert, nothing that could pass for independence and courage. First in innocence, but later to please her vanity, she had trapped him into a security of her love, a certainty that she would marry him. The one courageous thing about the affair was her refusal of him, and even that might perhaps proceed from obstinacy and not from virtue. She looked back into the past two years and saw a dozen times when she had falsely encouraged Robert, and a dozen more when she had laughed at him, slighted him and teased him. And always, it seemed, it had been when Rufus was there. Rufus had played the Mephistopheles to her Faustus. If she had thrown away something precious, Rufus had been the chapman, pressing cheap things upon her in its place. She couldn't forget Robert's face, with the look of doubt on it, and then of surprise, and at last of hurt pride and disappointment. And, for all his forbearance, it was impossible that Robert should not feel some contempt for her and be conscious of a lessening of his regard for her, and, what was worse, she deserved that he should feel this. She thought of the faint smile on his face when she had cried out, 'Don't go away,' like a spoilt child, giving nothing and demanding everything. Even in the darkness, alone, the colour came hotly into her face as she thought of it, and she cried for a long time, miserably and quietly, because she was ashamed, and nothing could ever alter it.

## CHAPTER 14

It was quite true that Robert had talked to Mary Shakespeare later on that Christmas evening. He had told her briefly that Joanne did not feel that she could be happy married to him, and had added in his quiet and compelling fashion that he hoped that she would not mention the matter to Joanne, as he didn't want her to be distressed.

'Distressed!' exclaimed Mary to her husband later. 'I'd give her "distressed!"'

She had never been angrier with anyone in her life. She was so indignant about Joanne's obstinacy and vanity in refusing the one good offer of marriage which she was ever likely to have that she could hardly speak to her. It was a tribute to her strength of mind and to Robert's impressive personality that she never did open the subject with Joanne. And then, Robert had made it clear to her that it would be useless for John to exert his authority and insist that Joanne should marry Robert. It was extraordinarily stupid of Robert, Mary thought. He should know that young girls never knew their own minds in such matters. Unless they felt an immovable dislike of the man, it was only kindness to them to make such decisions for them. But still, since he refused to allow this reasonable course, there was nothing for it but to hope that Joanne would in time come to her senses. Mary recognized in Joanne a good deal of her father's stubbornness. If she tried to persuade her, she would only make her more mulishly determined. But if she let her alone, Joanne's affection for Robert might overcome whatever odd notions she had in her head.

Meanwhile, Mary's mind was distracted from Joanne and her follies by Anne's illness. This had been increasing since Christmas, but so gradually that Mary had hardly realized it. Mary herself was engrossed in New Year entertainments and busy in the house, and two weeks went by before she thought with a guilty start that it was some time since she had visited Anne, although William when his father met him in the town had said that she wasn't well. She hastily packed a basket with food ready prepared, put in some sweetmeats for Susanna, and set off full of good intentions. But when she got there, she found that she was too late. Judith Sadler was there, helping Anne with the midday meal, her own baby playing with Susanna on the floor, and a general air about her of being very much at home. Mary, who had come to take charge of a disordered household, to relieve Anne of all anxiety and to perform a Christian and motherly duty, found instead that she was an intruder upon two young married women who evidently wondered why she had come. Her presents were gratefully accepted by Anne, and immediately laid aside. Susanna pulled away when she was told to kiss her grandmother, because she wanted to go on playing with her small visitor, and Anne removed the sweets, saying that she mustn't have them before dinner. They all sat and talked, pleasantly enough, but still Mary had the

195

feeling that Anne and Judith were only waiting for her to go, so that they could go on working and talking together. She asked if there was anything she could do for Anne, and Anne politely answered that she wanted nothing, and then, a moment later, when Judith was putting on her cloak to leave, Anne asked her to buy something for her in the town. So Mary, after lingering a little longer, walked back to Henley Street with her empty basket. She felt slighted and indignant (and no less so because she felt that she had been remiss), and she felt lonely too. She saw other women who, visiting a young household, advising the young mother and indulging their grandchildren, renewed their own married days and kept still some claims of interest in the future. If Joanne had been a true daughter, thought Mary, she too might have hoped for such pleasures, or if little Anne had not died, or even those two first daughters, Joan and Margaret, who had died in infancy but who still had a place in the family for Mary, though for no one else. But instead of that affectionate and confiding daughter who would have so delighted her, she had instead Anne for a daughter-in-law, Anne with her awkwardness and silence, and, worse still, with that indefinable air of being defenceless and easily hurt, so that one always left her with an uncomfortable feeling of not having been kind enough.

And Anne was looking very ill, thought

Mary. She would never agree that Anne was a good wife for William, and was sure that he would have been much happier if he had never met her, but still, she would not have Anne die. The strong light of death shows a truer image than was ever seen before, and even its glancing flame, flickering near, strikes off a poignant, momentary likeness. So now, as Mary walked home with that disquiet in her mind, she was conscious of some faint stirring of affection, not for the familiar Anne who always exasperated and disappointed her, but for that small and tender creature who stood behind and who moved her compassion and gentleness.

As so often happens, after the long waiting, the time for the birth of Anne's baby seemed to come at the end very suddenly, and she was very ill. 'You mark my words,' Mrs Hart had said, 'it'll be twins,' and it was one of her most annoying traits that she was always right when everyone wished that she wasn't. Judith took Susanna away to her own house and gave William his meals there, and Mary and the midwife spent night and day with Anne, until at last the twins were born, first the girl, a lusty, strong child with a powerful cry, and then the boy, who was so little and puny that Mary's first concern was that he should be baptized before he died.

She went downstairs to ask William what the children were to be named.

'Hamnet and Judith,' William replied.

Mary looked surprised. She had hoped very much that the twins might be called John and Mary, or even Robert and Agnes. 'If it was a girl,' William explained, 'Anne wanted her to be called Judith, and if it was a boy, Hamnet. Judith has been so good to Anne since we were married, and especially during the last few months.'

'Yes, of course,' Mary agreed, and went back upstairs to the sick room, thinking that no matter how much you did for young folks, they never thought as much of you as of their own generation. All her forbearance, the long months when she had housed William and Anne, and all her care of Anne when Susanna was born, all this went for nothing besides a little gossip and friendly assistance from Judith Sadler. And, thinking this, she entered once more whole-heartedly into the struggle for Anne's life.

It was some days before Anne was out of danger, and some weeks before she was able to get up and move about. And, even then, there was a startling change in her. She had looked before like a strong, healthy country woman, with a good colour and a sturdy figure. Now there were hollows under her cheek-bones, and there was a pallor in her face which made her look, oddly enough, much more of a lady, so that it was almost strange to hear her voice still unchanged, with its rounded vowels and country phrases. She seemed to have lost, too, that suppressed energy which always lay behind her look of indifference and calmness, ready always to show itself in a sudden burst of love or anger. William told himself that this change was only temporary, and that when she had recovered her health, she would recover also her old strength of will and her vehement likes and dislikes. But meanwhile he found this smoothness disconcerting, almost chilling. His pride in his son, so dearly longed-for, was checked by the fear that the birth might have taken from him and from Anne something which could never be recovered.

In April, Gilbert was to return to Stratford for a visit, and everyone looked forward to the event with eagerness. The absent member of the family, he had acquired disproportionate and undeserved merits in the eyes of those who remained behind. Anne had never met him, and thought of him as a second Bartholomew, a new brother, who, as the nearest to William, would finally welcome her into the Shakespeare family. John and Mary thought of him as their new eldest son, full of wisdom and the maturity which only travel and London could give. Richard welcomed a new companion in such engrossing occupations as fishing and shooting at the butts, and Edmund confidently expected a handsome present. But, above all did Joanne long for his arrival. Since William's departure from

Henley Street she had missed him very much, and she hoped that Gilbert now would take his place as an ally against her mother and as a companion of nearly her own age.

Gilbert arrived at Henley Street on the day he was expected, was warmly greeted, and disappointed everyone but Edmund. He *had* brought him a present and since Edmund, who had been only two when he went away, remembered nothing of his brother but the name, he was perfectly contented. Gilbert had gone away a boy, tall for his age, and unusually mature, but still a boy. He returned a young man, with a small, curling beard and moustache, and dressed in neat, beautifully-tailored London clothes. And he was very silent. Either he was more silent than when he went away, or else they had forgotten how silent he was. They asked him questions and told him the family news and the Stratford gossip, and he replied briefly with a detachment which, surely, was greater than when he went away—or had they forgotten how detached he had always been?

In the evening, he strolled round to the cottage to visit William, who alone remembered and expected Gilbert exactly as he was. Gilbert greeted Anne politely, looked at the sleeping children with a manifest lack of interest, and talked to William exclusively of business and politics and the likelihood of serious trouble with Spain. And Anne watched

William's face lighting up, watched him travelling gratefully away from Stratford and his narrow world of mischievous pupils and household accounts, into the great affairs of the realm and the great folk of London, and she felt that she would like to take hold of Gilbert in her two hands and put him out of the door and bolt it against him. Before he left, Gilbert said, casually, 'I saw Robert Brown in London. What follies has Joanne been committing here?'

'Nothing has been said,' answered William, 'but we think that she has refused his offer of marriage.'

'Something *will* be said,' Gilbert remarked, 'and about time too! Robert isn't a plaything, to be tossed about by a young girl's fancies.'

Anne, who had herself thought that Joanne had been greatly mistaken, was moved to say, 'If Joanne felt that she couldn't love him, then perhaps she was right in what she did. It is a matter which concerns her, after all.'

Gilbert looked at her coldly for a moment, and then said, with a faint smile which was more like a sneer, 'And perhaps you'd say that it was her own concern if she took it into her head to take her own life? She's always been too much indulged, ever since Anne died, and this is the result.'

He stood up and added, with a change of tone, 'Well, Will, it's good to see thee again. I'll wait for you when school is closed tomorrow.' He went to the door, with William behind him, and paused there to look back at Anne, sitting unmoving by the fire. He seemed to hesitate for a moment, and then made her a polite little bow, and said, 'Goodnight.'

Anne bent her head and gave him an unsmiling 'Good night' in exchange, and listened to his firm footsteps in the lane. William closed the door and came back to stand beside her, looking at her with an enquiring lift of his eyebrows.

'Let's go to bed,' said Anne, and went quietly upstairs, while William put out the fire.

'Gilbert has never had the trick of showing his affections,' William said, tentatively, when he came upstairs.

'Oh?' said Anne, engrossed in taking down her hair.

And then Judith began to cry loudly, and Hamnet woke and added his thin wail, so that they didn't speak of Gilbert again.

The next morning was market day, and Mary Shakespeare went out early, leaving Joanne with several tasks to do at home. Gilbert lounged about, and then, when Margaret went through into the kitchen, he came to stand beside Joanne, watching her in silence.

'No doubt it's very nice to have nothing to do for a change,' said Joanne, tartly, 'though, from what Robert said——' she paused for a fraction of a minute, but recovered herself almost at once and finished, 'your master doesn't make you work too hard in London.' Gilbert didn't answer, and she glanced up to find him looking at her with a very grim expression.

'The air of London must be melancholic,' she remarked, laughing. 'Ever since you've been home, you've looked quite jaundiced. If you ask Mistress Hart, she'll give you a draught for it, with plenty of good conversation to help it down.'

'Tell me, Joanne,' said Gilbert, slowly and softly, 'why did you say to Robert Brown that you wouldn't marry him?'

She flushed and answered too quickly, in the manner of one trying to forestall an attack, 'Did *he* tell you?'

Gilbert continued to look at her with narrowed eyes.

'I saw him in London,' he said. 'He was in low spirits, and he never mentioned you, so I guessed what the trouble was and taxed him with it, and he confessed at once.'

'Anyway,' said Joanne, rallying, 'it's no concern of yours.'

'Ah,' said Gilbert, slowly nodding his head. 'So that's the way the wind blows. No concern of mine. But it will be my concern, I suppose, and Will's too, when you're old and penniless and we must provide for you because you were too proud to take an honest husband. For God's sake, what more do you want? Robert is a gentleman, he'll be a wealthy man when his father dies, and he loves you, though that, by heaven, is no recommendation to his wit! What are you waiting for? With your face and fortune, my girl, you can hardly look for anything better than this, and you should count yourself lucky to have got as good an offer. In fact,' he added, thoughtfully, 'as a friend of Robert's, I suppose I should try to persuade him to do better for himself than to marry a scold with no portion.'

'The affair is between him and me,' Joanne said, breathing rather fast, 'and you can keep your long nose out of it.' Gilbert was a little sensitive about the length of his nose, so that this was a shrewder blow than it seemed. 'And, anyway,' Joanne went on, pressing home her advantage, 'who are you to advise on such matters? They say that there are plenty of heiresses and rich widows in London, but none seems to have fallen into your net. You're ready enough with your talk of providing for me in my old age, but if you're not already dead of the spleen, which I expect you will be, you won't have much money to endow me with if you're going to spend the rest of your life as serving boy to Master Harrison.'

Gilbert drew his breath in sharply at that, but after a moment's pause, he said in his usual drawling, sardonic way, 'Very true. No doubt I shall have none to spare, and you may starve in the streets for all I care. But perhaps it won't come to that. After all, there's always William Hart. I'm sure we could bribe him to marry you. He'd probably cut a throat for a shilling, and a crown would be enough to make him marry. Kings have married for the sake of Crowns, so why not Rufus?'

He glanced at Joanne, and was encouraged to continue.

'And what a match!' he said admiringly. 'An idle, swaggering good-for-nothing, the mock of the town, puffed out with his own vanities, and thinking that men are laughing at his wit when in fact they're jeering at his folly. A jester, a fool, fit to make my lady smile and then to be whipped because he oversteps his bounds. Now there's a fit husband for you. You did well to refuse to marry Robert Brown, and I'm sorry that I abused you for it. I shall tell Robert that you were wiser than either of us, and that you knew better the kind of husband you deserved. Marry Rufus. If you get hungry, you can always eat words, and you can warm yourself at hair of the fool's colour. Marry Rufus. Then Robert will escape a wife he little merits, and you will get a husband who exactly matches your deserts.'

Having said all this in the same pleasant, smiling way, Gilbert turned on his heel and went quietly out of the house, leaving Joanne blind with rage, her hands shaking so much that she dropped Mary's Venetian glass on the floor, and saw it break into a hundred pieces.

And she was suddenly afraid, too, because, for all her defiance, she couldn't take Gilbert's opinions lightly. She had never yet known his judgement to err, and she respected it more than she would ever admit.

When Mary came home and scolded her for breaking the glass, Joanne found herself blaming not Gilbert but Rufus.

It was on the afternoon of that same day that Rufus strolled into the house and found Joanne alone there, doing some mending which she hated and which her mother had insisted must be done then for the sake of the daylight, although she had hoped to pay a visit to Anne.

'Why aren't you at work?' she demanded, as Rufus sat down by the window and put his feet comfortably up on a stool.

'Hush!' said Rufus. 'Do not profane the quiet day with such wicked blasphemies.' He grinned at her disapproving face. 'My good master has told me to call at several houses on his account, and I'm now calling at one house on my own account. You're glad to see me here,' he added cheerfully. 'You know you are. You were very dull here until I came.'

'Not at all,' Joanne answered. 'I was enjoying my own thoughts, which are better worth listening to than your babbling.'

Rufus stretched lazily and yawned, looking at her from underneath his lashes with an air of enjoyment.

'I've hardly dared to come near the house lately,' he remarked. 'Your mother always looks at me grimly, and now there's Gilbert home. I met him this morning, and he looked so sour that I thought he must be ill, and asked him if it wasn't early in the year for him to be eating crab-apples.'

'Probably the sight of you turned his stomach,' said Joanne, viciously tugging at the needle which wouldn't pull through.

'No,' Rufus answered, blandly, 'he said it was the Stratford air which didn't suit him. He thought there was too much brain sickness about.'

Joanne said nothing. She worked in silence, and Rufus watched her. Then he said, still with that unmistakable air of self-satisfaction, 'You know, Joanne, I thought that you would have been married before now, or at least betrothed.'

She glanced up at him briefly and then down again.

'My mother was quite sure of it,' Rufus went on, chuckling. 'She kept saying, "Mark my words, Joanne will have married Robert Brown before midsummer next." She's quite ill-used about it. She'd decided what you'd have for the wedding breakfast, and the only thing she couldn't make up her mind about

207

was what name you'd give the first boy—whether it would be Robert, or John, or William.'

He was still grinning at her with the old teasing, baiting look which she could remember since she was a small girl and used to fly into tantrums with him. She kept her eyes obstinately on her work.

'Still,' Rufus went on, with a shade more seriousness, 'I'm glad you're not marrying Robert. He's such a dull fellow. I can just see him in ten years' time, with a large stomach and a good red face, and a "Hrmph!" every time before he speaks. You'd do far better to marry me.'

Joanne looked up at him sharply and seemed about to speak, then let her breath go and said coolly, 'And what would we live on?'

'Sweet words, and honeyed kisses,' Rufus answered, but, oddly enough, he looked quite sober now.

'Hah!' Joanne snorted.

'Well, you love me,' Rufus remarked, calmly.

Joanne laughed at that. 'Do I?' she said, contemptuously.

'Certainly,' answered Rufus. 'What other reason could you have for not marrying Robert?'

'I thought he was such a dull fellow!'

'Oh yes, so he is. But, after all, so are most husbands. No, that wouldn't have been enough to make you outface your mother and refuse a worthy fellow like Robert. The reason was that you loved me. So, you'd better marry me.'

There was a long silence, and then Joanne put her work aside, and folded her hands in her lap. She looked at him with bright eyes and flushed cheeks, as he lolled in the window-seat, and she spoke very quietly.

'Marry you?' she said, gently. 'Do you think I am mad? Marry you, whose very name is enough to make all the town laugh? How do you think I could feel any respect for myself, when I couldn't feel any respect for my husband? You may jeer at Robert as much as you like, but he is respected and admired wherever he goes. What does anyone admire you for? Oh, perhaps you're admired in the taverns because you drink your glass of ale faster than the next man!'

'Lord, Joanne,' said Rufus, still lounging in the same position, 'you must have been listening to too many Puritan sermons. You never used to set such a value on respectability.'

'Oh well,' said Joanne, 'an idle good fellow is well enough for a plaything, or at a Christmas party, but for a husband I should want someone I could be proud of. What should I reply to the children when they asked me what notable deeds their father had done? "Let me see, children, there was that time your father went deer-stealing with your

Uncle William, and he ran away without striking a blow and let your Uncle be taken." '

Rufus started to his feet, the blood suddenly in his cheeks, and stood over her in a fury.

'If you were a man, I'd kill you for that!' he said between his teeth.

Joanne looked calmly up at him. 'Killing with words is easy,' she said. 'There's none so valiant as the man who kills with "ifs".' Rufus swung round on his heel and went to stand with his back to her, looking out of the window. Joanne took up her work again, but her hands were trembling a little, so that she only pretended to sew. There was another long silence. Time rocked and jolted under their feet, like a horse charging in battle, and the words which could never be unsaid stood between them like slanting stakes stuck in the ground, to prevent them from ever retracing their steps. Rufus turned round at last and looked at her, and it was a Rufus she had never seen before except for fleeting, half-mistaken moments. He looked perfectly grave and lowering, not angry, but as though there was a blackness upon him, a sudden thunder sky.

'Idle,' he said, 'how could I be anything but idle? Ever since I was a child, my mother told everyone that I was idle, and laughed about it, and so did they. What do you expect from me? Did you expect me to become a sober man of business like Gilbert?'

'Yes,' cried Joanne, 'if you were *man* enough, but you're not. What a womanish thing to do, to hide under your mother's skirts! What is it to you, what she says of you? Did you have to make it all come true?'

Rufus stood and looked at her still, with the same dark intentness. Then he said with a sudden violence, 'I promise you one thing. I swear by the Blood of God, that I'll never ask you to marry me again!'

'You didn't ask me,' said Joanne, and tried to say it lightly.

Rufus gave a short, rough laugh. 'Then you can rest assured I never shall,' he said.

He turned and strode to the door, jerked it open, went out and slammed it behind him. Joanne saw him for an instant as he went quickly by the window, looking straight ahead, like a stranger. Then she closed her eyes and sat for a long time quite still, in an acuteness of suffering that was almost like vacancy, as though her mind and body dissolved under it, leaving only a heart's pain that filled the universe. She had never loved Rufus as dearly as then, and every word she had spoken struck back at her, loving him. And yet, through it all, she knew that she had been right to refuse him, that it was the only thing for her to do. And, knowing him as well as she did, she knew, too, that he would never retract the oath he had sworn. He would never again ask her to marry him.

When he passed the window, he had gone
from her as surely as any stranger, seen for a
moment and then vanishing into unknown
paths.

## CHAPTER 15

After the birth of Hamnet and Judith, there
came a time of great tranquillity for Anne and
William. It had none of the ecstasy of their
first summer love, nor the tender, clinging
quality of the first months at Henley Street,
but, for the first time, they lived their life
entirely together, with interests shared, and all
the trivial pleasures and concerns brought
together for their mutual discussion and
enjoyment. It was true that William left for
school early in the morning and didn't return
until after the prayers at five o'clock, but in
the evening he would describe the small events
of the day until Anne felt that she had taken
part in them. She even knew the little boys by
name, how James was the ringleader in
mischief, and how Nicholas always arrived
late and always with a new excuse, and how
Cuthbert and Anthony had had a fight because
each of them claimed that he was the better
scholar, and how the matter was settled by

Master Aspinall, who beat them both for the sin of vanity. She knew which boys stayed to dinner, coming from outlying parts, because it was William's task to take the meal with them and to correct their table manners, and he would describe their conversation, with its childish boastings and schoolboy speculation about voyages of exploration, and whether the men who lived in America really had two heads, as it was said, and whether if you sailed far enough you could come to an enchanted land where time had stood still and where men still lived who remembered Alexander the Great and Caesar.

In return, Anne would tell William her own small pieces of news. Susanna, their pride, had picked up one of Master Aspinall's great books and had sat all morning with it open on her knees, turning the pages and pretending to read. Hamnet, all unprompted, had confided to Mistress Hart, 'My father goes to school, but he doesn't learn there.' Judith, in one of her blind and mysterious rages, had flown at Susanna's doll and broken its head off and stamped on the decapitated body. Mary Shakespeare had called, and had spent the whole visit in criticizing Anne's method of making preserve. Hamnet Sadler had been knocked down by a horse and had broken his arm, and the elder Judith had fainted when he was brought home, and then scolded him when she was revived.

In the summer evenings, William would sometimes help Anne in the garden, where she spent happy hours cultivating cottage plants, and the children would try to help her with their clumsy, ineffectual little hands. (But, if Anne got too engrossed, Judith would sometimes run screaming on to the flower-beds and trample down the flowers, and then stand and look at her with that dark, secret look of hers, while the other two stared in astonishment.) On holidays they would usually take the children to Henley Street, although these were times of very mixed pleasure, with the danger of the children's misbehaviour with their grandmother, and a certain jealousy between Mary Shakespeare and Joanne, while Edmund could always be relied upon to lead the children into mischief if he could. And then they would return gratefully to their own little house, walking slowly down the garden path, with Anne lingering to point out a plant newly shooting green, and with the children running on ahead, shouting, glad to be home and free from the restraint of Henley Street. With these quiet, friendly, domestic occupations, Anne, at least, was quite contented.

For William, there were other pleasures which came from his work at the school. Master Aspinall had taken a great liking to his young usher, and William would often go back to his house after supper, to play chess, or to borrow a book, or to talk about a book he was returning. More than once he was invited home to take supper with the parents of one of his boys, and several times he was asked, with Master Aspinall, to take wine at some of the big houses round Stratford. Once, he was actually invited to dinner at Charlecote, and Sir Thomas Lucy treated him with dignified kindness, and offered to lend him any books he desired from his library. His poetry was everywhere the means of opening doors to him, and he had started to write a long poem on the subject of Venus and Adonis which Master Aspinall greatly liked. Anne had no understanding of his poetry, but she knew that it pleased Master Aspinall and the other gentlemen, and also that writing it made William happier and more contented.

In all this time, there was only one real shadow upon them, and that was the health of little Hamnet. They thought at first that he was outgrowing the delicacy of his babyhood, but, although he seemed a reasonably sturdy, healthy little boy, still he was periodically overtaken by these spells of sickness which neither the wisdom of the physician nor the experience of Mary Shakespeare could explain. For a few months they would think that he was cured, and then the flush and the fever and weakness would come upon him in the same frightening way, and every time Anne was afraid of losing him. It seemed to make it worse that, in between the bouts of illness, he was so dauntlessly determined to behave like other children. He adored Edmund, and would follow him unquestioningly into any dangers from tree-climbing to chasing cows. He loved to wrestle with his father or with Richard, and, even when he was ill, always demanded to know what mischief the boys had been doing that day, and was eager to go to school himself. When he was three, he could repeat the alphabet, and at four, he could point to all the letters on the cross-row. In the months when he was free from the sickness, he was so full of life and energy that it seemed ridiculous to worry about him, but then, during each attack, Anne would think, '*This* time he might not recover. This might be the end.' She did not see how she could have borne it without William. It seemed as though all his love for his son turned to courage and invincible faith when Hamnet was ill, so that even these grieved and anxious nights brought their own strange happiness as they watched together.

As for Judith, Anne was quite sure that the Devil was in her, and William said, laughing, that with Judith they never knew whether to whip her or to send for bell, book and candle.

One evening in September, when the twins were five years old, William came home slightly earlier than usual, brushing past Hamnet in the front garden, and hurried inside, calling for Anne. She came out of the

216

kitchen, wiping her hands on her apron.

'I'm going out to Charlecote, Anne,' William called, as soon as he saw her, 'with Master Aspinall. Some players from London are giving a performance there tonight, and Sir Thomas has asked us to go.'

'Oh, Will, you can't go tonight!' cried Anne. 'You promised to take Hamnet to see the archery. He's been out there for an hour and more, all ready and waiting for you.'

'I'll take him tomorrow,' said William. 'I must hurry, or I shall be late.'

He turned and went quickly out into the garden again, where Hamnet fell in beside him, running along and looking up into his face, saying eagerly, 'Are we going now, father?'

William stopped short. 'You stay here, Hamnet,' he said firmly. 'I'll take you out another day, but I'm busy this evening.'

'But—but, you said——' began Hamnet, the eagerness faltering, but hope still there.

'Not tonight,' repeated William. 'Stay with your mother.'

And he almost ran down the path, banging the gate behind him and going quickly down the lane. But still, as he went, he could hear Hamnet's voice raised in half-incredulous, horrified tears as he realized that his father was really breaking his promise and going without him. When William glanced over his shoulder, he saw Hamnet standing still in the middle of

217

the path and crying bitterly, while Anne hurried to kneel down beside him and take him in her arms. He hesitated, but then went on his way, knowing well enough the buoyancy of Hamnet's spirits, and telling himself that he would make up to him for the disappointment another time. And yet, there was a shadow on him which lasted even until he arrived at Charlecote.

It was late that night when William reached home and got quietly into bed beside Anne. She woke up when he came in, and knew from his breathing and small movements that he was awake for a long time afterwards, but she didn't speak to him, because she was angry that he should disappoint Hamnet for such a foolish thing as a play. In the morning, William slept late and was forced to eat a very hasty breakfast and hurry immediately away, in order to be in time for school. It seemed to Anne that his manner was odd, and he didn't look at her when he kissed her goodbye, but she thought that he was merely tired, and anxious not to be late.

'Will father take me out this evening?' asked Hamnet, looking after him.

'I don't know,' replied Anne. 'Now, stop worrying, Hamnet,' she added sharply. 'Your father has more important things to do than to play with little boys. You must be patient.'

And then her heart misgave her, as she saw Hamnet's face fall, and knew that she had spoken crossly because she was still annoyed with William.

Once more, Hamnet got ready to go out and hung on the gate waiting for his father. And once more he was disappointed. William came home so late that it was the children's bedtime before he arrived. He went upstairs to say goodnight to them while Anne put the supper on the table. She heard Hamnet say,

'Father, will you take me to see the archery tomorrow?'

'I don't know, my son,' William answered. 'I must make no promises to thee, for fear of breaking them.'

'Mother said that you were too busy to take me,' said Hamnet. 'You won't always be too busy, father, will you?'

'No, no, of course not,' said William, hastily, and came downstairs almost at once, though usually Anne had to call him away for his supper.

'Well,' said Anne, when they were sitting down, 'did you enjoy the play? How was Sir Thomas?'

'Very well,' answered William, absent-mindedly. He laid down his knife and looked at her. 'Anne,' he said, 'I'm going to London.'

'To London?' Anne repeated, in confusion. 'When? What for?'

'I must leave in a few days' time,' said William.

'But—how long will you stay there?'

'I don't know.'

Anne gazed at him in astonishment, but could find no words for the questioning in her mind. The suddenness of it had quite overthrown her. She could only think of some flight from justice. William was in debt, perhaps, or had quarrelled with someone and stabbed him. With these desperate thoughts, it was strange to find William continuing calmly, 'The company of players at Charlecote last night were the Admiral's Men. The chief of them was Edward Alleyn, the great actor, and I talked to him. He said that he'd take me into the company as a hired man.'

'But, *why*, Will? Why should you want to go?'

'I've always wanted to go to London,' said William. 'I should have gone instead of Gilbert, but for our marriage.'

'But, to become an *actor*,' Anne protested, 'when you are here a schoolmaster. How can you give that up to become an actor?'

'I should only start as an actor,' said William. 'They have great need of new plays. I should begin as a hired man, playing small parts, and then, if I wrote a play which suited them, they'd pay me for it. And, anyway, the stage would be only a beginning. Once I'm in London, I can find a patron for my poetry.'

Anne was silent. She did not really understand anything he was saying, except that he threatened to leave her. Out of her bewilderment, she said, 'But, why must you go now, Will? Why *now*, when we've been so happy?'

'*You*'ve been happy,' he corrected quickly.

'Oh, Will!' cried Anne, on a sudden, high note of pain.

'No, no, I didn't mean that,' said William, remorsefully. 'I've been happy too. But, Anne, I knew that it couldn't last, that I couldn't settle down here for the rest of my life in such a calm. You might as well build a ship and keep it in harbour, until it rots.'

Anne sat motionless and looked at him. You were born, you married and had children, and at last you died and were buried. It had happened to her father, and to his. They had never thought of going off to London for no reason at all and leaving their families. She said suddenly, seizing upon the one irrefutable argument, 'But you can't just go away and leave me and the children. How would we live?'

'I've talked to Gilbert,' said William, with an air of relief. 'He'll look after you while I'm away. I can send money to him here, and, after all, I shan't be gone for long. I shall be back for visits. London isn't so far away, and the roads are quite good now.'

Anne was driven to desperation by the note of certainty in his voice, as though it was all decided and sure. She gathered herself together, and with a great effort she broke through the calm of weariness which had held her ever since the birth of the twins, clutching at that power of love which she had once had over him.

'Ah, Will, Will, don't go!' she cried. 'If you ever loved me, if you ever truly loved me, Will, you can't leave me now!'

'Anne,' said William, with a note of pleading in his voice.

'No, Will,' said Anne, rejecting it. And then, not guile, but instinct leading her from the lover's argument to the wife's. 'How can you leave the children, Will, when they love you so much? How can I bring them up without you? And Hamnet—what if he should be ill when I was alone here? I couldn't bear it. What if he should die, Will? What if he should die, calling for you, and you not there!'

'Anne, Anne,' said William.

She saw in his face that she had won. He would stay with her. She would always be able to keep him, not by his weakness but by his strength, by that in him which not only knew what she was suffering, but also suffered it with her, and subdued his own emotions to hers. She knew that she had won, and in the same instant she knew that she had lost. She had it in her power to make him stay, and she must let him go. She remembered the afternoon in the upper room at Hewlands when he had said, gravely, 'I'm not "other folks", Anne.' Through their married years this moment had been waiting for her. She looked at their life together, and saw it turn sour and pitiful in the knowledge that all the time William had been only as quiescent as a wild creature held in the hand, outwardly calm, but ready always to slip sideways and out into freedom. She could tighten her grip and hold him. Perhaps, at last, she could almost make him forget that he had wanted to be free, but if she did, then she would kill that quality in him which was so much a part of him that without it he would be nothing—a man like other men, a good, honest husband, but not William. She had loved him before, when she kept him with her arms round his neck and her tears on his cheek. She loved him much more now as she sat with her hands clasped and let him go, freeing him at last and for ever. He would never come back. As he was about to speak, she stopped him.

'All right, Will,' she said. 'If you must go, you must.'

William looked at her, long and steadily, and into his face came slowly a look of exultation. And yet the triumph was not for himself, but for her, as though she had won, after all, and not lost. And then came a look of great sadness, and yet still not on his own behalf but hers, as though he knew with her the loss and loneliness and bewilderment.

Anne got up from the table, and suddenly William had slipped back into himself again and was smiling at her with eagerness and excitement.

'It won't be for long, Anne,' he said. 'As soon as I have some money and have found a place to live, you and the children can come and join me.'

'No, no, Will,' said Anne. 'You've married the wrong wife if that's what you want. You won't get me up to London, with all its dirt and wickedness. No, Will, I shall stay here with the children, and when you're finished with London, you'll come home again.'

They looked at each other, already divided by the miles that lay between Stratford and London.

'I must go, Anne!' said William, as though he called an urgent message across a widening space.

'Yes, Will, I know,' said Anne, wearily.

William went round to Henley Street to tell them of his plans, and he found there the same amazement and opposition. Mary was at first almost speechless with indignation.

'And what of Anne and the children?' she demanded at last. 'How will they live when you're gone? You know in what a state your father's affairs are. He has too many debts of his own to charge himself with your burdens as well. You were ready enough to marry a wife and get children.'

William glanced at Gilbert, sitting quietly by with an abstracted look on his face.

'All the money I have, I'm leaving with Gilbert,' he answered. 'When that's gone, he'll spend from his own pocket, and I shall repay him later.'

'He knew what you planned, then?' said Mary, quickly.

'I talked it over with him this morning.'

Mary's anger was temporarily diverted.

'Well, *Master* Gilbert,' she said, 'I suppose you think that because you've been to London, you can advise your brother better than his parents can! You haven't been so very successful yourself. We expected great things of you in London, and if you'd been diligent, your master might have made you his partner. And what happens? Master Harrison sends you down here to look after his interests in this part of the country, and you're no better than if you'd never left here.'

'He didn't send me,' Gilbert remarked, betraying a certain lack of interest in the conversation. 'I asked him if I could come.'

'You *asked* him?' cried his mother in astonishment. 'But why?'

'I don't like London,' Gilbert replied, coolly. 'Too much noise, and too many people. I have enough money for my needs, and a part-share in some of Master Harrison's ventures, and I can always go back to London if I want to. But I prefer it here.'

His mother gazed at him wordlessly. Then, quite defeated, she abandoned him and turned

225

back to William.

'Will Anne follow you there?' she enquired. 'How long are you staying? Do you expect Anne and the children to come and live in London with you?'

'I don't know,' William answered, showing at last some irritation. 'I must go first and see what possibilities there are of advancement. Sir Thomas has given me a letter to the Earl of Southampton, but he only knows him slightly. There's not much hope of profit from writing plays, except to make a bare living, but I shall hope to find a patron for my poetry.'

'Well,' said Mary, 'how you can give up a good, honest place here, just to go and kick your heels in the hope of patronage and to pick up crumbs at some rich man's table, I don't know!'

'Oh, come, wife,' broke in John Shakespeare, 'if Will has made up his mind to go, we mustn't let him be too downcast. There are many great men in London who are patrons of letters. We must admit that poetry is not our trade, but His late Majesty wrote some, and they say that Her Majesty enjoys it. It may be that Will might get a place at Court by it. It's been known to happen before.'

'Yes,' said Mary, 'but you forget that he's starting as a player. There won't be much hope of advancement when that is known.'

'You didn't mind when I acted in plays at school,' said William.

'That was different,' said his mother. She looked at her two sons with annoyance. 'The trouble with the world nowadays,' she said, severely, 'is that young people no longer do their duty. It was Gilbert's duty to stay in London and to justify his father's confidence in him. But, no, he "prefers it here". And William goes veering off to London, when it's his plain duty to stay here in the place which Sir Thomas was kind enough to obtain for him, and to support his wife and children.'

'Mother,' said Gilbert, with immense courtesy, 'I will serve God and honour the Queen. So far will I do my duty. But stay in London I will not. There is no angling there worth the name, and they do not know how to cook carp.'

The days before William's departure came and went like hurrying servants before a feast. Anne and William had nothing to say to each other. She could no more talk over his plans with him than she could have discussed with a mariner the course he proposed to sail. She did not even know what this poetry was which he talked about. Once she found some papers of his that he had left out on the table, ready to pack. She picked up the top sheet and looked at it, running her finger along the lines of writing, as though by that means she could draw out some of its mystery. That ability of hers to write her name—how it had enraged

Joan Hathaway! A friend of her father's had taught it to her when she was young, but in fact it had meant very little more than making her mark. She used to be able to form the word, Agnes, rather uncertainly, with the copy before her, but now she had lost the copy, and she no longer remembered how it went. As she ran her finger along William's writing, she came upon the first, big sign of her name, at the beginning of the fourth line, and for an instant the recognition gave her an illusory sense of comprehension. But the next bit was different, and at once even that tiny fragment of knowledge served only to show the extent of her ignorance. She stood for a long time looking down at the paper, feeling that she was gazing into a whirlpool which relentlessly drew William away from her by some force which she could neither resist nor understand. As she stood with it in her hand, she heard voices outside, and put it down quickly, as though in guilt. There, coming up the lane were William and Edmund, William looking down at his brother and laughing, walking with a young, light step. But for the difference in Edmund's age, it might have been the young man she had met in the market, those eight years before. It was as though all that had happened in between had been delicately removed, like a flaw in a piece of cloth, and the two ends had been invisibly joined, according to the original master plan.

It was early in the morning when Anne and William, with the children, walked through the town to the inn where William had bought the horse which he would sell on arrival in London. There they found the entire family assembled, together with the two Stratford men with whom William had arranged to travel. Hamnet was soon following Edmund into the stables and, perilously, round the horses' heels, John was discussing politics with one of William's travelling companions (who would much rather have been over-looking the preparations for his journey) and Mary was begging the other to take care of William.

'Is there much danger of footpads, sir, do you think?' she was enquiring.

'No, no, Mistress, not on the road we shall be taking. And, anyway, we're well armed. They'll get a warm welcome from us if they try it.'

'I'm glad that you know the road well,' said Mary. 'My son has never been to London, and I was so afraid that he would lose his way if he travelled alone. But, with you to look after him, he'll be all right.'

'And some say that the Spaniards will try it again,' said John Shakespeare, 'but, myself, I don't think that they will.'

'Ay, sir, ay, you may be—Boy! take care with that!—you may be right, but—boy! Tie that in front!'

'—and that you know the inns, and will be able to choose a good one,' Mary continued, earnestly. 'For I hear that some of them are no better than robbers' dens.'

'When you have escaped the footpads and the innkeepers,' Joanne remarked to William, who was standing frowning at this exchange, 'and the Spaniards who will, no doubt, be sailing up under London bridge, then perhaps you will have leisure to enjoy the journey.'

William's face cleared and he laughed. Then, as they stood together, he asked quietly, 'Have you heard anything of Rufus?'

'No, why should I?' cried Joanne, lightly. And then she met William's eyes and replied in a low voice, 'I've heard nothing.'

'Well, well,' called the anxious traveller, 'are we all ready? Time we were off. Ready, sir? Are you ready, young sir?' William kissed Joanne and his mother and father, ruffled Edmund's hair, patted Richard on the shoulder and shook hands with Gilbert. He kissed the children, lifting them in turn up in his arms, feeling for that instant the young delicacy of their bones, the small clutching of their fingers on his shoulders, the wet simplicity of their kisses on his cheek. And then he turned to Anne, and his eyes met hers. She looked back at him steadily, in the manner of one who has passed through all pain and grief and is now without hope, meeting the future with a calm despair. He took her in his arms and was blinded by a rush of tears, and heard her whisper, 'Will!' as though she awoke in a sudden panic in the middle of the night. But when he drew away and looked at her, she wasn't crying, and her lips were pressed together. When he mounted, the other travellers were already moving out of the inn yard, and as his horse turned its head to follow them, he called, in a choked voice, 'Gilbert, look after them for me!'

He heard Gilbert's cool reply, 'Trust me. I will.'

He saw them once more standing all together, dear, honest, reliable beyond measure, the only people in the world who would always love him simply because he was Will, careless of what success he had gained, unchanging in their love for him. He rode out into the street with the tears running down his face. His life was here in Stratford, and he was leaving it. Nothing forced him to go. No bitter necessity drove him away. No edict of banishment separated him from everything on earth which he held dear. Of his own free will he rode away, as though a prisoner captive to himself.

They turned into the open road. The other travellers jogged on ahead and William wiped his eyes and urged his horse forward. It was a bright morning with rich September colours in the trees and a freshness in the air. The horse stepped out bravely, shaking its head and dancing a little. William felt in his heart a gentle, rising surge of excitement. This was the conclusion of something begun a long time ago. From all the fleeting moments of ambition and aspiration, from all the fumbling, ignorant reaching after fame, from all the long, anguished struggle between restlessness and love, came at last this journey. With his eyes still aching from the tears of parting, William rode forward, smiling, to London.

But in Stratford his family looked round upon each other like strangers who have been thrown together in some great danger, but now, when it is all over, find nothing to say to each other.

'Mother,' said Hamnet, when they were back in the cottage, 'will father ever come back?'

He looked up at her seriously, and the two little girls, too, paused and looked up at her, waiting. Anne saw in their faces the same bewilderment which she felt herself, and saw that they thought that she understood it all and could reassure them.

'Yes, of course he will,' she answered. 'Now, children, go and play. I have work to do.'

But as she moved about the empty house, hearing the children's voices coming from the garden, clearing up the last meal which William had eaten with her, and putting away the few possessions which he had left behind, she found herself repeating over and over again, 'He will never come back. He will never come back. He is gone. He will never come back.'

# CHAPTER 16

An added reason for Mary Shakespeare's indignation over William's departure for London was that she felt that, just as with the deer stealing, he was following Rufus into mischief, even though it was four years now since Rufus had left Stratford. He had collected his wages from his master, good old Sharp, and to every one's amazement the old hatter seemed to be heartbroken at the loss of his disreputable former apprentice.

'I told him,' said Master Sharp, with tears in his eyes, 'I told him that if he would stay with me, he should have the business when I die, but he said—do you know what he said? He said, "When I return, I will *buy* the business from you." But how can he when he has no money? Dear, dear. I fear I have been rather a hard master at times, and he has been a good lad, especially when I was ill. He was a good craftsman, when he took the pains, and never out of temper. And now, when I die, the shop must go to a stranger.'

233

'The man must be mad,' said Mary Shake-speare, when this was reported to her. 'He knows that William Hart was the plague of his life when he was his apprentice, and has been in danger of dismissal every day since. If Master Sharp has no relations, he had better leave the shop to the town, to be sold for the relief of the poor, for if William Hart had it, he would only pour it down his throat.'

Rufus told his mother that he wanted a little travel, before his feet took root in Stratford like a rotten elm. He added that he was not quite sure whether or not he would accept the post of Lord Mayor of London if it was offered to him, but he supposed a man must not be too particular when he had his living to make.

The only real farewell he said was to William and Anne. He came to supper with them and talked nonsense all through the meal. Afterwards, when Anne was washing the dishes, William went upstairs to see that the children had not tossed their covers off, and Rufus, as though in mere idleness, went upstairs with him.

Susanna lay in the nook by the chimney, quietly folded up like a kitten, her delicate, round little face turned away from them. Her hair was pure golden, as Edmund's had been at her age, but her beauty was less angelic than his. Or rather, she was perhaps the sort of cherub you might find in a country church, but Edmund a gilded cherub in a cathedral, sure that his trumpet was making more noise than the Archangel's. At the foot of the big, four-poster bed, lay Hamnet and Judith, Hamnet in Edmund's old cradle, passed down the family since it was first made for Joan Shakespeare, William's elder sister who had died in infancy. The great oaken hood seemed to make the fragile features paler than ever, so that William leaned over, as he and Anne had done so often in the past year, to make sure that his son was still breathing. Beside him, Judith, in the lighter cradle which Hamnet Sadler had made, looked immensely strong, with flushed cheeks and curling dark hair, taking deep, strong breaths, her hands clenched as though she had a good grip on life and never meant to let it go. Rufus stood beside William, looking down at the children, and sighed. And then he grinned at William quickly and turned in haste to go downstairs again.

They sat down by the fire and remained there in silence for some time.

'What will you do in London?' asked William at last.

Rufus shrugged his shoulders.

'I have an uncle who's a merchant in the City. If he has some interesting employment for me—good. If not—I'll try somewhere else.'

'Rufus,' began William, and hesitated.

Although he was seemingly so talkative and unreserved, Rufus had always kept his own counsel and managed his own affairs in a manner which did not invite interference. Rufus looked at him enquiringly. 'If you're leaving because of some trouble in Stratford,' William went on, 'if there's anything I can do——'

'Lord, Will, there's no trouble,' said Rufus, cheerfully, 'except that this duckpond is too small for me. I want to go and paddle in a larger pool and fish in more troubled waters.'

'If that's really all——' said William, doubtfully.

'It's—nearly all,' said Rufus. He poked the fire and as he leaned forward his hair shone red in the flames, but his face was in shadow. He said in a low, uncertain voice, 'I can do no good thing while I'm in Stratford. I have such a reputation for idleness that it seems I—must—be—idle, and my mother——' He stopped short. William drew a quick breath of self-reproach.

'And I thought that you were content that it should be so,' he said.

'So did I,' answered Rufus, softly.

Then Anne came into the room and Rufus got up quickly and took his leave, talking and laughing. He was checked at the door, when Anne, with that country simplicity of hers, kissed him on the cheek and said, 'God keep thee, Rufus.' He smiled at her.

'Say a prayer for me sometimes, Anne. It may be that you're more familiar with heaven than I am.' He laughed and was himself again. 'As for me,' he called back, as he set off down the path, 'I shall light a candle to Lucifer, and so keep a foot in both camps.' He paused at the gate, 'Tell Joanne that no man deserves her,' he said, still laughing, 'and let her take it which way she will!'

He ran down the road, took a flying leap over a puddle, and so disappeared round the corner. It seemed to William that it was his own boyhood and youth which he saw vanishing out of reach.

A year went by, and another, and there was no word from Rufus. William went to London, and wrote at once to say that all was well, but it was as though Rufus had plunged into a great sea and never reappeared. It seemed that he had intended to cut himself off entirely from the little ship of Stratford, and that it was useless to ask for news of him. The mysterious ocean of the world could swallow up ten million men like him, and give no sign. Mistress Hart seemed quite unconcerned.

'I'll tell you what it is,' she said, sitting comfortably by the fire, while Mary looked longingly at the linenfold whose contents she and Joanne had been shaking out and replacing with fresh lavender. 'I expect Rufus is just waiting for his heiress. He said to me years ago, he said, "Mother, when I grow up, I shall marry an heiress, and then I shall never have to work." I expect that's what he's waiting for.'

And she laughed heartily. Mary smiled, grimly and politely.

'Yes, I dare say,' she said. 'Very likely. But I should have thought that it was his duty to stay at home and support his mother.'

'Ah well,' said Mistress Hart, tolerantly, 'he wanted to travel, and I always think it's good for young men to see something of the world. And I'm well provided for. I have the cow and the chickens, and, of course, before Rufus left he gave me all the money he'd saved.'

'He did?' said Mary, disconcerted. 'I thought—I thought that he just—went off.'

'Oh no,' said Mistress Hart, smiling placidly. 'He'd really saved quite a lot, considering, and he even walked to London, to save the cost of the carriers. He sold everything he wasn't taking with him and gave me the money for that as well. Only he said that I mustn't tell anyone, because if it got known that I had a lot of money in the house, thieves might break in, so I haven't mentioned it at all.'

'But, aren't you worried at not hearing any word from him?' enquired Mary. 'It must be—what is it?—nearly five years now since he left.'

'Oh no, not really worried,' answered

Mistress Hart. 'He won't come back until he has some success. He's like his father in that, he keeps his own counsel. I expect he'll come back and bring his rich wife with him. My husband used to say that he was born to be hanged (only for a joke, of course) but I always said, Oh no, born to marry a rich wife, and I shall be right, you'll see.'

When Mistress Hart had gone, Joanne escaped upstairs and sat for a long time by the window, looking down into the empty street. She told herself that after all these years, she had finally put Rufus out of her heart—if indeed he was ever really in it. He had gone away without a word, and if he should ever come back, it would be with a rich wife. When Robert asked her again, she thought, she would agree to marry him. She smiled and thought how pleased her mother and father would be, and Gilbert, and how pleasant it would be, after all, to be no longer solitary. Rufus seemed a shadowy figure, like one long dead.

But that night for the first time, she dreamed of him. He came up to her where she was standing in the market place, and kissed her, and at first she was glad to see him. But then she cried out, 'Oh no, Rufus, you mustn't. I'm going to marry Robert.' Then his face was suddenly angry and violent above her, and he walked away from her, saying over his shoulder, 'I'm going to London.' And then she was on the Banbury road, running after him and begging him not to go. It was dark and lonely, and she ran and stumbled and called out to him, but he took no notice but walked on ahead, very quickly, and she couldn't catch up with him. She woke up sobbing, his face vividly before her, and she could hardly believe that it had been a dream. The shadow of it hung over her for weeks afterwards and she couldn't forget it, as though his departure for London had really been like that, with her running after him and crying.

A few weeks later, Gilbert returned from a brief business visit to London. Joanne was out and came home to find him sitting by the fire telling his news. She paused inside the door, hanging up her cloak, and she heard Mary Shakespeare exclaim, 'What! So he's actually married!'

'Yes,' Gilbert answered, 'married, and with the dowry in his pocket.' He laughed. 'Mistress Hart knows all about it. She called to me as I came through the town.'

'I wonder where she heard it,' said Mary.

'Perhaps he wrote to her,' suggested Gilbert.

'Oh, yes!' cried Mary, sarcastically, 'very likely! She'd be the last person he'd write to.'

Joanne could feel her heart beating wildly as though she had been running. She lingered by the door, pretending that her cloak had slipped down and that she must hang it up again.

'Well,' said Mary, 'and what did Mistress Hart have to say about it? Some malice, I'll be bound!'

'No,' Gilbert answered, lazily. 'She only said that she wondered what Joanne would think of it.'

Joanne came composedly into the room, saying calmly, 'And why should I be concerned in the matter?'

'Why, indeed?' Gilbert agreed, but his mother broke in impatiently, 'Since you refused to marry him——'

Joanne, taken unawares, shot a surprised glance at her mother. She had thought that Rufus's proposal and her refusal had remained quite secret.

'Well,' said Mary Shakespeare, 'I suppose you are satisfied now that he has found a better wife in London.'

'Oh, I'll not grudge him his good fortune,' said Joanne, lightly.

Mary looked at her in exasperation, but made no reply.

'Well,' said Gilbert, 'anyway, he will be bringing his wife home next week, and then Mistress Hart will be able to satisfy her curiosity. She longed to know what colour Mistress Brown's eyes were, and she'll never forgive me because I was forced to say that I hadn't noticed.'

Joanne, who had sat down, looked sharply up at him and then away again. 'Mistress

Brown'? It was Robert! It was only Robert who was married! She clasped her hands tightly in her lap and the colour came into her cheeks at the thought of what she might have said. She knew that Gilbert was watching her, and was aware of a slow smile of dawning comprehension on his face, but he said nothing.

'Well, and what of William?' asked Mary. 'When is he coming home?'

'He expects to come soon,' Gilbert answered. 'There's a good deal of plague in London, and if it gets any worse there may be a complete inhibition of plays.'

'And is that to be the only reason for him to return?' said Mary, bitterly. 'Are his wife and children nothing to him—or his mother?'

Gilbert hesitated. Since he never excused himself, he found it difficult to make excuses for William, or, indeed, anyone.

'They need him to act in the plays,' he said at last, 'as well as to help to write them.'

'I suppose that one player is much like another,' said Mary. 'I should think they could spare him for a few weeks.'

'There's the cost of the journey too,' said Gilbert.

'Oh, and what of this great nobleman we hear so much about?' Mary demanded. 'Can't he put his hand in his pocket?'

Gilbert shrugged his shoulders, evidently thinking that he had said all that could be expected for William. Joanne, sitting silently by, hardly hearing what they said, was startled to find herself sick and weak as though she had just escaped some appalling physical danger.

'Well, well, so we're to meet Robert's wife today,' said John Shakespeare at breakfast a week later. 'Gilbert, you're the only one who's met her. Is she very fashionable?'

'She dresses in the London fashion,' said Gilbert. 'You know the saying there, "The man dresses like the master, and the master like the King". So by her dress and manners you'd think she was a lady and not a merchant's daughter.'

'We'll soon teach her better judgement,' said Mary, with satisfaction. 'I can't bear to see folks dressed above their rank. But she'll soon see that such London ways aren't well thought of here.'

'Do you think so, mother?' said Gilbert. 'I'd lay a wager that in two weeks half the good wives of Stratford will be changing their gowns and their headdress to match hers.'

'If she can make Mistress Hart change her dress, she will be very welcome!' cried Joanne. 'She's been wearing that same gown for so long that I swear if it walked down the street everyone would stop and talk to it, and only wonder that it was so silent!'

'And what of Mistress Brown's fortune?' enquired John.

'Robert seemed satisfied with it,' Gilbert replied. 'Her father died some years ago, and her uncle laid the money out for her at a good rate of interest.'

'What, Gilbert,' said his father, laughing, 'hasn't she a sister for you? Could Robert find such a wife, and not you? You'll have to go back and try again.'

'And take Joanne with you,' Edmund suggested, looking at Joanne sideways under golden lashes. 'Perhaps she could find a husband in London, although she can't find one here.'

'I wish *you* would go to London yourself,' exclaimed Joanne, suddenly flushing, 'and be hanged there!'

The clock had only just struck eleven when there was a loud knock at the door.

'Heavens!' cried Mary, basting the birds at the fire, 'surely that's not them already!'

'It sounded like Robert's knock,' Joanne answered.

Mary hurried out, smoothing her dress and tucking up a wisp of hair. She opened the door, and found there Robert, and beside him a lady whom at first sight she took to be the Queen of England. They came inside and Robert presented his wife, while Mary curt-seyed in numbed silence to red hair, tightly curled and bound with ribbon, a crimson velvet petticoat, a high ruff, and a white satin gown. With difficulty she collected herself sufficiently to say, 'You are heartily welcome, Mistress. It is very kind of you to come and see us so soon—that is——' She stumbled a little, but went on with determination, 'It is only a family party which we have for you. We're simple people, and don't stand on ceremony.'

'No, no,' answered the bride, dropping another elegant curtsy, 'it is I who should thank you.'

There was a pause. 'Won't you come over to the fire?' asked Mary. 'Perhaps you are a little chilled.'

'Oh no, I thank you,' replied Isobel Brown. 'I am quite warm.'

'But still, there is something of a nip in the air,' said Mary, firmly leading the way over to the fireplace, which, indeed, when the tables were set out, was the only clear space in the room. At that moment John Shakespeare kicked the door open, tramped into the house with the wine for dinner under his arm, stopped short and exclaimed, 'What, here already!'

'I hope we are not too early,' said Isobel.

'No, no, never too early,' said John cheerfully. 'But we did not expect you until noon.'

With that, he went on into the kitchen. Isobel turned her round, serious eyes to Mary and remarked earnestly, 'My uncle is always offended if his guests don't arrive before noon.

He says that the time before dinner should always be occupied with good conversation, and if his friends do not come early enough, he always says, "Ah, so we do not talk well enough to please you. You come only for our food, and not for our company." '

'Yes, very true,' answered Mary, distractedly, thinking that unless she could return to the kitchen, they were likely in this instance to get company alone, and no food. Searching her mind for some good conversation, she could only think of remarking that ten of Mistress Hart's chicks had died, and this, she felt sure, would never have satisfied Isobel's uncle. Into the silence, however, came Richard, walking in hatless, stopping short, and exclaiming, 'Oh, are you here? I must change my doublet.'

'Hush, Richard,' said his mother in exasperation, 'what does that matter? Come and pay your respects to Mistress Brown.'

'Well, I'm afraid it is rather torn,' said Richard, 'but, you see,' he added, carefully, 'I didn't expect that you'd be here so soon, or I would have changed it before I went out.'

'I'm afraid we have come rather early,' said Isobel.

'No, no, never too early,' said John, returning at that moment, and speaking with the same heartiness as before.

Mary, quite exhausted by the good conversation, escaped to the kitchen, and sent

Joanne out to bear her part in it.

Joanne hesitated in the doorway, annoyed to find her heart beating faster than usual and her mouth dry. She was very conscious of the fact that her face was flushed and damp and that there was a spot of grease on her gown. And yet she was more anxious on Robert's behalf than on her own. She remembered his voice saying, 'There has never been anyone but you. There is no one else for me,' and she thought what a cruel embarrassment it would be for him to meet her for the first time with his wife.

As she went forward into the room, they were talking to Gilbert, who had just come in, and she stood unnoticed for a few minutes. Then John Shakespeare presented her to Mistress Brown. Isobel acknowledged her curtsy in a civil but perfunctory manner, and turned back to Gilbert, and in Isobel's unconcern, Joanne saw herself mirrored for the first time as someone quite unimportant. No deliberate insult could have so completely overthrown her. She glanced quickly up at Robert, expecting to find his eyes on her face, expecting that he would be troubled and grieved at his wife's coolness to her, ready to reassure him with a smile. But Robert was not looking at her, but at Isobel. There was on his face an air of bland pride, like a farmer, thought Joanne, who has brought a pig to market and knows that it is the fattest in the county. She felt a sudden chill, as though death had laid its hand upon her, as though she knew already what it was to be buried and forgotten.

When they all sat down to dinner, Joanne began to rally her courage. She had lived too long as the only surviving girl among four boys, as William's sister and confidante, and as the wittiest girl in Stratford, to be now set down as an inconsiderable unmarried woman of twenty-two. And it was somehow necessary to her self-esteem that Robert's wife should like her. She began to smile again as John Shakespeare told Robert that he must find a wife in London for Gilbert.

'Oh, Gilbert will never marry,' she cried. 'He'll never find anyone who deserves such an honour.'

'I will never marry,' said Gilbert, 'until I find a woman who is both wise and good.'

'And that will be never,' said Joanne. 'For if she is good, she's too good to be wise. And if she is wise, she's too wise to be good!'

'Oh I cannot allow you that,' said Isobel, with a stare of immovable dislike. 'I know more than one woman who is wise and good, I assure you. There is my aunt, to begin with. And what of the Queen? Now *she* is wise and good, you must agree.' Joanne suddenly flushed and fell silent.

'Ah yes,' broke in John Shakespeare, blessedly unobservant, 'I suppose you have seen the Queen?'

'Yes, indeed,' said Isobel, in her finicky London voice, 'many times. We saw her one evening just before we left.'

'And how did Her Majesty look?' enquired John.

'Very well, I believe. She looked very well indeed. She bowed and smiled most graciously. Really, I could almost think that it was at *me* she smiled. My uncle had heard that she was coming to Parliament at five in the evening, so we were there at four o'clock, and my uncle found a good place, and when she came, we were there, right on the corner of the street, and my uncle called out, "God save your Majesty", and *that* was when she bowed her head and smiled. But, of course, she might know my uncle by sight, because he always discovers when she is to come abroad, and stands where he can see her.'

Joanne took no more part in the talk, and when the guests had departed she exercised no wit on Mistress Brown. Alone in her room that night, she knelt down to say her prayers. The moon was sailing between rich silver bars of clouds, with that giddy air of moving very fast and yet staying still. The face in the moon seemed compassionate and yet mirthful, as though it wept at human follies, but must needs find them laughable. It was a night to comfort lovers, reminding them of all those famous lovers of history who had suffered for love's sake. But Joanne had no such comfort.

She could only ridicule her own vanity for thinking that Robert's love for her was perpetual and enduring. She was ashamed to think how she had pitied him, and how graciously she had meant to reward his faithfulness at last. But worst of all was that, now that this vanity was cast down, Robert himself wore a different aspect to her. Now that he no longer looked at her with kind and loving eyes, she had a sudden picture of him standing in front of the fire with a large stomach and a good red face, and a Hrmph! every time before he spoke. She smiled unwillingly as Rufus's prophetic description of him came into her mind, and then put her face down in her hands and whispered, 'Rufus. Rufus.' She was carried away on a great tide of tears, bearing all before it, breaking down the sea-walls of pride and self-deceit. She cried quietly and bitterly, but without restraint. She loved him, she loved him, and he was gone. As long as she lived, and wherever he was, a part of her would be with him. Robert had been the shield to conceal her weakness. Now that he was no longer there, she was revealed as totally unarmed and defenceless—and without hope.

# CHAPTER 17

It was only when she had news of William that
Anne realized how far he was gone from her.
It seemed as though he was until then out of
sight just round the corner where she had seen
him last, but now she knew that he was many
miles away, caught up in a mysterious
cloud called London.

She was working in the garden of the
cottage when a hoarse voice called out, 'Ohé,
Mistress!' She looked up, startled and suspicious, and recognized William Greenway,
the carrier.

'I got a message for you from Lunnon.'

She stumbled to her feet and ran to the gate,
crying breathlessly, 'Oh, *yes!*'

'I brought a letter for Master Shakespeare,
and one for Master Gilbert, and a message for
you.'

'Yes,' said Anne, hardly able to speak.
'Come in. Tell me.' She put her hand on the
gate to let him into the garden, but William
Greenway planted his legs firmly apart, took a
deep breath, staring straight in front of him
like a man taking an oath, and declaimed,
'Your husband told me to give his love to you
and to the children.'

And then, with an air of great relief, he started to turn away.

'Oh, wait! Don't go!' Anne exclaimed. 'Is he well?'

Greenway paused. 'Well?' he said, blankly. 'I dunno. He *looked* well enough. 'Course, no one can't keep well in Lunnon. Turrible unhealthy place it is, turrible. 'Course, *I'm* all right, 'cause I don't live there. I jus' stay a night there, or mebbe two, but mos'ly I'm on the road. No. Full of sickness, Lunnon is, I always says. No wonder all the folks as live there is as white as whey.'

'But—did he seem in good spirits?' asked Anne. 'Was he cheerful?'

'Cheerful? Lord yes! I cracked a few jests with him, you may be sure. I always say, you can laugh when you will, but you die when you would not, so you might as well laugh while you can.'

He gave a great shout of laughter on the spot. Anne looked at him in growing hopelessness. 'Lord yes, Mistress,' said the carrier, beaming with self-satisfaction, 'I had a drink with him, and we cracked a jest together. I always say, I can't abide a hang-dog fellow. If a man can't laugh in my company, then hang him, let him leave it, that's what I say!'

As though she tried to beat through a barrier of goosefeathers, Anne tried once more.

'Did he seem prosperous?' she said.

Greenway thought the matter over, frowning. 'Well,' he said, doubtfully, 'he had the price of the ale in his purse.' A sudden thought struck him. 'And he gave me half a groat,' he said, 'for bringing the message to you. Ay, ay, he's prosperous enough!' And he gazed at Anne triumphantly.

'When you see him next,' said Anne, 'tell him that we're all well.' She hesitated, struggling against that deep conviction that emotions should not be spoken of. 'And give him our love,' she added in a low voice, 'and say that—that we miss him.'

But William Greenway had already set his feet apart, an anxious look upon his face. 'Tell him that you're all well,' he repeated. 'Tell him that you're all well. Ay, I've got it now. I shan't forget it. Tell him you're all well.' He set off down the lane, saying cheerfully, 'Good night, Mistress,' over his shoulder.

'Good night,' said Anne. 'And—thank you.'

She still stood by the gate. Her longing for William was like a physical pain, like the pangs of childbirth, so that she had to hold on to the gate to keep from throwing herself about and crying out. For an instant the path was no longer beneath her feet and everything that was most essentially herself flung itself out towards William, trying to meet his spirit and hold it through all the miles between them. And then once more she was aware of the first grey winter chill on the sky, and the smell of wood fires in

253

the air, and the early night stepping quietly in upon her like a lonely enemy, and she was alone by the gate, and she could not reach him.

Even when Gilbert returned from a visit to London a year later, in the spring, he did not help her much more than Greenway. He came into the cottage and was warmly greeted by the children. Anne could never understand why they were so fond of him when he hardly ever spoke to them.

'Uncle Gilbert,' cried Hamnet, 'see my cart. When I grow up, I'm going to be a carrier. Wouldn't you like to be a carrier, Uncle Gilbert?'

'No,' Gilbert replied, 'it has never been the chief of my ambitions.'

'I would,' said Hamnet, undeterred. 'I shall have a horse and cart and I shall go up to London and see father.'

'Yes,' Gilbert agreed, 'and then when you return you can go round and tell everyone the news about him, and then *I* shall not have to do it.'

He glanced at Anne, half-smiling, but she looked back at him with expressionless coldness. She offered him a chair and sat down herself by the table, waiting.

'Will sent his love to you,' said Gilbert.

'Is he well?' Anne broke in, brushing aside this greeting, as though Gilbert had no right to bring it.

'Very well,' said Gilbert. He paused. 'And he's beginning to prosper,' he said. 'He's found a patron for his poetry. He's a good actor, and the company has acted one of his plays, and they've asked him to write another.' He paused again. Anne made no reply. 'It's no small thing,' Gilbert said, after a moment, 'to achieve so much in London, when there are so many University men trying to earn their bread by their pens.'

'Where is he lodging?' asked Anne. 'Has he found a good place to live?'

Gilbert smiled faintly, but answered, 'Yes. He was in a very poor place at first, but now he lodges with another actor in the house of a widow near the theatre.'

Anne saw the smile and resented it. She asked no more, telling herself angrily that Gilbert must know what she desired to hear. Did Will often speak of her and the children? Did he ask about her garden? Had he bought any new clothes in London? How did he spend his leisure hours? What would he be doing at that moment? Would he be having dinner, and, if so, where? Would he be in the theatre? It was all pitifully beyond her reach, as though she tried to follow him beyond the grave. As with Greenway, her questions, unspoken this time, once more fell back unanswered. Did he still love her? Did he look tired, or discouraged? Could he be truly happy away from her? Ah, could he? For at last all her questions could be answered by one. But Gilbert spoke only of those things which had taken William away from her, the theatre and his poetry. With his passionless calm and coolness he sat silently before her, implacable and impenetrable, like that London which she could never enter or comprehend.

'Will told me to tell you,' he said at last, 'that he hopes to come home——'

'Soon?' cried Anne. 'Now? Is he coming soon?'

'Before many months,' said Gilbert, and there seemed to her to be reproof in the restrained caution of his voice. She looked out of the window, and when she turned her head back she found Gilbert watching her. He said hesitantly, 'Anne, he'll come—as soon as he can.'

'Well, of course,' said Anne, irritably. 'I know he'll come as soon as he can. But I want to know when that will be.'

Gilbert smiled suddenly, as though in relief, and said cheerfully, 'Of course. Well, I hope it will be before very long.' He stood up and added, 'I must be on my way.'

The children, who had been standing by in silence, knowing that they must not interrupt the conversation of their elders, at once fell upon him, begging him not to go and following him to the door. Anne came to stand in the doorway and watched him go down the path. She hated to see him there in the sunlight, with the children clinging to his sleeves and laughing up at him. It should be William there, she thought, and not Gilbert, and she blamed him for it.

All the time that William was away, Gilbert was coolly faithful to his trust. He made sure that Anne was never in need of money. He arranged for Hamnet to start his schooling. He arranged for the repair of the roof of the cottage and paid her rent for her. But he did it all in such an impersonal manner that Anne, never good at acknowledging favours, found it easy not to be grateful to him.

When William returned to Stratford, more than two years after he had ridden away with that visionary look upon his face like a young saint going forth to build a church in a country he has not yet found, he came, as he had gone, suddenly, with no warning. And once more, Anne, to whom emotions, like ideas, came slowly and tenaciously, found it difficult to turn her mind and heart to the event. She was making a new shirt for Hamnet, cutting it down from an old one of William's, when Edmund ran into the cottage, crying out, 'Anne, he's here! Will's home!' Anne looked at him for a moment blankly, as though she pretended not to understand him.

'Where is he?' she asked at last.

'At Henley Street,' replied Edmund,

257

laughing. 'He's got a new suit of clothes, Anne, and a beard!'

'A beard!' cried Anne, horrified.

'He looks like a lord,' said Edmund. 'There must be a lot of money in London. And he's got a new horse. He says he's going to keep this one, not sell it when he goes back.'

Anne caught her breath. Somewhere in her mind, never quite acknowledged, had been the hope that when William came home it would be for ever, that he would find himself, after all, unable to live away from his family— and away from her. And now she was suddenly stiflingly angry that he had gone to Henley Street first, instead of coming straight home to the cottage. She asked, shortly, 'Is he coming here?'

'Yes, he's coming,' said Edmund, happily. 'You can see him coming up the lane. I ran on ahead to tell you.'

Anne went to the door and opened it, and saw William, walking slowly, his eyes on the road. He reached the gate, and saw her, and stopped. Something which Anne could not understand and therefore could not combat held her motionless until he came to her and leaned down and kissed her, and even then it was as though they lived far apart from each other, and only planned to meet but could never really do so.

'Where are my babes?' cried William. 'Where's my boy?'

But the children, standing together inside, had not been prepared for his coming and were shy and awkward, puzzled, too, by the unfamiliarity of his short, curling beard, and by the London clothes and the jewelled ring on his finger. Even Susanna, with all her nine-year-old composure, drew away from him, glancing up at her mother. To Anne, the strangeness was not in his appearance, but in himself, as though William, in fact, had not come back from London at all, and she had only momentarily been deceived into thinking that he had. He stood and looked round the small, low-ceilinged, dark, untidy room, with the pieces of white linen tossed, apparently at random, on the table, and Hamnet's wooden soldiers lying massacred on the floor, and then he turned back to Anne, and the silence itself was like a chasm between them.

They were saved from that chill moment by Edmund, delighted by William's return, and gratified to have been the first to bring news of it to Anne. He started up from the window seat crying, 'Will! Did you bring me a present from London? Where is it?'

William's stiffness relaxed, and he laughed at him. 'What if I forgot to bring you one?' he said. 'Shall I have to ride all the way back to get it?'

'Yes, and take me with you,' said Edmund promptly. 'I want to go to London. Where is it, Will? I know you brought me one.'

259

'At the inn, with my baggage. Do you want to walk round with me and find it?'

Hamnet, never shy for long with anyone, came forward at that and enquired, 'Did you bring one for me, father? Can I come too?'

'You can all come,' said William. 'There's a present for each of you.' He turned back to Anne, and said, 'We're to have supper with mother tonight. Shall we go round there now?'

'Supper?' said Anne, sharply. 'What about the children?'

'They can come too, surely. They're quite grown up now, aren't you, Sue?'

She smiled at him, blushing, and he laughed and put his arm round her. Anne said nothing but turned away and began to tidy the room.

'Are you coming, Anne?' he said, after a moment.

'You'd better go on,' she replied, without looking up. 'I must clear up here first.'

'Shall we go too, mother?' asked Susanna.

'Yes, yes, go along with you, all of you!' said Anne. 'And we're not going to stay too late, or Hamnet will be sick.'

They all hesitated for a moment, and then went out of the door and down the path, and Anne went to the window to see them go. Susanna and Judith each held William by the hand, while Hamnet ran ahead with Edmund, laughing excitedly. The children were real and unchanged, but it was as though she saw them clinging to a stranger.

Anne did not hurry to Henley Street, and when she arrived she found them all waiting for her, with the table set out for supper and Mary Shakespeare out of temper.

'Come along, let's all sit down,' said Mary, almost before Anne was inside the door. 'Will, you sit here. Susanna, Judith, you here——'

'I want to sit next to Uncle Gilbert,' said Judith.

'No, Judith, you sit here,' said Mary.

'No, no, I won't!' Judith shouted, with that horrifying sudden violence which had increased in her during William's absence from home. 'I want to sit next to Uncle Gilbert!'

'Judith, hold thy tongue and sit here,' said Gilbert, coolly, and he picked her up and set her down at the table. She looked up at him, met his eye, and smiled suddenly, a dreadful, defenceless smile, like a baby standing swaying on unaccustomed feet in front of an open fire. And Anne felt for the first time a quick glow of gratitude towards Gilbert.

'Come on, Will, tell us,' said Edmund, when at last they were all settled, 'what's it like in London?'

'It's full of people,' said William.

'Huh! there are people in Stratford,' said Mary Shakespeare.

'Ah, but not so many!' cried William, laughing, 'and of a different kind.'

'Folk are much the same all the world over, I should have thought,' said Mary. 'Why

261

should London folk be different from any others?'

'They are, though,' said William. 'Ask Gilbert. He'll tell you.'

'How are they different, Gilbert?' enquired Joanne.

'Every man in London,' said Gilbert, 'stands on a scaling-ladder, set up against the walls of a fortress. Most of them don't know what the fortress is, or what they will do with it if they capture it. They only know that they must take it or die.'

'You didn't take it!' said Joanne.

'Nor did I die,' replied Gilbert.

William looked at him across the table and asked soberly, 'Shall I take mine, Gilbert?'

'Oh yes, you've made a breach in it already,' said Gilbert smiling. 'But then, you know the name of your fortress.'

'What is its name?' asked Joanne, softly.

'Fame,' said Gilbert.

'And what was yours?' asked William.

'I never found one worth the taking,' said Gilbert, 'Besides, every fortress, whatever its name, is in the hands of Fortune, and every man who tries to scale the walls, whether he wins or loses, is taken prisoner. Not choosing to become Fortune's slave, I came home.'

Mary and Joanne, who alone had understood the conversation, looked at Gilbert with troubled faces. William regarded him steadily, and smiled a little, and said, 'You are quite

262

right. But once our feet are set upon the ladder——'

'Then, like all besiegers, you must take the fortress or die.'

They both laughed. John Shakespeare broke in from the other end of the table, 'And what of the theatre, Will? You still like it? You're not tired of it yet?'

'Tired of it?' William exclaimed. 'It's my life!'

Anne looked up at him quickly and then down again.

'And have you fought many battles on the stage, Will?' asked Edmund.

'Oh, fought many battles, and killed many men—on the stage,' he answered.

'When I grow up,' said Hamnet, solemnly, 'I shall be an actor, father.'

'Will you, Hamnet?'

'Yes. I was going to be a soldier, but it's better to be an actor, isn't it? Because if you really *are* a soldier, then you might get killed. But if you only *act* one, then you can get up again at the end of the play.'

'Would you rather be a shadow, then?' asked William. 'Would you rather be a shadow of a man than a man?'

Hamnet thought it over carefully, and then replied, 'I would rather be a live shadow than a dead man.'

They all laughed, except Anne, who said, 'Eat up your supper, Hamnet.'

263

'*I* shall be an actor, too,' said Edmund. 'I needn't wait until I grow up, though, need I, Will? I could play women's parts now. You could take me back with you when you go.'

'Oh no,' said William. 'My fame couldn't bear comparison with yours. The light of your Zenocrate would dim my Tamburlaine. Besides, if you were playing women's parts, you wouldn't be able to fight any battles.'

'All right, then,' said Edmund. 'I'll wait until I'm a man. And then I shall wear a velvet cloak, and a sword, and I shall live in a great house in London, and——'

'That's quite enough from you,' said Mary, emphatically. 'Let's have no more talk about you going to London. It's bad enough to have Will making a show of himself.'

'But, mother——'

'I said that was enough, Edmund. What are your lodgings like, Will? Is the linen clean?'

And there was no more conversation about the theatre.

After the meal, they sat round the fire, talking. William seemed tired and restless, and he complained that the chimney was smoking and said he thought it needed sweeping.

'Nonsense!' cried Mary, crossly. 'The chimney has always smoked when the wind's in this direction. You know that as well as I do, and unless you want to climb up the chimney and blow the wind another way, you'll just have to bear it, like the rest of us!'

And yet, in spite of that, he lingered after Anne had taken the children home, saying that he wanted to talk to his father. She was in bed and pretending to be asleep before he came at last and got into bed beside her.

In the early hours of the morning, Anne was awakened by the sound of Susanna's voice calling her. With the familiar pounding of her heart, she ran into the children's room, and found Hamnet flushed and gasping, and Susanna sitting up and watching him anxiously. Judith, who always slept very heavily, was breathing evenly and deeply in the chimney-nook.

'Oh, God!' Anne whispered. 'Oh, God!' and she knelt down beside Hamnet's bed.

She had knelt so, alone and terrified, a dozen times during the past two years. The doctors could suggest nothing to help him, and it seemed that all she could do was to lift him up a little in bed, and hold him until the attack had passed. And always she thought that his body seemed too slight and frail to be racked by such a paroxysm, and that one night it would grip him until he died in her arms. She would kneel with tears running down her cheeks, suffering every pang with him, and saying only, 'God, God, God,' over and over again, more as though she spoke to a companion than prayed to a far deity. She was trying now to gather her courage together, alone in the darkness, when she heard a step behind her, and turned her head to see William.

'Ah, Will!' she cried, as though she saw him now at last, returned from London. And he, the true William, came and knelt down beside her and took Hamnet in his arms.

It was quite light when the coughing and gasping grew less, and Hamnet fell into an exhausted sleep. Anne got to her feet wearily and went back into the bedroom. She sat down on the edge of the bed and put her face in her hands, shaking.

'Oh, Will,' she said, as he followed her in, 'if he should die! One day it will kill him, I know it will.'

'He's all right now, Anne,' said William. 'You're worn out. Come to bed.'

Anne went to sleep with his arm round her, as she had on their wedding night, and she knew that they were not really divided. While they both loved Hamnet so much, and could share such grief and anxiety, they would never be quite parted.

But in the broad daylight, with Hamnet much recovered, and all the small matters of everyday life about them, Anne found that William's momentary nearness and simplicity had vanished. He seemed like a man divided against himself, as though a restless ocean tossed about within him, breaking up all that singleness which had once been so strongly

266

his. His poetry and ambition had always been a part of him. It had divided him from Anne, but never from himself. Now, in all he did or said there could be felt this hidden undertow, constantly dragging at him, drawing him away from his family, away from Stratford—away from himself. And, increasingly as the days went by, there lay between him and Anne a barrier which was too intangible to be removed; and Anne was too diffident and too unsubtle to endeavour to remove it.

Throughout the summer after William's return, the Plague continued very bad in London. Towards the end of September, Greenway brought news of the death of Isobel Brown's uncle. Isobel was horrified at this breach of good manners.

'My *uncle!*' she exclaimed. 'How could that happen to him?' No more would he stand upon the corner by Westminster, taking his cap off and crying, 'God save your Majesty!' No more would he welcome his guests to a fat capon, a leg of mutton and good conversation. No more would he enjoy the sermons at Paul's Churchyard and shake his head over the unread scurrilities of Martin Marprelate. He was gone, in a moment, without courtesies, like any uncivil man. Isobel's mourning dress was the admiration of all Stratford.

'More than a thousand dead, they say, in the first week of August,' said William

Greenway, with enthusiasm, pausing at the cottage gate to talk to William and Gilbert. 'And, they say, two thousand in the second week! Ah, but it might be more. 'Course, it must be hard to count 'em in Lunnon. Now, if 'twas Stratford, we'd know just how many it was, but in Lunnon, we-ell, there's so many people livin' there, seems like you wouldn't miss one or two, now would you?'

'I can think of one or two I wouldn't miss from Stratford,' said Gilbert.

'Ha, ha!' shouted Greenway, with his engaging welcome for any jest, however slight. 'You're right, sir, you're right! Now if we could on'y choose which was to go——'

'Ah, but Death is such an astute buyer,' said William. 'He will never take those at the front of the counter.'

'Well, hows'ever that may be,' said Greenway, 'he won't find *me* at the front of the counter. I'm on'y goin' as far as Oxford for the next few weeks. If Death wants me, he can come and fetch me, but hang him! I'm not goin' to meet him!'

He went off down the lane, and William and Gilbert strolled inside the cottage.

'I shall have to be going back to London soon,' said William. Gilbert made no reply. Anne, at the top of the staircase, paused to listen.

'The Plague always gets less in the winter,' said William, argumentatively, 'and I expect

268

the theatres will be opened again for Christ-mastime.' He paused. Gilbert said nothing. 'And anyway,' William finished, vehemently, 'I've business to see to. I can't stay in Stratford for ever!'

'I am not denying it,' said Gilbert, coolly.

William fell over something with a clatter and shouted, 'God's Blood! What's that?'

Anne came downstairs, with a look of reproof for his swearing, and replied, 'It's Hamnet's cart.'

'By heaven, this house is small enough without that!' said William. 'We shall have the hen-house in here soon! It should be in the yard.'

'He plays with it on wet days,' said Anne, pushing the box against the wall. 'He used to travel up and down to London in it to visit you.'

'He's getting too old for such games,' said William. 'He'd better do more work at school, and learn his Latin, and leave childishness like that to Thomas Quiney. Where's the book I left here on the table? I want it to take round to the school. By God, I can never find anything here! It is like living in a tavern!'

'I put it on the shelf,' said Anne. 'And if this is how you're going to be, the sooner you go back to London, the better.'

'I'm going in two weeks' time,' said William.

Anne looked at him for a long while without

speaking. That pride, which she had laid down so gratefully when she first acknowledged that she loved him, she now took up again, and hid her sorrow and disappointment and her longing for his company behind the old look of obstinate sullenness, more desperate because it came now from love and not from hate.

'Very well,' she said, and William took the book and turned on his heel and went out of the house.

For the next two weeks there was a false gentleness between William and his family—false because it did not mean that he was now less restless in their company, but that the struggle was over and he had already left them. The evening before his journey, Anne sat and mended a rent in his travelling-cloak, and he told stories to Hamnet and the girls, telling them about the theatre and London, and the road he would travel, with the good-humoured politeness of a stranger who entertains his host's children. The small room was comfortable and the fire burnt brightly, with a scent of apple-wood.

'Well,' said Anne, getting up, 'that's finished, and now I think you're all ready. You'd better be going if you want to visit Henley Street before supper.'

'Mother,' Hamnet broke in, 'may I go out very early tomorrow? Edmund's going out to snare rabbits and he said I could go with him.'

'Well, you don't want to go too early, do you?' said Anne. 'You want to be here for your father's department.'

'*Departure*, Anne,' said William.

He said it very quietly, and after he had spoken there was a silence. Then Anne turned and went out of the back door into the yard, closing the door gently behind her, and standing there quite still in the dusk, holding the cloak. She heard him call out rather awkwardly, 'I'm going now, Anne,' but she didn't answer, not from anger but because she was too dazed to speak. In that moment when he corrected her way of speaking, she knew that he had a mistress.

She put her hand against the doorpost to steady herself, as the truth beat against her and found easy admittance. She did not think, and draw conclusions from the facts—that everything she did or said irritated him, that he could no longer be content with his family, that he was returning to London although the theatres were closed, that they slept in the great bed together and never touched. She was not suspicious and jealous, slowly convinced that her suspicions were well founded. Indeed, she was not jealous at all, for jealousy brings with it anger and rebellion, and she felt none. She simply knew instinctively that William had a mistress, and she stood alone in the autumnal evening, while the knowledge took possession of her. Just as before she could use no wiles to catch a man, so now she could use no art to keep him or to bring him back. While he loved her, she could offer him a simple and boundless love in return, but she could not make him love her. She felt the old, stony anguish coming down upon her, and knew that it was useless to struggle against it. This was the end, then, of the love which had begun in the lane by Hewlands. She felt obscurely that Joan Hathaway and Catherine had, after all, gained the victory over her.

When William said goodbye to her next morning, Anne turned her face away so that he kissed her on the cheek. She stood and watched him as he rode away, remembering the last time he had left, and she wondered how she could then have thought herself unhappy.

## CHAPTER 18

One hot Sunday in August, they were all in the garden at Henley Street. William was home for his summer visit to Stratford, and they had all gone to church and then had dinner together to celebrate the great victory at Cadiz, sharing that comfortable glow of national pride which is like no other emotion

272

in the world. 'The Spaniards' whole fleet either taken, sunk, or burned,' said John Shakespeare, to whose optimistic spirit victories always came as a happy justification.

'It was the hand of God upon them,' said Mary.

'Certainly,' said John. 'For if our generals had succeeded in landing soldiers at the west end of Cadiz, where they first attempted it, they would have had great difficulty.'

'That's as may be,' answered Mary, repressively, 'but I think the minister was right. He said that our boats filled and sank when they tried to land there because it was a judgement on them for trying to land on a Sunday.'

'Well,' said Gilbert, 'here is Dick Quiney trying to board us on a Sunday, and half-drowned in perspiration too, but still he comes on. Haven't we any arms to repel boarders?'

'I have left my sword at home, Uncle Gilbert,' said Hamnet, helpfully. 'Shall I fetch it?'

'Hamnet!' exclaimed Mary, scandalized. Then, quickly, 'Your Uncle Gilbert was joking, which was wrong of him on a Sunday. We're very happy to see Master Quiney coming to visit us.'

'Oh! Oh!' said Gilbert, under his breath, as Mary went forward to help Dick with the latch of the gate.

'Dick, we must look at you through our fingers,' Joanne called out. 'You dazzle our eyes!'

'My new suit of clothes?' said Dick, bridling modestly. 'I had them made for me by a London tailor, to the latest style.'

'And two peacocks died of envy as he rode down to Stratford,' said Gilbert.

Dick Quiney glanced complacently down at his handsome clothes and smiled. He knew that he looked very fine, and his wife had admired him and so had her friend Isobel Brown. Gilbert always dressed in such dull colours that it was no wonder he was envious.

'Will,' he went on, always pursuing his own purposes, 'I called to see if you would come and dine with us on Tuesday. The schoolmaster is coming, and we thought you'd like to talk to him.'

'In Latin?' asked Joanne. 'You'd better ask Edmund. He remembers more of his schooling than Will does.'

'Or Hamnet,' suggested Gilbert. 'He knows more Greek than Will ever did.'

But William answered seriously, 'I won't be in Stratford on Tuesday. I shall be going back to London tomorrow.'

'Back to London?' exclaimed Dick. 'But playing is prohibited. Why should you go back to London?'

William looked annoyed as all the family

stopped talking to listen, and only Anne, straightening Judith's cap, did not look up at him for his answer.

'I have some matters of business,' said William stiffly. 'And I have to see the Earl.'

'Ay, well, that's a pity,' said Dick. He thought it over. 'Gilbert, can you come instead?'

'To stand proxy for Will?' enquired Gilbert, grinning.

'And christen the conversation with Latin words,' said Joanne.

'No, no,' said Gilbert. 'I only *hold* the infant conversation. I shall sit by and admire the schoolmaster's learning, and eat my dinner, pausing once or twice to cry, *Haud credo*, or such wise sayings as, *Vir sapit qui pauca loquitur*—especially when he dines.'

'Yes, well, that will do,' Dick agreed. 'I shall expect you on Tuesday.'

He turned towards the gate.

'Oh, must you leave us?' said Gilbert.

'No, I'm in no hurry,' answered Dick, turning back again. 'What do you think of the victory?'

Gilbert was speechless, but John Shakespeare answered cheerfully, 'Great news, isn't it?'

'I heard,' said Dick, confidentially, 'that there was such trouble among the leaders of our fleet at Plymouth, that some wondered if they'd ever set sail at all.'

'Dear me,' said John, always as interested as Dick in gossip about the great ones. 'We heard nothing about that here.'

'Yes,' said Dick. 'Rufus said that if all the fighting was to be between our generals, he wondered why they troubled to go to Cadiz to do it.'

Joanne found her hands trembling, and clasped them in front of her. Rufus. Rufus. In the years since he had left, this was the first news of him, and the name flamed up for her in the idle conversation like a beacon on the coast. But, with a sense of fevered unreality, she found that John had noticed nothing and was saying wisely, 'Ah yes, it's a great pity when these jealousies arise between the leaders. But what happened? Did the Queen intervene?'

'No,' Dick replied, 'I think that the Earl of Essex ordered that Sir Francis should have the precedence of Sir Walter on land, and he by sea, so all was smoothed over.'

Dick turned to go once more. Joanne looked away towards the road. She could feel the colour burning in her cheeks and knew that if she spoke she would betray herself. And yet, to know no more than that, to ask no questions and be told nothing, when she was half-sick for news of him—!

As Dick reached the gate, Gilbert asked, with a quiver of amusement in his voice, 'So you've just seen Rufus? Has he been in London?'

'Oh yes,' Dick answered. 'Didn't Will tell you? Rufus told me he'd seen him.'

'Did you, Will?' asked Gilbert.

'Did I what?'

'See Rufus?'

'Oh yes, didn't I tell you? I saw him before he went to the fleet.'

'Yes, Rufus went to Cadiz,' said Dick, 'in the force of Sir John Wingfield, who was killed there. I believe he's come back with plenty of plunder and booty, too. Anyway,' he added, with satisfaction, 'he gave me a very good dinner at the Black Horse tavern.'

'Well, well,' said John. 'I'm not surprised. Do you hear that, wife? Rufus was at the battle and has brought back much wealth with him.'

'Oh?' said Mary, belligerently. 'Well, I dare say. I don't suppose he has ever done an honest day's work in his life, but I don't doubt he would make a good pirate.'

'Lock all the doors and windows,' said Gilbert, smiling, 'for there was treason if ever I heard it. Have we all been celebrating piracy?'

Mary, for once, was silenced.

'Rufus said he'd been on several voyages,' Dick went on, 'and once he was lucky to escape only with his life, but the last one to the Indies and this one have brought him a good sum.' He sighed. 'Did you tell Mistress Hart, Will, that you'd seen Rufus?'

'No, I haven't seen her since I came down.'

'Then I shall have to go and tell her about him,' said Dick. He sighed again, and said, with that unintentional humour which had always delighted William, 'And I know that Mistress Hart won't listen to me.'

'Never mind, Dick,' said Gilbert. 'If you can silence her long enough to tell her one half of your news, we'll have all the church bells rung again to celebrate another victory.' He paused and looked at Joanne. She could feel his eyes on her face, although she looked away, and she knew that he was smiling. As Dick opened the gate and went through, Gilbert called, idly, 'Is Rufus coming down here?'

'No,' Dick answered. 'He'd come straight up from Plymouth, and he was only spending two days in London and then going back there to see to his affairs.'

'And did he send no messages to—to his mother?'

Dick shook his head. 'Only to tell her that he was not hanged yet, but there was still time.'

Mary made an indignant noise, and Dick went off, saying solemnly to Gilbert, 'Don't forget Tuesday, for dinner.'

'*Pax vobiscum*,' said Gilbert, loftily, waving his hand, and Mary couldn't decide whether this response, being in Latin, was still blasphemous or not.

278

'Dick reminds me in time,' said William, 'that I must see the schoolmaster about Hamnet. I'd better go round this evening.'

'What about Hamnet?' asked Anne, quickly.

'We must be thinking about sending him to the University,' William replied. 'He's well past his eleventh birthday, isn't he?'

'The University?' said Mary Shakespeare. 'Why should you want to send him there? *You* never went there.'

'Ah,' said William, 'but what was good enough for me isn't good enough for Hamnet.'

'I can't imagine why not,' said Mary, indignantly. 'You haven't done so badly, I should think.'

'Oh, I shall always be just the player turned poet,' said William, 'but, Hamnet—he's the true prince who'll inherit all that his father usurped, and make it good.' He looked across at Gilbert and smiled and added, 'The true sun rises when the false moon sets.'

'Your image is a poor one,' said Gilbert, answering the smile. 'It's the moon who derives her light, not the sun. So the sun is the father, and has the true light, and the moon is the son and is only the reflection.'

William laughed. 'Well, Hamnet's to be sun and moon, gentleman and scholar.'

'Also the carrier, a soldier, and an actor,' Gilbert agreed. 'A man of parts.'

'I know one thing,' said Anne, watching Hamnet chasing Edmund round the garden, 'if he doesn't stop running about like that he'll be ill.'

'Oh, Anne, he's all right,' cried William, irritably. 'You cosset the boy too much. You'll make a girl out of him.'

Anne said nothing, but pressed her lips together, as Hamnet stopped and leaned against the tree, gasping for breath.

'Here, children,' called Joanne, suddenly bustling about, as though to show that she had not spent the last five minutes in silence and abstraction, 'come inside with me. I made some sweetmeats for you yesterday.'

'I think that I deserve a sweetmeat more than anyone,' Gilbert observed softly, but Joanne pretended not to hear him and went quickly into the house.

Joanne spent the afternoon with Anne and the children and then went back to the cottage to keep Anne company, since William was having supper with the schoolmaster. She was glad to escape from Gilbert's sardonic amusement. It was as though once more she and Rufus stood alone and looked at each other across a room full of people. But this time Gilbert was there to watch them with a mirthful and dispassionate eye, and this time it was she who was at a disadvantage, and not Rufus. He came this time, not out of breath and dishevelled from an inglorious escapade, but fresh with the dignities of travel and danger and the great victory in which he had taken part. And she, too, was changed. No longer was she a gay young girl with two suitors for her hand, but a plain woman of twenty-seven with the reputation of a shrew. And yet the grief she felt was not for what she had lost in herself, but in Rufus. When she heard of his return, sensible, honoured and wealthy, she suffered the anguish of a sharp and cruel bereavement. All the evening she mourned the loss of the Rufus she had loved, idle, laughing and irresponsible, the Rufus she would never see again.

# CHAPTER 19

'Will,' said Anne, at breakfast the next morning, 'I wish you wouldn't go to London today.'

William replied without looking up, 'Why not? I've arranged to go now.'

'Hamnet's not at all well. I've kept him in bed.'

'He was all right last night,' said William.

'No, he wasn't. You weren't home until late. And this morning he's so short of breath that if he moves it seems to choke him.'

'Well, I'm sorry,' said William, 'but there's nothing I can do for him. He'll be all right in a day or two.'

'Wait until tomorrow,' said Anne.

'There'd be no sense in that,' said William. 'What could I do if I did stay?'

Anne looked at him in the dumb resentment which with her took the place of argument. She did not tell him that when Hamnet was ill he always called for his father, or that when William was there to hold him the paroxysms seemd to be less violent, or that Hamnet slept more easily in William's arms than in hers. 'Why should I say that?' she thought, angrily. 'He knows it quite well himself,' Nor would her pride allow her to beg him to stay for her sake, or to tell him that the terrors of the illness were trebled for her when he was not there.

William stubbornly finished his meal and went out of the house. When he returned from the inn with his horse, the two girls were busy about the house and he packed his saddle-bags and dressed for the journey. He said goodbye to his daughters, Susanna gentle and affectionate, Judith unpredictable, sometimes violently loving, sometimes even hostile, but today they both seemed to him to kiss him reproachfully, and he went unwillingly out into the yard where Anne was hanging out the washing, and called, 'I'm going now, Anne. I won't go up to Hamnet in case he's asleep. Say goodbye to him for me.'

Anne came towards him with her sleeves rolled up above her elbows and a wet shirt hanging over her arm. She said in a voice of ill-humour and complaint, 'Don't go today, Will. Don't go while Hamnet's ill.'

'I must, Anne,' William answered, very reasonably.

She stood and looked at him, and for a moment it was as though she saw him flinging himself headlong down a rocky precipice. It was in a strange terror for him that she suddenly caught hold of him and screamed, 'No, you shan't go! I won't let you go!' William turned his head away, standing stiff against the doorway. Anne clasped him in her arms with all her strength and sobbed, 'You must stay, Will. You must stay!'

'Let me go, Anne!' said William furiously. He wrenched himself free, the wet shirt falling to the ground, and he said with the terrible obstinacy of the man who is determined to resist his wife's demands, 'I'm going up to London today. Let's have no more talk about it.'

He turned and went through the house and Anne heard the front door close behind him. He was gone. He had left his son in sickness and ridden away to the London woman who tormented him and destroyed his peace. Anne leaned against the wall of the cottage crying bitterly, and yet it was not because he had left her, but because his going was an insult to the William she had married, whose love and faithfulness she had trusted beyond anything in the world.

Through the open door, Anne heard Hamnet calling. She pressed her hands against her mouth and closed her eyes, and at last subdued the violence of her emotion and went through the room, past the two girls who looked at her with serious, frightened faces, and up the stairs, where she found Hamnet. He was standing outside the bedroom, white and shivering and gasping for breath, the tears streaming down his face.

'Where's father gone?' he said. 'I called and called him, but he didn't come. Where's father?'

'Hush!' said Anne. 'He's gone to London. He'll be back before long.'

'No, no, he couldn't!' cried Hamnet, still choking and trembling. 'He couldn't go without saying goodbye to me. I don't want him to go to London.'

Anne knelt down and put her arms round him, laying her face against his body in an acute tenderness which was almost unbearable. She loved Susanna dearly. She felt for Judith a troubled fondness. But for Hamnet she had always felt this love which was more like pain, in which his indomitable gaiety and the frailness of his body were sharply blended. As she knelt and held him, it was his grief which she felt with more poignancy than any of her own.

'There, now,' she said, drawing away from him, 'father won't be gone long. Supposing you was to come and sleep in my bed? You can see right down the lane from there, and you'll be able to tell us when anyone comes to call on us. Come along, my love.' She half carried him along the passage and helped him to climb into the bed, and he stopped crying and began to smile, always ready to be distracted into amusement.

'This is a besieged castle,' he said, 'and I'm the watchman in the tower. I'm watching for the relieving forces. Uncle Gilbert can be the relieving forces. Do you think he'll come today, mother?'

'He might,' said Anne. 'You just stay there and watch for him.'

But all day Hamnet's sickness increased on him, and that night was the worst that Anne had ever known. When morning came, she was so exhausted by suffering with him that she saw the dawn break like a prisoner in the torture chamber, holding his life in her hands like the fragment of truth still withheld from the questioners.

Joanne came in the afternoon and sat by Hamnet's side, bringing him a sweetmeat. He took it and looked at it with regret, but at last was forced to admit that he couldn't eat it.

'Shall I have it, Aunt Joanne?' asked Judith, eagerly.

'All right,' said Joanne. 'I'll bring Hamnet another one tomorrow, when he's better.'

'Two,' Hamnet suggested, rallying slightly.

'Two, because Judith had more than I did yesterday.'

Joanne laughed, and Anne was glad to be able to say, 'You're greedy children, the pair of you.'

Anne sent the girls to bed early and herself sat up holding Hamnet while the breath dragged to and fro reluctantly in his throat. Once, after a very bad fit of breathlessness he said in a sad, wondering voice, 'I wish that father was here,' but mostly he seemed too weary to talk at all. It was like holding in her arms his shadow instead of himself. At last he fell asleep and Anne slept too, lying fully dressed on the bed beside him.

In the early hours of the morning, Anne awoke and started up in fear, wondering what had disturbed her. The room was quite silent. She could hear nothing in the lane but the quiet rustle of the leaves in the summer breeze. And then she realized that Hamnet's breathing was no longer heavy and laboured, that there was no sound from him as he lay beside her. She leant over him in terror, thinking that he was dead, but he was still alive, his quick, light breaths like the last flutters of a butterfly's wings. She took the rush-light and brought it close to his face. It was no longer flushed but perfectly white and hollow.

'Oh, God!' said Anne. 'Oh, God!'

She went quickly through to the children's

room and knelt down beside Susanna and woke her up.

'Get up and go to your grandmother,' said Anne, steadily. 'Tell her that Hamnet's ill, and ask her to come round at once.'

'Yes, mother,' answered Susanna, always gentle and reliable, and she pushed back the covers at once and began to dress.

Anne went back and knelt down beside the bed. She put one hand under his head and the other on his heart which she could feel faintly beating. She heard Susanna go downstairs and heard her struggling with the bolts on the door. She heard her close the door very softly behind her, heard her run down the path, through the gate, down the lane. Anne stayed where she was, quite motionless, not daring to move her hand in case Hamnet's heart should stop beating, as though by feeling it, she made it still continue.

All the world contracted to that one heart beat. There was nothing outside the room, no town, no houses. She and Hamnet were alone together on the surface of the unpeopled world, her hand and his heart together, kept alive by its beating. If his heart should stop, then all the world would be ended. Nothing would exist any more. The little heart seemed very strong in the small body, as though it was stronger than its frame, as though it was the spirit of Hamnet, all that was left of him, indomitably beating, invincibly defying death.

She could feel the firm little breast-bone and the curve of his head under her hands, but it was the heart which was Hamnet, still there though the rest of him had gone from her into stillness and silence.

Like a wheel that turns once, and again, and comes to rest, Hamnet's heart stopped beating. He lay between her hands, dead, and nothing remained.

Anne did not hear any footsteps in the lane, but she heard the door open downstairs. She drew her hand very gently from beneath Hamnet's head and went to the head of the stairs. It was Gilbert who called out anxiously, 'Anne, how is he?' The human voice struck violently upon her ears, as though she had been dead with Hamnet and it brought her in agony back to life. She cried out and stumbled down the stairs and Gilbert came and caught hold of her and she burst into tears, her head against his shoulder.

'Anne, Anne,' said Gilbert, in a voice of compassion which she had heard before but never recognized. And then, 'He is with God.'

'Hamnet,' said Anne. It seemed that for the rest of her life there would be nothing else she wanted to say. 'Hamnet, oh, Hamnet, Hamnet!'

Later in the morning, Gilbert set off for London. The next day he found William at his lodging, and through the oppressive August heat they rode back together. Ten miles out of

Stratford it began to rain, heavy warm drops falling silently out of the sky. In the town they parted, without speaking, and William rode on to Chapel Lane, his horse stumbling because he had pushed it hard all the way. He dismounted and walked stiffly inside, and Anne met him inside the door.

'You are too late,' she said.

# CHAPTER 20

'Well, mother,' said William, more than a year after Hamnet's death, 'the purchase of New Place is concluded now.'

'H'm!' said Mary. 'I hope you can afford such a great house. It may be fine enough now, while things go well for you, but what if the time comes when you're not so prosperous? One of these days they might close the theatres altogether, and then what would you do?'

'Why, then, mother,' William answered, 'I should have to sell New Place again, or better still take it down and dispose of it, stone by stone, to buy our daily bread, thus disproving the Scriptures, because when my family ask for bread, I shall give them a stone.'

Gilbert and Joanne chuckled, and Mary

could not help smiling, though against her will. But Mistress Hart, who had called in for a brief visit more than an hour earlier, said solemnly, 'William, I don't know how you could buy that house! *I* couldn't live in a house where a murder had been committed. I hope you'll have it exorcized.'

'I don't think poor Underhill's ghost will haunt us,' said William.

'Ah, *his* ghost may not,' Mrs Hart agreed, 'but what of his son? Fancy a son to poison his own father, and in that very house! They say murderers return after death to the place where they committed their crimes. Why——', her face beamed with an awful delight, 'why, you might wake up in the middle of the night and see Fulke Underhill re-enacting the murder!'

'But don't you speak to him,' said Gilbert, 'because such things are always acted out in dumb show, and you might put the actor out of his part.'

'It's well enough for you to laugh,' said Mistress Hart, who was not very fond of Gilbert, 'but, it's as my husband used to say, "We know what we are," he used to say, "but we know not what we may be." Spirits do walk the earth, we all know that, and of course murderers don't lie quiet in their graves, for if they did what would be the use of being an honest man? So what I say is, there's no need to run risks, and if I know there's a murder been committed, then I don't go near the place. Why I remember when I was a girl there was an old man done to death in his house and they must've thought he had some money hidden, though where they thought it was I don't know for he only lived in an old hut with nothing in it but a stool and a bit of straw, but still kill him they did, and blood everywhere. Blood! And a little while after, not thinking of it, I was walking along that road after dark because it was the only road to get to our house and of course I wasn't thinking of the old man, Jack Silence his name was and silent he was poor soul when they'd finished with him, and suddenly there was a terrible noise from the hut like someone in his death agonies threshing about and beating against the walls.'

'Not so silent after all,' said Gilbert.

'Well, I took to my heels, I can tell you,' said Mistress Hart, encouraged by Gilbert's interest, 'and never stopped until I was home. And my father said there was an old white horse in the field used to shelter in the hut, but I said it didn't sound like a horse, I said, and if there was a white horse there, where had it come from? Well, anyway, I never went by there after dark again I can tell you, except once, and then as I ran by as fast as I could, I saw a dreadful white shape rising up out of the grass by the doorway of the hut and I was so afraid it would get me that I fell in the ditch and I arrived home mired up to my knees!'

'But, wasn't that the white horse you saw?' enquired Richard, anxious to understand the affair.

'Ah,' said Mistress Hart, mysteriously, 'that's as may be.'

There was a general silence. At last, William, seeing that Richard had turned the whole matter over in his mind and was about to announce his conclusion, said hastily, 'Have you any more news of Rufus?'

'Yes, didn't I tell you?' answered Mistress Hart, placidly. 'He sent me a message by Greenway to say that he'd be coming down quite soon now. Lord, Lord!' she added, laughing. 'I expect I shall find him changed. To think of the places he's seen, but then as my husband used to say, a man can travel all the world over and still remain a fool, not but what William never was a fool, though he often played the fool I will say that.'

'Does he mean to stay in Stratford?' asked Mary.

'Oh, I shouldn't think so,' Mistress Hart answered, with the same air of cheerful unconcern. 'Because after all he's got all that money to spend, hasn't he? And I don't expect he'd want to spend it in Stratford. And then he hasn't found his rich wife yet, and there are better wives to be found in London, I'll be bound, than in Stratford. I can't think of anyone he could marry in Stratford except Joanne, of course, but she wouldn't have him,

I know that.' And she smiled amiably at Joanne.

'Oh, I don't know,' said Edmund, softly, from the window seat, 'beggars can't be choosers.'

'But it seems that Rufus is no beggar now,' said Gilbert, politely misunderstanding him.

'And when *I* beg a husband,' said Joanne, 'it will be a proper man, not a long-legged idler.'

'He idled to good purpose at Cadiz,' said William, 'and he fought in the battle, you know.'

'Bah!' said Joanne. 'I will eat all he killed!'

They had said all this in undertones, out of consideration for Mistress Hart's feelings, but she heard enough to say, laughing, 'Yes, yes, it's strange to think of my William fighting in a battle. But I'll wager he got out of it as soon as he could. He always used to say he'd never be a soldier because fighting is such hard work. Well, I must be going, I suppose. Why, Edmund, how you've grown. You've become quite a man. We shall have you going off to London soon, like the others.'

'No, no,' said Mary quickly, 'Edmund is staying here. There's to be no talk of *him* going.'

'Ah well, perhaps he can find enough here to keep him busy,' said Mistress Hart, with that flash of malice which sometimes glinted through her foolishness.

Edmund smiled at her sweetly, with narrowed eyes, and William quickly opened the door for her and speeded her departure.

'What did she mean by that?' asked Mary, suspiciously.

'Does she ever mean anything?' said William, smiling.

'Yes,' said Mary. 'Usually she means mischief.'

'Well, Will, you've given her some pleasant gossip to spread,' said Joanne. 'Now she can tell everyone about New Place.'

'I hope you know what you're doing, Will,' said Mary, diverted from Mistress Hart's hint. 'What about all the repairs needed, and the furnishing? All that's going to take money. Suppose they get tired of your plays in London?'

'I shall still be a Sharer in the Company,' answered William. 'And besides, I shan't do all this at once. As the years go by, we will gradually furnish it to our taste, and when I die——' He stopped, and then finished quietly, 'and when I die, the girls will inherit it.'

There was a moment's silence, and they all thought of the young prince who would never come into his kingdom, of the bright little sliver of a new moon which had never come to harvest.

'Yes,' said Gilbert, his voice sliding as though by chance across the silence, 'and then they might inherit the ghost, too, and see William Underhill rising out of the floor crying, Revenge! Revenge! like the ghost in the old play.'

'You'd better buy a white horse, Will,' added Joanne, 'and then Mistress Hart will be able to see it too.'

The ghosts at New Place held no terrors for Anne. She had her own small ghost who was with her all the time. Wherever she turned, she saw Hamnet. It was a long while before she remembered to set out only two bowls at table instead of three, and even then she looked for him each time in his familiar place. In the mornings it seemed strange not to have to hurry him off to school, and in the evenings it seemed strange not to welcome him home. At every moment of her life there were now small vacant places of loss and heartache, and she filled them by remembering him, by seeing him there still. When she went to plant flowers on his grave, she almost expected to find him there beside her, thinking how much he would have enjoyed helping her, how he would have stood by with the water, and how he would have wandered about, reading the gravestones.

As the last load was carried out of the cottage and it stood bare and echoing and strangely neutral, Anne stayed behind to make sure that nothing was left. Here was the children's room. Here she and William had knelt—how many times?—to see if Hamnet was still breathing. Here was their own room. Here the great bed had stood. Here Hamnet had been born, here he had died. Downstairs in the living-room Hamnet had worked at his books. Here he had sat at table and she had reproved him a hundred times for talking with his mouth full and for being greedy. Here his satchel used to lie, and here his cart used to stand, in this corner. From the empty cottage the memories thrust against her until she went outside and closed the door, as though to shut them all inside. Here Hamnet used to swing on the gate. The marks of his feet were still there. She went down the garden path and through the gate. She had come to the cottage with Hamnet, unborn, within her. It was as though in leaving it now she left him there behind her. Hamnet, Hamnet, oh, Hamnet!

'Will must have made a lot of money in London,' said Edmund one day, sitting in the window seat at New Place and watching Anne sew the hangings. William was in the study, his very own study, full of books, which, Anne knew, meant more to him than all the other rooms in the house.

'He's worked hard enough for it,' Anne replied.

'Oh, acting isn't work,' cried Edmund, 'nor writing plays. You can't call *that* work!'

Anne was silent. She would once have

agreed with him, and even now she wasn't sure that he was wrong. And yet she remembered all the times when William had sat up writing late at night by candlelight, and still more the look on his face each time he arrived from London, a look of burning weariness, like a man with a fever which animates even while it exhausts him. But because she did not understand this, she never spoke of it.

'I wonder why Gilbert came back so soon,' said Edmund. 'Everyone says he's cleverer than Will. If he'd stayed, he'd probably have made a fortune.'

'Money isn't everything,' said Anne. 'If you went to London, you wouldn't find anyone to love you as you're loved here.'

Edmund shook his shoulders restlessly. 'I'm tired of being treated like a child. I'd like to be my own master for a change.'

'No man is his own master,' said Anne. 'We're all in the hand of God.'

Edmund chuckled, with that dear, wicked look she remembered from his childhood.

'Then I'd rather be in the hand of God in London. It doesn't grip quite so hard there!'

'You ought to be ashamed of yourself,' said Anne, but smiling, because even now when he was a long-legged young man, the glance of innocent devilry from under his eyelashes was still irresistibly charming.

'And what about that girl in Bishopston?' she enquired.

'Oh,' said Edmund, 'have you heard about her?'

'Yes.'

'And has mother?'

'I hope not,' said Anne, severely.

Edmund laughed. 'So do I!'

'Are you going to marry her?' asked Anne.

'Not if I can avoid it,' said Edmund.

'You don't love her then, Ned?' asked Anne, seriously.

But Edmund answered, still laughing, 'I love myself. Too much to want to run my head into that noose!'

Anne shook her head at him, and yet she was thinking that this would not be a fit wife for him.

'Well,' said Edmund, getting up, 'I must go home or I shall be late for supper.' He stood beside her for a moment, as though in some indecision, and then bent down and kissed her, saying, 'Goodbye, Anne.'

'Ned, Ned,' said Anne, smiling, but with tears suddenly in her eyes, because Hamnet had loved Edmund so much that it seemed that there would always be a part of Hamnet in Edmund, to catch at her heart, to remind her that Hamnet was dead while Edmund was still alive, and yet to make her feel that, in Edmund, Hamnet yet had some faint hold on life.

It was late in the afternoon of the next day when Mary came in to New Place, calling out, 'Anne, Will, have you seen Edmund?'

'Not since last night,' said Anne.

William came out of his study and enquired, 'What's the matter, mother?'

'It's Edmund,' said Mary. 'He hasn't been home all day. When Richard woke up this morning, he wasn't there, and I thought he'd gone out after rabbits, but he's not home yet and I'm afraid something's happened to him.'

'I shouldn't worry, mother,' said William. 'I expect he's just gone farther afield than he meant to, and it's taken him longer than he thought to get back.'

'I don't know,' said Mary, clasping her hands together. 'His father's very angry and says he's just playing truant again, but it's not like Edmund to miss his dinner, or to go out for so long without telling me. He'd know how much I should worry about him.'

'I'll go out and see if I can find him,' said William. 'He probably goes to much the same places as Rufus and I used to.'

'Yes, I dare say,' said Mary. 'I suppose I should be thankful that you didn't teach him to steal deer as well.'

William laughed, but at that moment John Shakespeare came in, out of breath and distressed, calling, 'Mary, are you there?'

'What is it?' cried Mary. 'Something's happened to Edmund! What is it?'

'He's gone,' said John. They all looked at him blankly. 'Hamnet Sadler saw him going down the street early this morning, carrying a bundle. And I saw William Greenway. He says Edmund left some things with him two weeks ago to be carried to London for him.'

'Why?' said Mary. 'Why should he go?'

William turned away to look out of the window. He said in a troubled voice, 'He used to say he wanted to be an actor. But I'm going back myself in a week's time. He knew that. Why didn't he wait for me?'

'In a week!' cried Mary. 'You'll set off this minute and find him and bring him back!' Her voice rose in a sudden fury. 'This is to your account!' she said violently. 'You're to blame for this! You were the one who would go strutting about on the stage making a show of yourself! If any harm comes to him, it is you who have done it.'

William drew a deep breath and closed his eyes for a moment in pain. Anne, by her stillness, seemed neither to defend him nor to disagree.

'London——!' cried Mary, but she was interrupted by John Shakespeare, suddenly grey-faced and panting, his hand to his side, gasping, 'Wife, wife——'

William turned quickly, and he and Anne lowered him into a chair and Anne fetched him a glass of wine. With the colour gone from his cheeks and the cheerfulness from his expression, John looked very old and tired. Mary never moved. She stood and gazed at William with hatred and said, 'London! It's

300

like the plague, and you have brought it here!'

Like a child carried off by gypsies at his play, Edmund disappeared from Stratford. William returned to London the next day and wrote soon after to say that Edmund had not called at his lodgings in Bishopsgate, nor at the theatre where his company was now playing, and that he could get no news of him. To them all it was almost incredible that Edmund, ingenuous and confiding, who had seemed until now to exist only in being teased and loved and spoilt by them, should now vanish overnight from their lives. It was as though all the time, unknown to them, this secret place had waited for him and he now stepped silently back into it and was gone. Once more it was painfully proved upon them that each life is a solitary pilgrimage undertaken in a throng of people, and that death is only the final assertion of this evident truth.

## CHAPTER 21

The days passed warily for Joanne, as though she lived secretly in an alien country, awaiting a message from across the seas. It was Richard who brought the message at last, tossing it down carelessly at dinner.

301

'I saw Rufus in the town. He was so changed, I'd hardly have known him.'

'Yes, dressed very rich, but sober,' said Gilbert, 'and talking to old Sharp as serious as a lawyer who's afraid the case is going to be settled out of court.'

'They say he's made enough money to buy half Stratford,' said Richard, opening his pleasant, credulous blue eyes very wide.

'Oh, all the town's talking about him,' Gilbert agreed. 'Mothers point him out to their children and tell them to mark him well, and one day they too might become great men. When he goes abroad, we shall all be expected to stand on the street corners and wave our caps to see him pass.'

'Huh!' said Mary. 'I hope we can all find something better to do than to stand gaping at William Hart! When all's said and done, I dare say he's done no better than Will!'

'Ah, but how much more unexpectedly!' said Gilbert.

All the afternoon, Joanne longed and dreaded to see Rufus, but with the dread more strong. The dream in which she had run after him crying in the darkness on the Banbury road lay heavily upon her mind as a portent of grief, and this new stranger Rufus was an enemy both to herself and to the old Rufus she had loved.

It was late in the evening when she came into the sitting-room and saw him at last, standing outside the window with his back to her, talking to John Shakespeare and Gilbert. She stepped quickly back behind the kitchen door so that she could watch him without fear of being seen, half hoping that after all he would not come into the house that day, that she could keep for a little longer the memory which he had returned to destroy. But at that moment he turned and they all three came inside, smiling. Joanne stepped forward into the room and Rufus paused, and their eyes met. And suddenly it was as though Joanne awoke after a long illness and found herself recovered. It was Rufus. Rufus, unchanged, unchanged!

'What, are you returned already?' she cried. 'We were just beginning to enjoy your absence, and here you are back again!'

'Woman,' said Rufus, 'are you still talking? You were talking when I left, and I swear you've been talking ever since, unless you stopped at night. But no, I expect you talked in your sleep even then.'

'And a good thing if I did,' said Joanne, 'for now you're back, I shall be lucky to find a space to speak a word!'

They looked at each other, laughing but cautious, like fencers, and then fell apart as Mary Shakespeare came into the room. She greeted Rufus with some reserve, but John insisted that he should sit down and tell them of the taking of Cadiz.

'Weren't there a great many knights made?' enquired Gilbert. 'We hoped that you might return Sir Rufus.'

'Knights!' cried Rufus. 'How I escaped it I don't know! If I had tripped over the tail of my cloak, I should have been lost. There were so many that I, being unknighted, walked like a king among them. There were two cooks and a rat-catcher knighted as they went about their business, and a Nubian slave whom they took to be a sunburnt gentleman modestly rolling his eyes, and a fellow who had come up for judgement as a pickpocket, but they knighted him by accident instead. Knights! King Arthur's Round Table would have to have been set out in Saint Paul's to accommodate them, and then some of them would have been in the churchyard. I tell you, I knelt down to take a stone out of my shoe, and I was almost knighted before I could get up again, but luckily a Dutch gentleman fell over me and so the honour lighted on him instead!'

'Fifty-seven made, I heard,' said Gilbert.

'Fifty-seven Englishmen, perhaps,' said Rufus. 'But what of the foreigners?'

'Well,' said John Shakespeare, 'I'm sure you deserved it as much as any of them, Rufus.'

'Certainly, sir,' Rufus agreed, 'for I ran as fast as any.'

'Towards Cadiz, or away from it?' enquired Joanne.

'Towards it,' Rufus answered. 'I remembered that you were behind me, in England, and I never stopped running until I was safe inside the walls of Cadiz.'

'Well, now that you're back again,' said Mary, tartly, 'will you stay and have supper with us?'

Joanne found herself holding her breath in the hope that he would say yes.

'I should like to stay,' said Rufus, 'but my mother is expecting me.' He grinned. 'I told her to kill the fatted calf for me, but she said she had nothing but an old boiling fowl, so I must hurry home and begin to sharpen my knife. Judging from the feathers which I saw on the table after she had plucked it, I think it must be a bird I remember as being in its middle years before I left. If you hear no more of me for three days, you'll know I'm still trying to gnaw a wing of Methuselah.'

'Take care he doesn't turn and gnaw you,' said Joanne.

'No, no, never fear,' said Rufus. 'I shall never be henpecked!'

And he went off triumphantly. Joanne moved to the window to watch him go, striding down the road with that same light, insolent walk. She smiled as she watched him, but then she thought how in the old days he would have invited himself to supper, placing himself next to her with that familiar assurance which used to enrage Mary, and how he would never have thought of going home however much his mother might expect him. She thought that, after all, it would have been better if they had both laughed a little less and shown a little more constraint. She stayed by the window until he was out of sight, and all next day she waited for him, but he didn't come.

Some weeks had passed since Edmund's departure, and it was only now that they had any news of him. Even so, it was only a brief note from William to John Shakespeare, saying that Edmund was 'with another company of players'.

'Is that all he says?' cried Mary, indignantly.

'I'm afraid Will isn't very satisfied with Edmund's position,' said John.

'Edmund's voice is too soft for him to make a good actor,' said Gilbert, 'and he'd never take the pains to learn his lines.'

'No doubt he must start in a small way,' said John. 'Will doesn't say much about the company that he's joined.'

'The truth of the matter is,' said Mary, 'that William is too busy acting before the Queen and other foolery of that sort to write a proper letter.'

'If Edmund prospers in London as well as Will has,' said John, 'we may well be thankful. But I agree with Gilbert.'

He got up and went slowly and heavily into

the workroom, and Joanne, watching him, thought with pain that this was the first time she had heard him speak quite without optimism, as though age at last had come upon him.

' "Prosper as well as William"!' said Mary, when the door had closed behind her husband, 'of course he will, and better too, I dare say. And what's all this about Will encouraging this other fellow who writes plays—this— what's his name? Ben Jonson. Will will turn round one day and find this Jonson writing all the plays and himself pushed aside.'

'I don't think you need worry, mother,' said Gilbert, smiling. 'Will has won himself such a place in London now that it would take more than Ben Jonson to push him aside. When I was up in town last, people could talk of nothing but his play of Henry the Fourth, and his fat knight, Oldcastle.'

'Didn't the Queen ask him to write another play about Oldcastle?' enquired Joanne. 'That's what Dick said. So that she could see Oldcastle in love?'

'So the rumour goes,' said Gilbert. 'I didn't ask Will about it. But if he does, it'll make the Oldcastle family more angry than ever. Will changed the fat knight's name to Falstaff later, but people still talk of him as Oldcastle.'

'Ah, there you are!' cried Mary, triumphantly. 'Will writes all these plays for the public stage, and one day he'll offend some great man and find himself in the pillory with both his ears cut off!'

Gilbert broke into a shout of laughter, saying, 'Well, mother, you're determined that he shan't be too proud.'

'No, I thank heaven,' said Mary, smiling a little, but not yielding, 'I may be pleased when my children do well, but I hope I may never encourage them to think too well of themselves.' This time Joanne joined in the laughter.

'It's all very well for you to praise William,' said Mary, 'but it was thanks to him that Edmund went to London. But for his tales and boastings, Edmund would still be here.'

'I never yet heard Will boast,' said Gilbert.

'Well, it's all the same,' said Mary. 'Buying that great house, as though London was made of money. And why hasn't Edmund written to his father? It's as though he was trying to hide from us. How could he go off and leave me so, without a word!'

Joanne and Gilbert were silent, recognizing here, undisguised, their mother's bewildered grief.

'I'm sure Edmund will be all right, mother,' said Joanne at last, more tender than Gilbert, and less cautious. 'Look at Rufus. He went off with hardly a penny in his pocket, and see him now!'

Mary recovered herself in an instant. 'Yes, it may be all very well for Mistress Hart,' she cried, 'to allow her son to go running off and not to know where he is or what he's doing, but I'm not that sort of mother, and—thank heaven!—my sons aren't like William Hart, either! They have more sense of duty. I expect if the truth be known, Edmund has done very well for himself, and William has been so busy playing the fool with this Ben Jonson that he knows nothing about it!' And she went energetically away to her store-room.

'Let that be a lesson to you,' observed Gilbert. 'When the lioness is angry with one of her cubs, never interfere, because she only wants an excuse to bite someone else instead.'

'You'd think,' said Joanne, pensively, 'that mother would be less critical of Rufus, now that he's done so well.'

'What, because he's proved her wrong?' asked Gilbert.

'Oh—well.' She looked up and saw Gilbert's expression, and faltered. 'He proved you wrong, too,' she said, after a moment, rallying.

'And you?' Gilbert suggested, and got up and went out, looking back at her with the same sardonic amusement.

Joanne stayed where she was, thinking uncomfortable thoughts. When Rufus returned unmarried to Stratford, she had felt tolerably secure in him. He had gone away to prove himself worthy of her love. He was now returned and should have his reward. But since that first, brief visit, he had hardly been to the house at all, and when they met by chance there was nothing loverlike in his manner. She wondered now, after all, whether it would not have been better if he had come back greatly changed. He had not *before* deserved her regard, she could say, but now, for her sake he had cast off his folly, and therefore she could admit her love for him. But, ah, the truth was that Rufus had not changed, but she had. He still treated the world as a joke and work as an insult. He still abused women and plagued his friends. Joanne had always thought, with her mother, that life was a serious matter. Life was a battle between right and wrong, and men were ranged upon the one side or the other. But while other men were throwing down their gages, Rufus stuck his in his bonnet and dared anyone to get it, and it was perhaps for this reason as much as any other that Joanne had refused to marry him. She was now prepared to admit that she had been mistaken, that she had arrogantly thrown away what she now ardently desired. But did Rufus wish her to admit it? She remembered, painfully, that he had never said that he loved her. He had asked her to marry him because she loved him, which was simple truth. But what of him? Had he, after all, any very strong affections, or did his laughter stand between him and true feeling? The only time he had spoken to her in sober earnest was when he had sworn that never again would he ask her to marry him. Across the lonely years, Joanne saw that oath alone as undeniable reality, and all the rest delusion.

Just before Christmas, Rufus's purchase of Master Sharp's business was completed, and the town could talk of nothing else.

'Ah yes,' said Mistress Hart, meeting Joanne outside New Place and keeping her talking on the windy corner for twenty minutes, 'yes, everyone's quite amazed with it, and I'm sure I am, too. Dear, dear, I can't imagine Rufus making much of a success on his own, though. He always had to have someone behind him or he'd never do a stroke of work. I said to him, I said, Rufus, you'd better marry a good, sensible wife, I said, who'll make you work. And he said, Well, perhaps I will, mother, he said. I might find some merchant's daughter in London, he said, who'd hold the strings of my purse and melt down the candle-ends and scold me when I was idle. Now, that'd be a wife, he said, to make a man happy and prosperous. So I said, it sounds as though you've seen someone you fancy, I said, but you know what Rufus is, Joanne, he'll never tell you anything if he's no mind to. But anyway, I dare say he'll surprise us all one day and come home with a rich wife.'

'Yes, I dare say,' said Joanne, her teeth chattering with cold.

'He said to me, See how the righteous flourish, he said, but I said, oh no, Rufus, it's the wicked who flourish, I'm sure of that. Of course, he never worries, Rufus doesn't. Never has. That's why he looks so young, you know. Never lets anything upset him. I remember when he was a boy, he lost a little knife he was very fond of, well, it was my fault that it was lost really, because I'd borrowed it for something and then it must have fallen out of my pocket. Well anyway, I couldn't find it again, and I said to him, I said, I'm afraid you're going to be upset about it, Rufus, I said, but he only looked grave for a minute and then he said, Well, mother, if it's gone, it's gone, and that was an end of it. And I said then, well it's lucky he doesn't feel things too much, because the truth was, it was his father gave him that knife just before he died, and I was afraid he might feel it rather, but there, it's a blessing to have a short memory, isn't it?'

Joanne walked home, weary and sick at heart, Mistress Hart's words jingling in her mind, true coin and false mixed up together, the sum of that which she had blindly accepted to deny her love, so long ago. She went slowly down Chapel Street and High Street, and so into Henley Street, and in the town where she had lived all her life she was a stranger, as lonely as any vagabond walking homeless through its streets.

She pushed the door open and went inside,

turning shivering towards the fireplace, and then stopping with a sudden catch of the breath as she saw Rufus standing on the hearth, looking at her.

'Well, and what do you want?' she enquired, gathering her wits together, and speaking more sharply for that momentary betrayal. 'Have you come to sell us some hats?'

'No,' said Rufus, 'I've come to supper.'

'Then you can go away again,' said Joanne, 'because there isn't enough for you.'

Rufus moved away from the fire to allow her to come and warm her hands, but kept his eyes on her face, and, disconcerted, she said quickly, 'Gilbert and father are in the work-room, I expect.'

'And your mother's staying for supper at New Place,' said Rufus, politely informative. 'Hamnet Sadler burnt his bread this morning, and Timothea Parsons hit her husband over the head with a spit and told him he was an ass, which he didn't deny, being all blood and astonishment. And my mother thinks that I should marry a sensible wife who would make me work hard. There! Now we've told each other all the news of the town!'

'I'm cold,' said Joanne, suddenly miserable and unable any more to play her part.

She still stood with her head bent down, warming her hands, and Rufus leant his elbow on the ledge of the fireplace. There was a moment's unusual silence between them.

Then Rufus said, casually, 'Master Sharp has bought a house at the other end of town.'

'He could buy one at the other end of the world for all I care,' said Joanne.

'—And I've bought his business,' Rufus went on.

'God help it,' said Joanne.

There was another silence. Joanne straightened her back and turned away. 'Well,' she said, 'I can't stay here gossiping with you. I must go and get supper.'

'No, wait a moment,' Rufus commanded.

She paused, startled, and looked back at him. Though he still lounged against the chimney, yet there was something in his voice and in the directness of his gaze which exacted obedience from her, and it was the knowledge that this was so which made her put her chin in the air and say, 'Well?'

'Before I went away,' said Rufus slowly, 'I asked you if you'd marry me, and you said you'd have to be mad to do it.'

A tentative little flower of gaiety bloomed in Joanne's heart. She began to smile and replied, 'And you said you must have been mad to ask me.'

Without answering her smile, Rufus went on, 'I swore I'd never ask you again.'

'Well?' said Joanne again, but this time laughing.

'Joanne,' said Rufus, 'do you love me?'

'Who, I?' cried Joanne, taken by surprise,

'Why, here's a question!'

'And a question deserves an answer.'

'Oh no, not always. A question would like an answer, but there's many a question that doesn't deserve an answer. Besides, which of us gets his deserts in this world?'

'And yet,' said Rufus, 'I want an answer to this question.'

'You want it. That means you lack it. And so you shall, for me.'

She laughed up at him, but he was quite serious, as she had only seen him serious once before.

'Do you love me?' he asked again.

'Why should you think I'd answer that?' cried Joanne, between amusement and indignation.

'Because unless you do, I shall go away,' said Rufus. 'And this time——' He paused. '——And this time, although I shall stay in Stratford, I shall go farther away than Cadiz.'

'Oh, riddles now!' said Joanne, impatiently. 'First questions and then riddles. You should go to the Wise Woman.'

'And instead I've come to a foolish one,' said Rufus, 'but she's the only one who can give me the answer to this question.'

'She can,' said Joanne, 'but will she?'

Rufus stood waiting, looking at her intently.

'You've forgotten something else,' said Joanne, desperately. '*I* said that if you asked me to marry you, I should say, no.'

315

Rufus's face darkened. 'I've forgotten nothing that you said that afternoon.' He said again, relentlessly, 'Do you love me?' Joanne searched about her for a way of escape and found none. She must submit, or lose all, and, like a good fighter, Rufus would give no inch until she surrendered. She must put her hand under his foot and declare herself defeated, and this time he promised her nothing in exchange—not even the assurance that he loved her. She came very close to making the admission, but it was too much for her pride to bear. That quality in her which had met and matched his quality from the first was too fine to be so broken.

'Why should I answer that?' she cried, 'I won't!'

'Very well,' said Rufus, no less unyielding.

He turned and went towards the door, and Joanne watched him go with a feeling of doom, as though this had been ordained from the beginning, had happened already in the mind of God, and as though he had already gone out into the street, never to return. So that, as he reached the door and opened it, it was with no hope of preventing him that she made a sudden, anguished movement, and cried out, 'Rufus!'

He stopped and turned to look at her, and then he closed the door and came back across the room and took her in his arms. In the firelight, Joanne saw his face close above her,

316

as though for the first time, with all its warmth and emotional energy. He smiled down at her, and she knew the truth at last—that laughter was not his weakness, but his strength. Robert Brown had existed for her only while he loved her, his sober honesty illuminated briefly by that passion which had no true place in him. But Rufus, though he had died a pauper in London or been drowned in the sea off Cadiz, would have remained unchangeably himself, unchangeably her love. Beggar or rich man, soldier or merchant, Rufus was indestructible, for the man who could laugh at life or death was in the end the only conqueror.

'Well, I'll say it first,' he cried in a voice full of laughter. 'I love thee, Joanne, I love thee! And now will you answer an honest man's question?'

'No,' said Joanne, with the tears running down her cheeks. 'Why should I, when you know the answer already?'


# CHAPTER 22


'Mother,' said Susanna one day, 'there's a man at the garden gate asking to see you.'

'Who is he?' asked Anne, looking up from the first roses which she was cutting to take round to Mary.

'I don't know,' Susanna answered. 'He looks as though he might be a gardener. But he said he wanted to speak to you most particularly.'

Anne walked back through the garden and saw a man by the gate, and she said 'Bartholomew!' in a voice of wonder, because, standing there with grizzled hair and a red, sunburnt face, he yet brought all her childhood with him in his hands, like a summer's memories in the scent of dried rose-petals. She invited him inside and he came doubtfully into the garden, looking round him uneasily.

'I only come because of *her*,' he said, jerking his head backwards.

'Her?' Anne asked, uncertainly.

'*Her*,' said Bartholomew again. 'She's ill. Isobella's bin looking after her, but she can't stay any longer. Catherine won't come. I don't like to ask you, seeing that——. But I don't know where else to turn. She's very sick. I think she's going.'

And Anne remembered that once all her life had been bounded by her stepmother, so that she would have known at once whom Bartholomew meant when he said 'her'.

She walked with Bartholomew across the fields to Shottery. Hewlands had its usual neglected look, and smelt stale inside, as it always had since Joan came to it. Anne went upstairs and found Bartholomew's wife sitting by the bed and Joan Hathaway lying with her eyes closed. Isobella stood up with the same nervous, doubtful look as Bartholomew and said, 'I hope you didn't mind, Anne, but we didn't know what to do, because I got to get back, and none of the others won't come, and we don't like to ask the neighbours because *she* didn't want us to.'

Anne glanced down at Joan, but the pallid face remained quite motionless.

'I'll stay here,' she said. 'It's very good of you to have done so much. If I'd known she was ill, I'd have come over before.'

'Well, Bart didn't want to ask you,' said Isobella again, 'but you see I can't stay. I don't think she'll last very long.'

Bartholomew and Isobella went away, riding on the same horse, and Anne was left sitting in the quiet, sunlit room, large and bare without the big bed in it. She felt relaxed and calm, as though she returned after death to look upon the strange little world of life, or like a soldier who returns after long years to visit the battlefield and sees it stand vacant and silent in the sunshine. She went downstairs to shut up the hens, finding everything in its old place, but unfamiliar because she had been away for so long. In the garden, a thrush sang on the tree where he always used to sing, and the sky stretched impersonally beautiful down to the setting sun. She paused by the gate, dizzy with the passing of the years, almost waiting for William to walk over the fields from Stratford, William, young and loving and beloved.

When she went back upstairs again, Joan Hathaway was awake, looking at her suspiciously out of her little black eyes.

'Oh, it's you!' she said, in the old, disparaging voice. 'I thought Isobella was here.'

'She had to go home,' said Anne.

'Oh,' said Joan. 'I thought Catherine might come. But I s'pose she wouldn't. It's always the same. Look what I done for her. Bin like a mother I have to her, and never a word of thanks.'

'Would you like me to get you something?' asked Anne. 'Would you like anything to drink?'

'Oh no, thank you,' said Joan affectedly. 'Don't trouble, I'm sure. I don't want to give any trouble.'

She stirred uneasily and groaned, and Anne sat down again, thinking how strange it was that Joan, who had always pretended to be ill when she wasn't, should now really be in danger of dying, and yet seem just the same.

The night passed slowly. Anne slept a little on a truckle-bed, but Joan was constantly demanding attention, a drink of water, or to be lifted up in bed, or more covers, or less. She was in great pain and groaned most of the time, stopping only to say that no one cared what became of her, and that Catherine would have sold the house over her head if she could.

'Don't you let that Mistress Bowman in here,' she said once, as Anne shook up her pillow. 'All she wants is to come and criticize, that's all she wants. Thinks she's so fine, with her rings and brooches and all. Where did she get them from, I'd like to know? Her and me aren't on speaking terms, and I don't want her poking around here when I'm ill.'

'All right,' said Anne.

Joan sank back with a defeated look and closed her eyes. But presently she opened them again to say, 'I s'pose when I'm gone Bartholomew'll see to everything. Of course, it doesn't matter to *you* what becomes of this house. Of course, *you* got a rich husband, even if you did have to marry him in a hurry!'

And she threw at Anne the same quick, sly look of hatred and malice, unchanged by the passing of time. It gave Anne again a strong feeling of being returned from the dead—that Joan should still feel such hatred, and that she should feel none.

As morning came, Anne sat by the window, listening to the bird songs and looking at the dew silver-grey on the meadow, and thinking of William. There, by the gate, he had kissed her for the first time. There he had come to find her as she crouched down in the stubble by the hedge and wished that the rain would drown her. Here at Shottery, here, here, in this very room, they had clung together as though on an enchanted island, they two alone real and everyone else in the world nothing more than shades and insubstantial spirits. And now it was gone, the love and the passion, vanished like the sunset clouds, leaving behind only sober greyness and the approach of night, and she and William lived each on his own island, alone, while the light failed. Their love for Hamnet which once had held them together when all else separated them, now parted them, it seemed irrevocably. Not once since his death had his name been spoken between them. Often when Anne was silent, it was because she was thinking of Hamnet. Often when William started to speak and stopped, it was because he had come close to speaking of him. Each silence enforced that first wordlessness of grief and guilt, until now it seemed that only some great stress of emotion would be strong enough to break through it and bring them together. And all strong emotions were ended now for them.

Sitting there, with that calm upon her, and with the violent passions and miseries of her girlhood clearly seen but far behind her, Anne thought of William's mistress. She had neither kept him nor given him back. Anne knew well enough that it was over, that he had left his mistress and ceased to love her when Hamnet died, and that that death which had so parted him from Anne had ended also that which had divided them. But just as the knowledge that he had a mistress had not made her angry, so the certainty that he had left her brought to Anne no exultation. Rather it increased her sadness and bereavement.

'It happened,' thought Anne, 'and we were parted. And it's over, and we're not together.'

Joan, who had fallen into a restless doze, woke up suddenly and called out, 'Anne!'

Anne came over to the bed, and Joan peered up at her as though she looked through a mist. 'Oh, you're there,' she said. 'I thought you was gone.' She lay back again, moaning, and then added ungraciously, looking up through half-closed eyes, 'You're not goin' away, are you? You're goin' to stay?'

'Yes, I'll stay,' said Anne.

And she felt an unexpected compassion for her stepmother, such as one would feel for a creature caught in a trap, which would bite if it were released but commands pity when it is helpless. In that demand for help, thus answered, they came to a sort of reconciliation, on both sides unyielding, and yet complete.

When the funeral was over and the neighbours had eaten the funeral meats and departed (Mrs Bowman, Anne noticed, wearing one very plain brooch of beaten silver and showing no curiosity whatever), Anne and Bartholomew discussed the inheritance, which was small enough and came only to Joan's own children, all now grown and living far away, except for the house which was willed to Bartholomew from their father.

'If there's anything from the house that you'd like to have, Anne,' said Bartholomew, doubtfully, as they stood by the gate, 'you've only to say so.'

Anne looked back at Hewlands. She heard again the shrill sound of women quarrelling and children brawling. In the peaceful beauty of the summer sunshine, the unhappiness and humiliation and cruelty seemed to hang about it like evil spirits.

'No,' she said, and, even after so long, she shuddered, 'no, I don't want anything from it.'

'Of course, you've got the bed,' said Bartholomew.

'Yes,' said Anne, 'I've got the bed.'

Anne walked back alone to Stratford, through the tall grasses and the meadowsweet, feeling a deep and settled sadness, for burying an ancient adversary seemed as melancholy as burying an old love, bringing with it the same sense of loss and parting and of the briefness of human existence.

# CHAPTER 23

With that simplicity and rightness that had marked all the events of her life, when she was twenty-four Susanna was betrothed to John Hall, the well-loved and greatly respected Stratford doctor.

'Ah, I see how it is,' cried Rufus at the wedding. 'Will thinks that if he has a doctor as son-in-law, he won't have to pay him any fees. Now, I wonder if we shall all benefit. I suppose that I'm a kind of cousin. Shall I be cured for nothing, too, or must I wait until John Hall has a son who can marry my daughter? See to it, Susanna!'

'I'll make a bargain with you,' said John Hall. 'If you make my hats for nothing, I'll cure you for nothing too.'

'No, no, that won't do,' said Rufus. 'I know that you'll wear out your hats, but I might never get sick. I might need a grave-digger before I needed a doctor!'

'Oh, doctors have to be grave-diggers as well,' said Joanne, 'don't they, John? You'd dig his grave for him with pleasure, wouldn't you?'

'Certainly,' answered Susanna's husband, 'and write his epitaph too.'

'No, Will's our poet,' said Joanne. 'Come, Will, what epitaph will you write on Rufus?'

And William replied immediately,

'Here lies Rufus whose hair was red.

'Once he was alive, but now he's dead.'

There was a shout of delight, and Joanne and Rufus turned to each other, laughing, and suddenly clasped hands, as though this was once more their wedding, as though once more they plighted their troth in love and mirth.

'Give my love to Edmund if you see him,' said Anne, as William mounted his horse to return to London at the end of the summer.

'I doubt if I shall see him,' William replied. 'We keep different company now.'

He sat looking down at her for a moment, reining his horse back. He wondered if she was thinking, as he was, of Susanna, truly their love-child, child of their first love, with garlands of country flowers in her fair hair, going with her husband to her own house in Old Town, and of how there remained at home with them now only Judith, their changeling, their bitter remembrancer, who had once screamed at her mother in a temper, 'You hate me because I'm not Hamnet! You've never forgiven me for not dying instead of him!' For an instant it seemed that even from the calm familiarity of their life together some words of almost accidental

326

tenderness should come, as two enemies imprisoned together must now and then discuss their situation. But the long habit of silence was upon them, that silence which can fall between husband and wife like the withdrawal of God's mercy from a sinner. William loosened the reins and rode out of the courtyard, turning in the saddle to see Anne standing at the door, waiting as she always waited, until he had passed through the gateway and into the street. And all the way along the familiar road to London, William found himself repeating the lines written by his friend some years before.

> Farewell, thou child of my right hand, and joy;
> My sin was too much hope of thee, lov'd boy.
> Seven years thou wert lent to me, and I thee pay,
> Exacted by thy fate, on the just day.
> O, could I lose all father now! For why
> Will man lament the state he should envy?
> To have so soon scap'd world's, and flesh's rage,
> And, if no other misery, yet age?
> Rest in soft peace, and, ask'd, say here doth lie
> Ben Johnson his best piece of poesy.

Early in the new year, William returned to Stratford. The buds were thickening in the hedges, the snowdrops were trembling in the grass, and only human death, it seemed, could not be quickened into life.

He rode straight to Henley Street and dismounted there, sending his servant on to New Place with his horse and the news of his return. Then he stood still for a moment before he opened the door, thinking how often he had gone through that doorway with Edmund on his shoulder, how often he had stood back while Edmund pushed in ahead of him, calling to his mother.

Mary Shakespeare was sitting by the fire, sewing, in John's old chair, and William, seeing her there, was aware of the change in her since his father had died. It was as though his death had come upon her, not as a violent shock, but as a steady and increasing deprivation. When she had married John Shakespeare, she had been a quiet, serious girl, with character quite unformed, and what she had become, she had become chiefly through her marriage with him, through the need to meet his optimism with carefulness, through the need of firmness in his moments of despair, through the necessity to provide for the children unyielding principles to balance his easy-going good humour. Her character had been strengthened equally by his weakness and his strength, and now she seemed to have no reason to be what she was. As she looked up, William seemed to see in her a new unsureness, as though she was uncertain now what part to play. But her glance was still quick and acute, as she said in surprise, 'Will! What are you doing here? We didn't expect you yet.' And then, before he could reply, 'It's Edmund! There's something wrong with Edmund!'

William was suddenly at a loss, like a man forced to fight before he is prepared. Mary said again, 'It's Edmund.'

William, whose trade was words, found none to serve him now.

'He's ill!' cried Mary.

'Yes, mother,' William answered, 'he's ill.'

'Then why aren't you with him?'

That old shrewdness of hers thrust aside all his tentative delays. She stood up in front of the fireplace and cried out in a voice of anguished rage, 'He's not dead! No! No!'

'Mother——' began William, and then, with painful calmness, 'Yes, he's dead.'

She looked at him, not with grief, but with fury and rebellion, as though he stood between her and Edmund, trying to hold them apart.

William remained where he was by the door, in cloak and spurs, and now he knew why he had tried to delay the telling of his news. It was because, that said, there was nothing more to say. For the Edmund who had died was for her the loving and engaging child who had staggered about the room on unsteady feet, who had cried, 'Ned come too!' weeping at the door, and who had returned always to his mother's arms. William could tell her nothing more about that child, but that he was gone for ever, and had gone for ever when he crept out of the house and set out upon the road to London. Indeed, perhaps he never had existed, because in every child are curled the tendrils of the later years, and to be blind to them is to deny life to the child.

Mary said slowly, 'Tell me about him. What had he been doing in London?' And then, the vainness of the question proving his loss, she sat down suddenly with her face in her hands and cried, 'Ah, my baby! My boy!'

William came at once to put his arms round her, but she stiffened and drew away from him and said, 'Tell me about him.'

'What can I tell you?' said William. He sat down and threw back his cloak and went on after a moment, 'He was employed by— various companies, as an actor.' He paused, glancing at his mother to see if she would understand what that meant, but she gave no sign. 'When he died, he was lodging in—in Southwark. It was a consumption, and there was nothing to be done. He's buried in Saint Saviour's Churchyard, in Southwark.'

What could he tell her? That Edmund had died in a tavern, tended by a whore. That Edmund had not fingered London daintily, but plunged both hands into it like a pirate at a

330

treasure chest, wasteful and improvident. That they had him written down in the parish register as 'a player' because that at last was his profession and his final mark—not little Ned, beloved youngest child, but Edmund Shakespeare, a player, of Southwark. And through William's mind rushed the tale of all those other poets and players of his London days, Kit Marlowe, his first London friend, stabbed in the eye in a Deptford ale-house; the Burbages, brawling with the Widow Brayne in the theatre, and Richard Burbage beating her friend Miles with a broomstaff; Ben Jonson killing another actor in Hoxton fields and afterwards boasting that *his* sword was ten inches shorter; or John Hampton, that first enchanter in the travelling company at Drayton, whom William had seen one day in a London tavern, looking as though he had been drowned in ale and was not yet revived. He had staggered in it, like a man just coming ashore, waving his hands feebly and talking in the sodden remnants of that voice which had rung across the village green, his audience now a landlord, a sharp-nosed boy, and two rotting soldiers home from the wars. This was Edmund's London, thought William, and Edmund himself a part of it.

'Why didn't he come home?' asked Mary slowly. 'Was he in need of money?'

'Edmund was always in need of money,' answered William, smiling, thinking of all his

London friends who were at all times in need of money, borrowing it from Henslowe, from each other, or from gullible citizens who hoped to see it again. But Mary didn't smile. She said with an ugly vehemence, 'I suppose *you* grudged giving it to him!'

William was once more sober and silent. He saw Edmund sitting on the corner of the table in his lodging, no longer with a look of golden freshness, but like a very fair young fallen angel, Lucifer's youngest companion, and heard him say, with a sideways glance of careless mischief, '*I* have a son to support now, Will—even if he is a bastard. I'm sure you'll dig your hand into your coffers for such a cause.' William remembered how in a sudden rage he had thrown his purse down on to the table and said, 'Take it, and go!' Edmund had picked the purse up with a look of surprise as though he had not expected William to recognize his intentional touch of cruelty, like a child who disobeys an order and then is astonished that he should be punished. He said, beguilingly, 'Come and have a drink, Will.' And, with a generous gesture of the purse, 'I have some money.'

'Go on,' said William, half-laughing, half in earnest, 'before I kick you down the stairs!' He added, 'I'm going home next week for Susanna's marriage to John Hall. Do you want to come?'

'Home?' said Edmund. 'Why should I want

to go home——' He tucked the money in his belt and chuckled, '—when I can find a home in every ale-house in London?'

William had stood at the window, looking down into the street to see him go. He saw him apparently accidentally jostle against a young woman carrying a basket of vegetables for sale, and saw him stand in front of her, putting his arms round her to steady her. William saw the girl laughing at his impudent compliments, and then she pushed past, looking over her shoulder to shout a pleasurable insult, and for an instant William had seen Edmund smiling back at her with exactly that piercing-sweet and irresistible smile which had delighted them all for so long.

'Ah, mother, mother,' he said now, sadly, 'you know that I loved him.'

'How did he die?' asked Mary, still with that coldness and removal. 'Were you with him?'

'Yes, I was with him,' said William, and thought by what a chance it had been so. 'And Gilbert, too.'

Then Mary asked the final question and the only one which mattered, as though the last instant before death could cheat eternity, compensating for all estrangement, all neglect and irrevocable parting.

'Did he ask for me? Did he send a message to me before he died?'

It had been in William's mind to lie to her.

So few words were needed to content her that, almost without considering it, he had resolved to tell her that Edmund had sent his love to her, returning him to her arms at the end. But now, as he cast about for the right phrase, he found that he could not do it.

For it seemed to him that there was in Edmund, in his life and death, a certain pattern which was hard but true. To lie now about the manner of his dying would be an insult to that complete, that sturdy, selfish, veritable Edmund, with all his faults upon him. William knew now that this was his ultimate faith which he must stand to, that it was not in false prettiness, but in the very, bitter truth of human nature and human life that hope and beauty lay, miraculously light in all the darkness. He could not now betray that faith, and dull the cold, clear flame of Edmund's departure.

It was in all knowledge of what his mother would suffer in hearing it that he replied in a low voice, 'No. He sent no message to you.'

Mary turned her eyes upon him, and said in the rigid voice of extreme rage, 'How could God allow this to happen? I've always trusted in Him. Why should He do this?'

She clasped her hands tightly in her lap. All the forced strength of her character expended itself in an instant to combat this sole event, and William saw the piety and faith of a lifetime crumble away, like a mummified body which has survived a thousand years and yet at a touch is gone into dust and nothingness. She said with terrible quietness, 'I will never forgive Him for this,' and for a moment William thought that she meant Edmund, but then knew at once that it was God.

In the room where their family life had whirred unceasingly round like a spinning-wheel, he listened with her to the silence, and it seemed, not that Edmund was dead, but that he himself no longer existed, that Gilbert, Joanne and Richard had all vanished, and that Edmund alone remained there with his mother in the house in Henley Street.

# CHAPTER 24

As he stepped out of the house, the untold story beat in William's mind and took possession of him, until Henley Street, High Street and Chapel Street became like a stage under his feet, invisible and unconsidered, subordinated to those events which took place in a far different scene. He saw the London tavern, and the drawers coming and going in their aprons, and heard the idle players' talk, that unchanging and yet always eager talk which he had listened to and joined in with pleasure for nearly twenty years, the talk of his trade, about the unlucky early breaking of a boy's voice, or the need for a change of costume between two scenes and whether a lengthened speech would make it possible, and, most important, what the takings had been that week. And, through this familiar talk, among his friends and in their own favourite tavern, William heard another sound, a sound also familiar yet which for the moment he could not remember—a sound like water running under the bows of a boat, followed by a thump like the boat coming to rest against the steps. He had turned round and seen an old man sitting at the next table, watching him, his gnarled fingers still curled round the handle of the empty cup.

'Why, it's——' he began, and hesitated.

'Crooked John,' the old man finished for him, and chuckled, his humped back shaking and bumping against the wall. 'That's what they calls me. I don't know why.' He gave William a sudden, odd, meaning look, and added, 'You do remember me, then?'

'On the road to Drayton,' said William, smiling. 'It was in an ale-house then.'

'Ah, an' you bought me some ale,' said old John.

William glanced into his empty cup.

'Can I buy you some now?' he enquired.

'Ay,' said Crooked John, with the same air

of one handsomely conferring a favour. 'Ay, you can.'

William beckoned the drawer and ordered the ale, pulling his stool across to the old pedlar's table.

'Well,' he said, 'and how's London? Better than it used to be?'

'Worse,' said Crooked John, 'worse. There's so many knaves in Lunnon, it's hard to find an honest man to cozen.' He grinned. Sitting so close to him, William could see now that he must have been much younger than he had thought when they saw him before—not more than fifty years old perhaps. But now his face was, not wrinkled, but tight-drawn, brown and knobbly, like the devil's face on a church door, and his narrow green eyes were still sharp but a little distant, as though he looked down upon the world from a stone niche instead of mingling with the concourse. 'How is it with you?' he asked, regarding William with the same wicked mirth that William remembered. 'I'll wager you 'as more trouble with pickpockets than you was used. Now, we that 'as empty pockets, they don't trouble *us*.'

'Hoo!' cried William. 'Are your pockets ever empty?'

'Well, not fer long,' Crooked John conceded, and showed his single yellow tooth again. He drank and looked round the room, and then brought his eyes back to William. 'I bin looking fer you,' he said. 'They told me I mought find you here.'

'Looking for me?' said William, in surprise. 'But how did you know my name?'

'Oh, I've knowed it fer a long while,' said Crooked John. 'I seed a play at the theatre, and you was playin' a small part in it, an' I says to meself, I says, that's the young man I seed in Warksher, I says. An' then I sees you onct or twice more, an' I asts what's your name. I've seed some of your plays, too,' he added, judicially, 'an' some on 'em was good.'

'Thank you,' said William, with genuine pleasure. This was Warwickshire speaking, this was a voice from his youth. Like the commendations of an old schoolmaster, this seemed more valuable than any compliments paid to him by those who had only known him in his later years.

Crooked John nodded over William's shoulder.

'That's Ben Jonson, en't it?' he enquired.

William glanced round at Ben who had just set Dick Burbage shouting with laughter at an extremely bawdy joke, and agreed that it was.

'I seen some o' his plays too,' said Crooked John. 'They en't bad, but seems like he says, Go on, he says, *laugh*, can't yer? An' then I begins ter say, No, I says, I don't think as I will laugh. An' I *don't*,' he finished, and nodded his head triumphantly, as though Ben

338

had been a magistrate and he had just scored a hit against him.

There was a silence, while William drank his wine and looked at his companion, and Crooked John once more looked about him with his shrewd, pedlar's assessing glance. Then he said, casually, 'You got a brother in Lunnon, en't you?'

'Yes,' William answered, startled. 'Two of my brothers are in London at the moment.'

'Ah,' said Crooked John. 'It's the wild one as I means.'

William was silent, waiting. It came to his mind, unpleasantly, that perhaps Edmund had had some dealings with this pedlar, and that Crooked John, finding that Edmund had a well-to-do brother, had seen this chance of reclaiming his money. Crooked John leant closer and, in his disappointment, William thought that there was a sly and leering look about him. He found it difficult not to draw away from the smell of the old man.

'I wuz in th' Red Bull, in Southwark,' said Crooked John, in a conspirator's tone, 'an' I hears the landlord say, he says, That young man as lodges upstairs, he says, I think he's a-dyin'.' William caught his breath. 'So the fellow he's a-talkin' to, he says, Get'm to make 'is Will, he says. Make his Will! says th' landlord (rascally sort o' fellow he is—a Cornishman or some such), Make 'is Will! he says. He's nothin' ter leave but a rotten doublet an' a pair of shoes all wore out, he says. Only a player he is, he says. So, knowin' a few players meself, I asts him, What's 'is name? I asts. An' he says, Shakespeare, he says. So then I thinks to meself, That mought be young Edmund Shakespeare, I thinks, because I saw'm onct, an' I guessed as he was your brother, because he looked something like you, but o' course, I seen at onct as he wuz a wild one.'

'I must—go to him,' said William, uncertainly. He put his hands on the table to stand up, but paused to ask, 'Where did you say it was?'

Crooked John drank the last of his ale, smacking his lips over his one tooth, and stood up.

'Th' Red Bull,' he answered. 'D'ye know where 'tis?'

William shook his head.

'I'll walk along with ye,' said Crooked John. 'I thought you mought not know it. 'Ten't much of a place.'

William stood up and put the money for the drinks down on the table. Crooked John twitched his shoulders, as though he hitched his hump into position, and moved towards the door like a pirate vessel nosing out of harbour.

They walked in silence for a while, and Crooked John had a blessed air of being entirely unconcerned over the whole matter.

No painful sense of officious sympathy hung about him. He trod steadily along at William's side, taking the middle path and evidently gratified to see people, as usual, hastily giving him room, with superstitious glances. Then he said suddenly,

'How's the little maid with th' cherries?'

'Married,' William answered.

'Not to the pale one?' enquired Crooked John.

'No, the other one.'

'What, th'one with red hair?' said the pedlar, and chuckled.

' "Like will to like, quoth the devil to the collier",' he quoted. Then he said, 'Are you married?'

'Yes,' William answered, 'some time since.'

'Yer wife in Lunnon?'

'No,' William replied, 'at Stratford.'

'Ah,' said Crooked John, with satisfaction, 'that's what I allus says. Keep yer whore in Lunnon, but marry in th' country. Country wimmen's like country shoes—they wears better.'

They came at last to the Red Bull, in a stinking alley where a dead dog lay crawling with maggots not far from the door. Crooked John led the way into the dark entrance, and paused, and shouted, "Ost!'

A little dark man came out, his face dead white under his stubble of beard, his mouth twisted downwards as though in perpetual disgust at everything that was said to him. He looked from Crooked John to William quickly and suspiciously.

''Ost,' said the pedlar again, 'where's th'young player as lodges 'ere?'

'Upstairs,' the man answered, with a jerk of his head.

The old man stood aside to make way for William, motioning with his thumb towards the staircase. 'Here,' cried the man, suddenly starting forward. 'Here, is this the young man's father? When do I get my money, eh? He owes me——'

Crooked John turned on the man, snarling like an animal and showing his one yellow fang, and the landlord shrank back into the doorway and fell dumb. William went up the stairs, his nostrils full of the smell of cheap ale and foulness.

On the dark landing, William paused, the floor-boards curving grotesquely away under his feet. He saw at the end of the short passage a sliver of light where the planks of a door had split apart at the top, and from behind that door there came, appallingly loud and startling, the sound of coughing and choking. William waited for a while, and then, when silence fell, he went up to the door and pushed it. It had no latch and swung open at his touch.

It was a tiny hutch of a room under the roof and what window there was was level with the bending floor-boards, but there was a truckle-bed and Edmund lay there with his eyes shut. A woman stood by the bed with a basin in her hands and a look on her face composed of indignation and distaste and love—the sort of look a mother wears when her child is sick. She was quite young and dark-haired, with a beauty only slightly marred by pock-marks and much more by a hardened acceptance of the worst that life could inflict upon her, and she turned her head, dully unsurprised, when William came in, and said nothing. After a few minutes, Edmund opened his eyes. He looked at William and slowly began to smile, watching him from under his eyelashes.

'Ned,' said William, coming to stand beside him. 'Ned!'

'I sent a message to your lodgings,' said Edmund, in a scratched whisper, 'but you weren't there, and they wouldn't send again.'

William nodded slowly, comprehending the jealous hate of the landlord and the jealous love of the woman. He saw Edmund smiling faintly before he closed his eyes again, and knew that he understood it too and was almost glad that his brother had come to London to learn so much.

There was a sound of heavy footsteps up the stairs and along the passage, and William, expecting the landlord, turned, preparing himself for a battery of foul-mouthed insults. But instead Crooked John came in, incongruous in the sick-room, and yet with his usual air of being sure of himself and master of the situation. He came and looked down on Edmund from the end of the bed and said, 'H'm!' He said it not pityingly or in embarrassment, but with an interested recognition of the state of affairs.

'I've dealt with that dog downstairs,' he said. 'You won't 'ave no more yappin' out'f 'im.' William found the maggoty dog and the landlord confusedly together in his mind. 'D'ye want me to fetch a doctor?'

'Yes,' said William, putting his hand to his head in a hopeless gesture. 'Do you know of a good one?'

'A good one?' cried Crooked John, with a hearty enjoyment which quite ignored the creeping presence of death in the room. 'There en't no such thing. They's all rogues, doctors is! But I knows one what's better'n most. A Jew, 'e is. Cured my woman onct. Called 'Lonso.'

'Does he live near?' said William.

'I'll fetch 'im,' said Crooked John. "E'll come fer me. 'E knows I dun't care if 'e's Jew or Christian. All's one ter me.' He looked at William enquiringly, and for an instant he didn't look like a hunch-backed, villainous old pedlar, living by cheating and men's fearful superstitions. His glance was momentarily direct, open and shrewd. 'Anythin' else you want?' he asked.

'My brother,' said William. 'If I could send

a message to my other brother——'

'The quiet one?' enquired Crooked John. 'I seen'm. Where does 'e live?'

William told him, and Crooked John went towards the door. William followed him, overwhelmed by incalculable and unrepayable benefits, and seeing represented in this old man all the strange and obstinate kindnesses which men, in spite of everything, still perform to men.

'Anything I have,' he said, 'is at your command.'

Crooked John turned and looked at him, the wicked zest back in his eyes. He smacked his lips and grinned, and said, in his wheezy, evil old voice, 'Say it's payment fer th' cherries. Or th' ale,' he added. He chuckled and went out, the door swinging to behind him. William heard him downstairs growling out suddenly, 'G-Gr, you cur! Was you tryin' ter listen, was yer, you lousy, whoreson dog!' and heard the landlord's terrified protest, and a clatter as though the landlord stumbled back over a hogshead, and then a silence. Crooked John had gone out into the streets of London, vanishing like a wary old wolf into the forest.

The little room was bitterly cold. The dirt and chill together made it seem like an antechamber to death, the dusty entrance to the tomb. The woman never spoke, and never seemed to question who William was or why he had come. It was as though she was incapable of thought, and acted only in that kind of brute tenderness which comes from an animal's instinctive care for its young. When William drew the scarred and rickety stool up to the bed and sat there with his head stooped against the sloping ceiling, she left the room, only returning some time later with the doctor.

Alonso nodded to William and went straight up to the bed and examined Edmund. When he had finished, he drew his gown about him and said calmly, 'It is too late.'

'Is there nothing to be done?' said William, urgently.

'Nothing,' replied the doctor. 'The consumption is too far advanced.'

'At least,' said William, 'can I move him to somewhere——' He glanced at the woman, standing motionless by the door, '—to my own lodgings? He would be warmer there.'

The doctor turned his eyes towards Edmund and replied with tranquillity, 'He has only a few hours. Let the young man die in peace.'

'Oh, God!' said William, under his breath.

Alonso regarded him steadily for a few minutes, his dark face with the big nose and brown eyes quite expressionless. Then he said, 'I must go now. I have other patients whom I must visit.'

He moved towards the door, and the woman opened it for him and stood back.

'For your fee,' said William. 'I haven't

346

enough money here, but when my brother comes, if you'll tell me where your house is——' The doctor turned at the door and looked back at him.

'There is no fee,' he said. 'Since my art was of no use to the young man, there is no fee.'

'But, your time,' said William, 'and your journey here——'

'I am my own master,' said the doctor. 'There is no fee.' He said it, not with kindness and sympathy, but with a commanding pride.

'But, is there nothing we can do?' cried William.

'Give him what he asks for,' replied the doctor, 'and keep him warm until the end.'

And he went out, still holding his gown close to avoid contamination from the walls and floor.

'Until the end,' thought William. 'Warm until the end, and then the cold earth and the cold stone above him, and only cold bones left at last.'

The woman had gone downstairs after the doctor, and Edmund still lay as though unconscious. William fell on his knees beside the narrow bed, his face among the rotten, evil-smelling coverings. In a strange and terrible way, the emotions which his poet's heart had imagined, his man's heart now felt. Once more he lay dying with Hamlet and saw with him the days not spent, the youth not yet worn out, the end inexorable. Once more

347

he knelt by Hamlet dying, and cried out against the waste and loneliness and the pity of it—ah, the pity of it! The chill crept about him, the early darkness fell on the frozen town, and Edmund's suffering and his merged into the anguish of humanity, all the world tormented and consumed within that little room.

After some time Gilbert arrived, bringing with him William's servant whom they sent out at once for warm coverings for the bed. The night wore away like a disordered dream, with Edmund torn by his disease, with the woman ministering to him with that silent, mechanical care, and with William and Gilbert, wrapped in their cloaks, sitting still and unsleeping, the rush-light flickering coldly in the darkness of the room.

William found the landlord's words beating in his brain. 'Is this the young man's father?' The words fell into a rhythm, like a marching-song. 'Is *this* the *young* man's *fa*ther? Is *this* the *young* man's *fa*ther?' They came back persistently into his tired mind. 'Is *this* the *young* man's *fa*ther?' And Edmund dying and Hamnet dying lay together on the bed, and he sat and watched them both, and sometimes it was as though Edmund was already dead, and Hamnet died now, and sometimes they both died now together.

In the early dawn, Edmund seemed a little better. He lay still for a while with his eyes open, and then he asked, with difficulty, 'Is that Gilbert?'

'Well, Ned,' said Gilbert, coolly tolerant, but kind.

'Edmund,' said William, leaning forward, 'the child—your son——?'

'Dead,' said Edmund. 'Died in August. Buried in Saint Saviour's yard.' He laughed, and choked, and managed to say at last, 'Burying him—took—the last of my money.'

The silence lengthened. The grey light spread across the room. Edmund raised his head very slightly and whispered, 'Give—give——' His voice failed, and William thought that those would be his last words. But then he finished, 'Give my love to Anne.'

'Ned, Ned!' cried William.

He was kneeling by the bed again, holding Edmund in his arms, the woman crouching close by the other side. They stayed there for a long time, and then the woman cried out, 'Oh, Jesu! he's gone!' and her voice which they heard for the first time was coarse and vibrant, full of the breath of life.

Gilbert said in a low, thoughtful voice, quite free from passion, 'God help us. God help us all.'

Half-dazed with grief relived, William found himself at New Place. He stood with his hand on the door, and he seemed to hear still the tolling of the great bell of Saint Saviour's, telling Londoners that a Stratford-born child had died in their city.

He went into the house and paused, and Anne came to the doorway of the garden-room and stood there, motionless, in that withdrawn, silent greeting to which he had become accustomed, anxious to hear from him why he had returned so soon, but mysteriously prevented from showing any pleasure at his return. It was as though he saw in her at that moment a perfectly lifelike statue of that woman whom he had seen in the dusk at Shottery with her hands resting on the gate. It was a statue dear to him for the sake of the living woman whom it commemorated, and yet in this moment of loneliness and loss, the very success of its portraiture was unbearable, to see the look of tranquillity which he remembered so well, and to know that he himself had destroyed the warmth of feeling which had once been hidden beneath it.

With a sudden rush of emotion, like a man laying his sorrows at the feet of an image in a church, he cried out, 'Anne, he's dead! Edmund is dead!' and yet with the same hopelessness of any response.

In the silence of the hall, she stood, unmoving, looking at him. And then, miraculously, her face changed, as though life flowed into it, life and sorrow and human pity. She took a step towards him and put out her hand and whispered, 'Oh, not Edmund! Not

Edmund, too!' They were close together, and William put his arms about her, and found with a sense of wonder and discovery that she was warm and breathing.

All the love which had lain for so long in silence and stillness stirred once more between them, not with that old passion and uncertainty, but with all the steadiness of long-remembered tenderness, as though it had burned all this time unperceived, and they now turned at the same instant and found it waiting for them.

And because in every death, each death is sharply repeated, Anne cried out, 'Edmund!' and then, 'Hamnet, oh, Hamnet!' Once more she knelt in the upper room at the cottage and there, alone in the darkness, she held the small body between her hands. Once more she felt the little heart stop beating and knew that Hamnet was irrevocably gone from her. Once more she stumbled down the stairs—and now into William's arms! The tears were wet on her cheek and she did not know if they were her tears or William's. They were drowned together in a great sea of sorrow, and the shared grief was like the bitter ecstasy of first love. In the death of Edmund, Hamnet died again, and they suffered it together, and together they felt the loss of the child in the market place, whose toy cart, clumsily pulled along on a string tied by Rufus, had brought them to this moment. The mystery of life broke over their heads with all its promise and defeat, its richness and squandering, and its final strange triumph in death.

They drew apart and looked at each other, and knew that London lay still at last in Edmund's grave. The house that William had built and Anne had lived in as a visitor was now their home, and, standing there in the hall, they entered it together for the first time. And where Anne had once come to William, helpless, demanding sanctuary, so he now, all ambition and all triumph left behind him, came home to her silent and unchanging love, finding now that sad, ironic, and yet hopeful truth, that the prison of youth is the gentle refuge of the later years.

He bent his head and kissed her, and Anne said in a voice of astonished joy, 'Ah, Will!' seeing him returned now at last to Stratford, and to her.